Show Me

a
Beautiful
Woman

HERU PTAH

SUNRASON BOOKS

New York   Charlotte   Kingston

ALSO BY HERU PTAH

Love, God and Revolution (poetry)

A Hip Hop Story

Sax and Violins

Michael Black

Published by
SUNRASON BOOKS

facebook.com/heruptah
http://www.sunrason.com

Ebook ISBN: 978-0-9852881-1-2
Book ISBN: 978-0-9852881-3-6

Published 2012
Printed in the United States of America

To . . . Perseverance

1

Was there ever anything more beautiful than a beautiful woman sleeping . . . yes . . . a beautiful woman sleeping in the buff.

Her body lay bare; bare back, bare thigh, bare bottom; her breasts pressed in, her breathing unbroken—it was a blessing. Being in the same bed with this woman was a blessing. But even blessings in overabundance will eventually taste like bile.

His hand slid down her spine, dipped at her lower lumbar, rested on her coccyx . . . and then pulled away.

Dressed to leave he stood by her living room window. Manhattan was his horizon. The city winked a sleepless eye. It was flirting with him. It was a daily dalliance they liked to play. The city was always calling him to bite the apple and no matter how many times he had already gone down on her, he was always obliging.

There was blue in his brown eyes—dawn was coming. Her hands came through his arms. He could feel her bare nipples on his back. She slipped an envelope in his jacket's inner pocket.

"Thank you," he said.

With her lips on his ear, "Do you have to go?" she asked.

He turned and faced her. He was handsome but that wasn't what made him special. It was an inner unstated charm and magnetism, something you couldn't quite put your finger on, it was intangible and it made you want to touch him. He was aware of it (of course he was) but even he himself couldn't articulate exactly what it was, but she knew. It was confidence—not conceit, not narcissism—just pure unabashed confidence. It was a quality so few people truly possessed but everyone desired.

He left her apartment and walked down the hall to the elevator wondering how many women's apartments had he left in the early morning? Too many to count, so many every hallway began to look the same. He pushed the button and waited, admiring the drab ecru walls as he did. He sighed. How many times had he seen a hallway painted this color, stepped on this grey commercial carpet, smelled this brand of lilac air freshener? He would swear the same management company was in charge of fifty percent of the buildings in the city.

The elevator door opened and there was a woman inside—another woman—and that was something he had learned a while ago. No matter how attractive or personable or pliable her lower lumbar there was always another woman, and she was just his type—beautiful. They looked as if they had both had the same night a fact which was not lost on either of them. They shared a conspiratorial smile as he entered. That was his invitation. As a general rule women prefer for a man to initiate and when he does for him to do so quickly. He wasted no time extending his hand. "Hey, I'm Alex." She shook it and smiled, "Helena . . . hi." The elevator door closed.

2

The season was fashionably Autumn. It was the fall you see in catalogues; just cold enough to wear a jacket and scarf but not a coat. Sorrel leaves blew down the block. The black Audi R8 drove over the cobblestone street. He was in Dumbo and you could see Manhattan in the backdrop. DUMBO was an acronym for Down Under the Manhattan Bridge Overpass. It was Soho in Brooklyn. It was artsy, cosmopolitan and gentrified. None of that mattered much to Alex but Dumbo was somewhere he had never lived before and that in and of itself made it attractive.

He pulled his car into the parking lot of the Apartment building on Water Street. The Security Guard never knew anyone to move in at five in the morning but it wasn't his job to ask questions. He handed Alex the keys to his apartment. Alex nodded and walked off to the elevator carrying all of his possessions: a leather-bound messenger bag hanging from his left shoulder, a garment bag swung over his right and a suitcase pulled in his left hand.

The apartment was eleven-hundred square feet of gorgeous hardwood floors, with a modern kitchen, a refrigerator built into the wood grain cabinets, exposed brick walls and fourteen foot ceilings. He was the first person to ever live here and when getting a pre-furnished flat that was always a must.

He dropped his bags and headed for the bedroom. It had a window with a ledge large enough to sit on and he did. It had a great view of the East River and Manhattan beyond that. He settled in, rested his elbow on his knee and he and the city continued their flirtation. Show me a beautiful woman, he said to her . . . and I will show you a man . . . she replied.

3

You rarely see stars in the night sky but the city lights made up for it. It was midnight and New York City was never more alive—and there was no other city like New York. Every other was just a facsimile; a simile here a simile there, always like it in some ways but never like the real thing.

Alex was dressed for a night on the town, stylish but never flashy, wearing brands most people never heard of nor could they afford. He popped the price tag off the nearly 3,000 dollar leather jacket, slipped it on and turned off the bedroom lights.

4

A thousand people packed into a two story warehouse. Three hundred of them were dancing, another three hundred were maneuvering from one spot to the next for no other reason than to appear occupied, and the other four stood around posing because that's what they were told cool people do—and then there was Alex. Like a predator he blended in and stood out concurrently. He made his way to the bar and called to the Bartender. "Gin, dry with a lime," he said to him. The Bartender acknowledged and went about making his drink. Alex turned his attention to the dance floor. Like a serial killer he was on the hunt and when at the club he always preferred the Girls who danced. They tended to be less pretentious. The ones who stood around fooling themselves into thinking they came to the club for any other reason than to put a For Sale sign above their cleavage would give it up as well but why go through the extra trouble if you didn't have to.

Six friends entered the dance floor. One of them caught his eye. She was easily the best of the bunch and one of the better looking women he had seen so far; a sienna complexioned Latina who wore a slinky fit red dress that had a habit of riding up her thighs when she danced. Consequently she had to fix her hemline every few seconds as well as push off the men who would intermittently creep up on her from behind and try to grind on her ass. *Yeah, you're the one,* he thought. He had his prey. He drank his gin and went to the dance floor.

He came at her surreptitiously, positioning himself just outside the girls' circumference. The song was mid tempo and he effortlessly matched his rhythm to the beat. Alex danced well without doing anything extravagant. She gave him a sidelong glance, a half second of eye contact. It was sufficient. He had his invite. He steadily maneuvered himself closer coming to her from the side. They brushed arms—an intentional accident. She didn't retract. That was his welcome. He steadily moved in behind her and when the song changed she stepped back and evaporated the space that separated their bodies.

5

Twenty minutes later they were at the bar.

"What are you drinking?" he asked.

"Tequila," she said.

"You know it's no fun if you can't remember it the day after."

"Okay then, what are you having?"

"Gin."

"Okay, I'll have that."

Alex looked over to the Bartender and held up two fingers. The Bartender nodded and went about making their drinks.

"So what's your name?" she asked.

"Alex—y tu?"

"Angie."

"Short for Angelica?"

"Si."

"Colombiana."

"Wow. I'm impressed. How did you know?"

"I know my women."

"Ahhh, you're one of those."

"Nah. I'm one of a kind."

"Sure you are. So tell me, Alex, what do you do?"

"What do I do? I . . . am . . . a Philosopher."

"A photographer, oh that's so cool."

"No. I do, do some photography for fun, but no I'm a Philosopher."

"A Philosopher? If you don't mind my asking what does that mean?"

"It means I do a lot of thinking."

"Thinking?" She smiled quizzically. "That's it?"

"Yep."

"And you get paid for that?"

"Not always."

"Are you fucking with me?"

He smiled slyly. "Not yet."

6

She looked like she was being tortured—in a good way. Her eyes rolled to the back of her head and her mouth went from clenched to ajar to clenched again. His hands caressed her breasts under her dress. She couldn't see his head but could feel his tongue. She gave him a standing crescendo. He came up from cunninlingus, turned her around, dropped his pants and lifted her dress, and the first thrust was always the best—and unfortunately it slowly got worse in succession.

She was sleeping. His hand slid down the small of her back as his fingertips did tiny circles on her skin. His touch was more scientific than loving. He was trying to find something, to feel something . . . anything.

He pulled his hand away, sank his head in her pillow and sighed through his teeth. What the hell was going on? This was becoming frustrating and admittedly scary. She was like a corpse lying next to him. She breathed but she was dead. Her flesh had become meat.

He inhaled and closed his eyes. Moments later he felt a hand tiptoe across his chest. He opened his eyes, turned and looked at Helena, the woman from the elevator. He swore a second ago he was lying with . . . what was her name again? He couldn't remember or even how he got here. It didn't matter. All his nights were the same and the women weren't any different. "What are you feeling?" she asked him.

"Nothing," he replied and belied it with a smile.

7

Alex returned to his apartment feeling empty. He was spent but this was due more to ennui than exhaustion. Before it took weeks to fade away, then it went to days, now it was a night sometimes just a few hours. It was all getting old too quickly and it was confusing the hell out of him.

He began stripping as he entered the bedroom. On the wall adjacent to the loo there were three wicker hampers labeled Ian, Church and Trash respectively. He took off his jacket and shirt and placed them in the Ian hamper. His jeans and boots he placed in the Church hamper. His t-shirt, boxers and socks he placed in the Trash. He then walked naked into the bathroom and entered the shower and as the water beat on his brow he came to a scary realization, *I think I'm losing interest in Women.*

8

"What?" Ian asked.

I think I'm losing interest in women, Alex thought but said, "Nothing." Not that Ian would have noticed, enrapt as he was with his new jacket, which happened to be Alex's old jacket, the 3,000 dollar Gucci from three nights prior.

"Damn this jacket is sweet. Are you sure you don't want it anymore?"

"Yeah, I'm sure."

"How many times did you wear it?"

"The usual."

"Damn. Thanks man, I appreciate it."

"No problem. It was either you or the Salvation Army."

If Alex were to have a friend it would be Ian. He was a bit older, a bit shorter and by his own admission a bit less handsome, which wasn't to say he wasn't attractive, just average; an average thirty-three year old with a paunch in his mid-section and a little less bounce in his swagger.

They had known each other for two out of eighteen years. They first met at Canarsie High School in Brooklyn and were best friends for most of freshman year until Alex moved to Long Island two months before the summer. Back then at their age it was hard to keep in touch and as most high school friendships tend to do theirs withered away.

Ian, however, was able to move on as back then he had a lot going for him. Beyond being the inveterate class clown he used to do stand-up at the school talent shows, riffing on students and faculty a like. People told him he could be another Martin Lawrence, Chris Rock, Chris Tucker or Bernie Mac—any of the above would do. They were all his idols as he had decided he wanted to be a stand-up comedian. Then at sixteen he got his girlfriend pregnant. That was a curve ball he never saw coming. He did go on to become a comedian but his career had been a series of strikeouts with a few walks in between.

Ian and Alex reconnected a year ago at the Laughing Stock, a comedy club on Manhattan's lower east side. After all those years it was great seeing each other again and they fell right back in where they had left off, recalling old episodes of the Simpsons and Martin they used to go on about back in home-room. Ian never usually liked running into old friends as his career wasn't where he wanted it to be and each encounter always devolved into a measuring stick. That was not the case with Alex. In fact he was impressed Ian was still doing stand-up. Ian was impressed with Alex overall, with how he looked, how he dressed and the damn near mutant ability the man had for picking up women. Alex deprecated and turned the subject back to comedy. He told Ian comedy was something he had recently thought about doing but could never see himself on stage. He had written a few bits and asked Ian if he wouldn't mind reading them. Already feeling like he was in the twilight of his career at thirty-two Ian was eager for new material—and they were good, they were very good in fact. Ian asked if he could perform one of them. Alex asked if he could perform them all.

Alex's laptop was on E*TRADE. He was watching the futures for the Dow Jones and the markets in Asia. Satisfied with what he saw, he minimized the web page and revealed a Word document. "Yo, I worked on a new bit. Come check it out," he said to Ian.

Ian got up from the sofa and walked over to the laptop. Alex turned the screen so Ian could read it.

"Oh shit . . . oh shit—that is funny."

"Yeah?"

"Hell yeah. In fact I'ma work it in tonight."

"Cool. I'll be there."

9

Dressed for the gym Alex exited his building and found Ian outside looking intently at something across the street. Curious to see what it was Alex looked in that direction as well. It didn't take him long to find it. Through the passing traffic he saw them; two barely legal, if legal at all, teenage girls walking down the block, giggling and carrying on in that way that young girls do. They were attractive and sexy, arguably too sexy for daylight, but there was something else about them that caught Alex's eye.

"Yo, Ian, you see those book bags they're wearing, it means they're still in high school."

Ian smirked. "Well you know what they say, 'if there's grass on the field, play ball.'"

"You trying to play in the prison league ma man. And don't you have a daughter that age?"

"No I don't." Ian shuddered. "Tiana is only sixteen. Those girls are at least . . . seventeen."

They both laughed.

"Yo, I'll catch you later," Alex said and departed with a pound.

10

Rihanna's Only Girl in the World played over the Gym's sound system. *Only girl?* How many times had he heard that before? How many times had he tried to fall for the platitude? How can something be special when there are millions of them? Like cornflakes no two are ever alike but just like cornflakes they all taste the same.

Alex rode on an exercise bike while flipping through pictures on his phone. His index finger went from one pretty woman to the next. He pulled the image back and his screen filled with thumbnails of a dozen women. His finger went to the bottom and an option for Delete All came up. He thought for a moment before pressing down. The screen went black and he felt empty, in a good way; evacuated, like he had his colon cleansed, also a bit light-headed; a little of the good always went with the bad. Melancholy he put his phone away and looked up.

You don't see beauty you feel it and once you've felt it you know it forever. It's the difference between artificial and sun-light, between oil and Photoshop. It's like inhaling pure oxygen. It gives you a little vertigo.

When he saw her the word that came to mind was elegant. She was an elegant creature, which was something you didn't see every day. And it wasn't because of her clothes. Like every-one else she wore sneakers, sweats and a t-shirt. It was the way her clothes fit her; slim but athletically shapely, hung like they were tailored, like the designer had her in mind when he drew it. And it had nothing to do with her hair. It was simply pulled back into a bun elaborating her rounded forehead. Nor had it anything to do with her make-up, because she wore none, didn't need to, her skin was a smooth bronze, a complexion people risk cancer for. Her elegance was in the abstract; in her gait, in her posture, even in how she breathed. All of the men took a breather when she walked by. Alex got the feeling she didn't want the attention. She wore headphones and kept her eyes straight. Still she could feel him calling from across the room. She involuntarily turned in his direction—eye contact for a half second—and then turned back and went on her way.

Seeing her was like drinking Gatorade after a marathon. She made him feel like he could run again, vivified and virile—very virile. He wanted to have sex with this woman. He was going to have sex with this woman. This he knew for certain. First he would have to approach her, but not just yet. There were others in front of him on line. Alex hadn't been the only man in the gym to take notice. Three of them walked over as she positioned herself to use the Leg Extensions machine. One of them decided to provide unsolicited assistance. "Now what you wanna do is slowly carry it up, and now hold it . . . hold it . . . now slowly bring it down." "Okay, thank you, I got it, I'm fine," she said. "Yes you are," he said and Alex laughed to himself. If they were his competition it was fairly, well . . . laughable.

11

A shadow came over her.

She both loved and hated doing leg curls. It was great for the hamstrings but also had the effect of propping your ass in the air. She knew some of the men were watching her, ogling like high school boys. *Do they never grow up?* She couldn't do anything about that but figured as long as they kept their distance they were tolerable. Now she could feel this shadow blocking out the light. This was her first time coming to this gym and if this was how the men were going to be it would be her last. She finished her set and started turning around intent on giving whoever this shadow was a polite piece of her mind, when "Excuse me," the shadow said.

"Look, I got it. It's not my first time at the gym. So thank you for your help but really . . ." she looked up and saw it was Alex, "I'm good." She recognized him from across the room and looked at him with slightly less annoyance than she would have if he had been one of the other men. She wasn't quite sure why she did that.

"Actually I was wondering if you could help me out." He was standing by a machine that worked out your glutes. "You seem like you know what you're doing, do you mind?" Granted the machine was a bit more complicated than the others at the gym, but it was nothing a novice couldn't figure out by taking a look at the guide at the side of the equipment, and Alex was certainly not a novice. This she could tell from his overall build and the definition in his arms.

"You really don't know how to work it?" she asked disbelievingly, knowing this was all part of his game and not wanting any part of it.

"I've never used it before."

"Then why start now?"

"I like trying new things. Don't you?" He looked at her with a winsome smile. It was charming but when she thought of the multitude of silly girls who had probably already fallen for it, it became repulsive. She sighed listlessly and began pointing at the machine.

"Fine. You put your elbows there, you put your knees there, you do one foot at a time and raise them till you feel it in your butt. Got it?"

Alex had been hoping for a more intimate instruction. "Yeah, I think so."

"Good." She was about to put on her headphones when he extended his hand.

"I'm Alex by the way."

She debated a moment before taking it. "Zawe."

"Zah-weh," he repeated. "That's a beautiful name," and he had heard it before or something quite similar. "It's Ugandan, I'm thinking."

"It is." She was impressed but didn't show it. Actually the fact that he knew reinforced her opinion of him—Player.

"Are you?"

"No. My father just liked the name."

"So, just an all American Girl."

"Who would really like to get back to her work-out. So, if you don't mind."

"Oh, no problem, and thank you."

"You're welcome."

She walked away and he let her go without pressing the issue. That was never his style. Also it was apparent her disinterest was disingenuous. Deep down he knew she wanted him. He saw it from across the room. She had given an invitation she couldn't take back—and she would come back to the gym and they would speak again, and eventually go out, and inevitably (sometime this week) he would look deep into her eyes as she orgasmed with her ankles wrapped around his neck.

12

Coming home from the gym Zawe climbed the steps of her Brooklyn brownstone. She had always loved brownstones and it had been a long held desire to own one. Now that she did, regrettably, it wasn't all she had built it up to be. The house didn't quite feel like home. In all fairness to the house she had only just moved in a week ago. There were still roughly fifty boxes scattered about that needed unpacking, the furniture hadn't been properly arranged, and she hadn't quite gotten used to the loo, which was important because it was where she got naked and did her most private things. There was nothing wrong with the bathroom. It was lovely as the entire four bedroom house was lovely but it just wasn't hers yet and it would take a good deal of work to get it there.

Most of this work she'd have the pleasure of doing alone. When she first saw this listing seven months ago buying this house by herself was so far from the plan. But as her Mother always said, 'Man plans and God plans and God was the best of planners.' Zawe never cared much for her Mother's maxims but that one always stuck with her. So was this God's plan, for her to be alone, like so many other women she knew? If she were to take a poll she'd wager sixty percent of her friends were either single or dating in non-committed relationships.

It seemed this was the generation of single women, single Black Women especially. She had read the articles and seen the specials and had been thankful she wasn't part of the epidemic. Being single was nothing to be proud of and no matter what she might say to assuage herself no woman ever liked being a bachelorette. Now at the precipice of thirty Zawe was about to dive back into the dating pool and it was a filthy pool that people regularly pissed in it. The idea of dating again was as appealing as a urinary tract infection. As Zawe entered the foyer and closed the door behind her she felt her cell phone vibrating. She reached into her bag and pulled it out. "Hey Emma."

"Hey Girl, how was the new gym?"

"Filled with a bunch of men who act like they've never seen a woman."

"Sounds great. I need to start going with you. Any hotties?"

Involuntarily Zawe thought about Alex. "I couldn't tell, wasn't paying attention, that's not why I went." Now that he was in her head she was having a hard time pushing him out. Why? He was good looking, she would admit that. However, there were other good looking men at the gym. They hadn't done anything for her. So why did Alex stand out? Why did she turn and look at him from across the room. There was a certain relaxed easy going way about him. Players are like that. Players are like one hit wonders. They're catchy and they're addictive and if you're not careful you'll end up drunk, table dancing the Macarena during spring break—not a good look. *God, I can't believe I ever did that.*

"Well maybe we'll see some hotties tonight. You are still coming right?" Emma asked.

"Ahhhh, Em, I don't know, I'm kind of—"

"Bitch you're not standing me up again. You're going even if I have to come over there and drag you out by your fucking hair."

"Okay, take it easy. I'll go."

13

"So I'm getting a divorce ya'll."

There were a few 'awwwws' in the crowd—mock sympathy. The audience was mixed but mostly African American as the comedy at the Laughing Stock was mostly geared towards them. White Comedians came through every now and again but for the most part this was a Black club and the preeminent in the city. Ian was on stage doing his stand-up.

"Yeah, it's sad. And the hardest part is that we have kids. And you know kids always take it especially hard because they don't know whose fault it is. And as parents you have to handle this right otherwise the kid could be confused. So my eldest comes to me, and he's nine, and he's near crying, and he says, (in a whiny child's voice) 'Daddy why you and Mommy breaking up, is it because of me?' And it almost broke my heart to see him like this. So I took him in my arms I looked at him directly and I said Son . . . yes it's your fault." The audience guffawed; some playfully aghast.

"The truth is things have never been the same between me and your Mama since you came. I mean everything between me and your Mom was beautiful before you came. We used to do it everywhere, on the living room floor, on the dining room table, over the kitchen sink, once did a 69 in the tub, damn near drowned. We even did it on the toilet—while I was taking a shit. And we was so crazy in love the stink didn't bother us. That's how good shit was before you got here. Once you got here all that changed. Couldn't touch the titties anymore, because the titties had milk and the milk was for the baby. Couldn't have sex all over the house anymore because you might see us. Could hardly have sex in the bedroom anymore, because you had to be a little bitch, talking about there's monsters in your closet so you had to sleep with us. And the truth is son that pussy has never been the same since you came. I mean that pussy used to be mine. It used to fit my dick perfect—tight. But after your big ass head came out it was a wrap. Lord knows I don't know how you got a head that big, because damn sure nobody else in my family got a head that big. Sometimes I look at you and I have to wonder if you really mine with a head that goddamn big. But all that being said, I want you to know that both Mommy and Daddy love you very much, and we gon' get through this as a family, okay. I love you. Hey I'm Ian Washington and that's my time ya'll, thank you."

14

Alex sat at a table by himself in the dark of the room. Ian's set had gone well. Even after a minute the audience was still applauding. Comedy is a funny thing. It can sound funny to you when you write it, even funnier reading it to yourself, but until you put it on stage and try to sell it to a crowd you'll never know if you're peddling pyrite or gold.

As he left the stage Ian was congratulated by members of the audience and his fellow comedians. Though he wrote the bit Alex wouldn't get any of the credit and neither did he want it. Comedians he believed were the closest thing to modern day philosophers. They posed questions and pointed out the ridiculousness of the world. Alex liked that. He liked showing people their own bullshit and having them laugh at it. For him this was like a social experiment and seeing the reaction from the audience was satisfaction in and of itself.

But this wasn't an experiment for Ian, this was life; a life lived in pursuit of a dream, a dream simultaneously within reach and out of grasp. He kept on reaching; he couldn't help reaching. He had been reaching for so long he didn't know how to do anything else—wasn't capable of doing anything else—and every once in a while his fingertips grazed the handle.

Troy Dixon, the owner of the club, came up to him and shook his hand. "Loved the set," he said. "Been really feeling the new material you've been doing. How about doing a regular on Friday nights?" Ian's broad smile was his reply and he held the owner's hand as if he was holding onto that dream itself. He spotted Alex sitting on the other side of the room and gave him a heads up that said hello and thank you all at once.

Alex understood and was nodding back when something, or rather someone, behind Ian caught his eye. It was the woman from the gym—the elegant one. What was her name again . . . Zawe . . . yes. All dressed up with her hair down she looked even more beautiful now. He had planned on running into her at the gym again, and if that didn't happen, he would bribe one of the workers to give him her cell number, input it into the GPS Locator app on his phone and then bump into her on the street one day and pretend it had all been inadvertent. He had never done that before and until he met her had never considered it, now he wouldn't have to. Seeing Zawe here was nothing short of fortuitous. After thinking he might be losing interest in women she did something very special for him. She gave him hope.

15

Besides work this was Zawe's first time going out in the last six months, and left on her own, her sabbatical probably would have extended to a year. She'd so much rather be home watching an episode of the Real Housewives of . . . whatever . . . and putting her house together right now. She came because Emma just about dragged her out and it would have taken more energy to argue with Emma than to go, so she conceded. Emma had been trying to get Zawe to go out since the break-up. She chose the Laughing Stock because Zawe made it abundantly clear she wouldn't go to any kind of club, lounge or bar. Emma was hoping comedy could keep Zawe's mind off the elephant in the room.

"Gavin called," Zawe said.

Or maybe not.

"Really?"

"Hmm-mm. He's been calling in fact."

"And how has that been?"

"You'd have to ask my voicemail, I never speak to him."

"And what's he been saying to your voicemail?"

"The same shit. He's sorry. He never meant to hurt me. It didn't mean anything, which really pisses me off. Because if it didn't mean anything why did you do it? Why would you throw away what we had because of it? What we had couldn't have meant that much then now could it?" Emma listened as she had been listening for months, however, after hearing the same thing again and again it had a habit of becoming redundant. Zawe stopped talking but Emma couldn't think of anything to say that wasn't something she had already said so she was silent. "What?"

"I didn't say anything," Emma replied.

"Exactly. You don't agree?"

"Zawe, you know I love you but, honestly, I think either you should give Gavin another chance—"

"Give him another chance, after what he did? Are you kidding me?"

"Or completely move on to someone else. You know what they say, 'the best way to get over one man is to get under another one'"

"Is that what 'they' say?"

"Yep—and believe me they know what they're talking about."

"Well, I'm not 'they.' And I'm so not ready for another relationship."

"Hey, I'm not telling you to get into another relationship, but a miscellaneous ménage a trois never hurt anyone."

"Menage a trois? Seriously? What, I just went from celibate to freak in zero to sixty?" Emma smiled. "And who am I having this threesome with?" Zawe looked at her and Emma just kept smiling. "I knew it, I knew it, you wanna fuck me don't you?"

"What?" Emma coughed up her drink. "Whatever. I don't even go that way. And if I did, you would be so lucky, okay."

"Okay. Ohhh—shit."

Zawe hadn't been able to get him out of her head all day—not that she had wanted him there. He was like a fleck of dust that had gotten under an eyelid and no matter what you do you can't get it out. You don't always feel it but periodically it pops up and annoys the hell out of you, and when you try to rub it, all you do is leave yourself with a red eye, which was kind of how she looked as Alex approached their table. Emma looked up and saw him; six feet tall, lean built, well-dressed and every woman's favorite shade of brown.

"Well hello," she said.

"Hello," he said to Emma, surveying her discretely; tawny complexioned with dark orange hair, which she wore naturally like an afro mop, which he liked, though overall he found her uninspiring. Emma was pretty—and fuckable, very fuckable—but she wasn't special. You noticed her but you weren't wowed by her. She was like a meal prepared from a cookbook. All of the ingredients were there in the right proportions but there was something missing that made the meal sing. Zawe had that something.

"Are you following me?" he asked her.

"Um, I was just about to ask you the same thing."

"Maybe it's just a coincidence," he said.

"I'm not a big believer in coincidences," she said.

"Well my boy was the last comic up, what's your excuse?"

"We just like comedy. And your friend was funny by the way."

"Thank you. I'll be sure to tell him that."

"And speaking of friends," Emma interjected feeling a bit left out and talked over.

"Oh—um . . ." Zawe stumbled having forgotten his name—or had she?

He smiled wryly feeling her forgetfulness was dubious. "Alex."

"Yeah, Alex. This is Emma."

Alex turned to Emma. "It's a pleasure to meet you."

"Likewise." Obviously Alex and Zawe already knew each other and Zawe had willfully neglected to tell Emma about him. Emma was curious why. "So how do you two know each other?"

He smiled again.

All of this damn smiling. Zawe imagined some women might find him disarming—saccharine was her impression. *He thinks he's such hot shit.* "Zee here is my new personal trainer," he said.

"Really? Zee. And here I thought you didn't meet anyone at the gym."

"I didn't. He needed help with a machine and I . . . I'll tell you later."

"What are you guys having? I'll get you another round."

Emma was game but,

"That's okay we can get our own drinks," Zawe declared for the both of them.

"Yeah but it's so much nicer when someone else offers," Emma said.

"What are you talking about? I'm always offering to buy your drinks."

"I meant someone with Y chromosomes. And thanks for telling him I'm a broke bitch."

"Oh my God, I did no such thing. In fact you just did that."

"Honestly, it's my pleasure." Alex said and signaled to the Waiter.

"Honestly, Alex, we're fine. And this is kind of like a Girls' night out."

"Oh. Sorry. Didn't mean to intrude. Well you Ladies have a good night."

Alex gave a nod to Emma and then walked away.

Emma watched him leave and the eyes of the other women in the club who were watching him as well. "What's wrong with you?" she said to Zawe. "He's the one decent man in here and he's fine as fuck and you run him off."

"He's alright," Zawe said and Emma gave her a look as if

to say, are you kidding me. "He's alright. And he's obviously a Player, and I don't have time for that right now."

"Well I do. Could you have let me decide that for myself?"

"Do you wanna call him back? Go ahead."

"Don't have to, I'm right here." A voice came from behind and gave Zawe a start.

"What the hell?" she remarked and turned around to find two men, Dexter and Ron, standing behind her. They both looked to be in their mid-thirties, but she could only imagine thought they were twenty years younger, as they had fro-hawks and wore skinny jeans that sat well below their waist; a look she found distasteful on teenage boys but on grown men was downright disgusting.

"So you ready to go?" Dexter asked.

"Excuse me? Go where?"

Dexter casually placed his car keys on the table. "Your place or mine, whichever works for you?" He then looked down expecting Zawe to do the same. She didn't. She could've cared less.

"Oh, you just gon' forget all about hello and get right to it, huh?" she said.

"I figure when we both know what we want why waste time with words, you know what I'm saying?"

"Hmm, actually no I don't."

"You're beautiful, you know that?" Zawe shook her head at how pathetic his game was. It wasn't so much the words as it was the delivery and the messenger. "No for real you're beautiful. Baddest chick in here." He looked at Emma. "No offense."

"None taken," Emma said with a mocking smile.

"Do you wanna get outta here?" Zawe asked her. "I've had enough comedy for tonight."

"I hear you."

They got up from the table and started walking away leaving Dexter feeling a bit dismissed. "Look at you, you don't even know what you're walking away from," he said.

"Actually I think I do," Zawe said and continued walking.

Dexter turned to Ron. "See, she don't know, she don't know. Stuck up Bitch."

Zawe heard him and debated for a moment responding but decided better of it. That was exactly what he wanted and he wasn't worth the spit it would take to curse him out. She and Emma continued walking and left the club, and from across the room by the bar Alex watched them leave.

16

Zawe and Emma walked down the lower east side avenue to the parking lot at the end of the block. It was a cool night but Zawe was hot inside. Dexter had really pissed her off. She was even angrier at herself for allowing him to piss her off. Where did he get off calling her, "a stuck up Bitch? Can you believe that?"

"Yeah I can believe it."

"Why can they never just accept no? I mean what the hell? And did you see his pants? I swear they were freakin tighter than mine."

"Don't even waste your breath. And really he wasn't even that bad." Zawe gave her a look. "I'm for real, he wasn't—" Emma continued when they heard someone calling them.

"Hey . . . Hey."

They turned to their right. A silver Mercedes Benz S500 had pulled up. Dexter sat in the passenger seat with his head stuck out the window and his friend Ron drove.

"S500. Have fun on the train Bitch," Dexter shouted, flipped them the bird then, as quickly as they had appeared, drove off.

Gobsmacked Zawe turned and looked at Emma. "Okay, maybe I was wrong."

17

The S500 Benz pulled up to a stoplight. Dexter and Ron were feeling pretty high on themselves after what they did.

"I bet them hoes feeling real stupid right now getting on that train," Dexter said while rolling a joint.

"That's cause they don't know real ballers when they see 'em."

"You know what I'm saying?" Dexter licked the tip, put it to his mouth and was about to light it, "Stupid ass trick gon' try an play—" when he heard someone calling him.

"Hey . . . hey."

Dexter and Ron turned to their right. A beautiful amber S55 AMG Benz (a 50,000 dollar upgrade to the S500) had pulled up beside them. Emma rode shotgun and Zawe drove. Emma stuck her head out the window.

"S55, AMG, get your game up Bitch."

The light changed and Zawe peeled off leaving Ron and Dexter looking,

"You are so stupid," Zawe said to Emma two blocks down, holding in her laughter.

"Did you see his face? Tell me you did not just love that?" Zawe couldn't help it. She broke out laughing. This was one of the reasons Zawe loved Emma. She said and did the things Zawe wanted to but never would. "Oh my God. This car is the shit," Emma shouted as they drove off, the radio blasting Beyonce's Run the World (Girls).

18

Thirty-five minutes later:

"This car is a piece of shit."

"Hey don't call my car that."

"I'm sorry but what the hell happened?"

"I don't know. It just shut off on me and now it won't start."

Zawe threw her head back in frustration after trying the ignition for the umpteenth time. She couldn't understand what was going on. This car was only four months old. She had never had any problems with it before. Everything had been going fine. They had left Manhattan and had just crossed the Brooklyn Bridge when they came to a red light. When the light turned green she tried to accelerate but the car was incredibly sluggish, unable to go beyond twenty miles per hour. It went like that for another two blocks before shutting down on the side of the road on Front Street, roughly ten blocks from her house. That had been seven minutes ago.

"This is not even cute," Emma said.

"I'll call Triple A—and you can get out and walk, see how cute that looks." Zawe was frustrated enough as is, having Emma nagging in her ear only made matters worse.

"Hey don't get mad with me because you bought a brand new jalopy."

"Emma, I swear right now I'm not in the mood." This was one of the things Zawe disliked about Emma. Sometimes she didn't know when to stop.

Just then a car pulled up beside them—a black Audi R8. It was Alex. "You guys need any help?" he asked.

"Hey—yes we do," Emma said equally surprised and happy to see him.

Having run into Alex for what would be the third time in less than twenty-four hours Zawe was decidedly less so. "What the hell? Are you really serious? Are you following us?"

"I don't know, but meeting up three times in one day it's beginning to look that way isn't it?"

"Yes it is."

"No, I'm not. I live in Dumbo. The fact that you're on this road I'm guessing you do too. We just happen to be going in the same direction." This was the truth. He had never stalked a woman before and if he did, he wouldn't have done it this way. It was a little too obvious. Granted after meeting her at the local gym he had surmised she more than likely lived in the area, and given he ran into her again at the club he could wager they'd be taking the same path home. However, he left the club ten minutes after they had and couldn't have planned on her car shutting down. It was simply a coincidence. Still this seemed a little more than serendipity. Perhaps it was fate.

"Hey, we're stuck. Do you think you could help us?" Emma asked.

"Do you want me to help you?" Alex asked Zawe directly.

Zawe looked unsure. She didn't want to trust him before because she knew he was a Player. Running into him now at the side of the road made him doubly dubious—like a stalker dubious. Still he didn't look like a stalker. Then again what do stalkers look like? Would anyone have suspected the guy from American Psycho was . . . well a psycho? While Zawe ruminated Emma answered for her. "Yes, we do." Zawe turned and looked at her sharply. "What? You're not the only one in the car and I'm tired and I wanna go home."

"Fine," Zawe conceded with an exhaustive sigh.

Alex thought to himself, this Girl is too much. She even made helping her appear as if she was doing you a favor. Alex drove a few yards ahead and parked. He then got out and walked back to Zawe's car. Emma had already gotten out and Zawe was about to but he stopped her and told her to pop the hood. She did as instructed then met Alex and Emma at the front. "It's a new car. I can't imagine what the problem could be." Zawe said.

After taking a cursory look at the engine Alex said, "It's nothing. The computer probably just shut down on you, more than likely it's a faulty relay."

"How do you know that?" Zawe asked.

"I had this car about six months ago."

"Six months? What's wrong with it, why did you change it?" Emma asked.

"Nothing, it's a great car. I just get," Alex leaned over and unplugged the battery, "bored quickly. Okay, I just disconnected the battery. I'll give it ten minutes then reconnect it and every-thing should be fine."

"Thank you so much. We really appreciate it," Emma said.

"No problem."

"Yes thank you. And you know you could just show us how to reconnect the battery and then you could go, if you want." Zawe said.

"Zawe?"

"What? It's late and we don't wanna keep him if we don't have to."

"You know you're right. I don't like being kept. Come on let me show you." He directed Zawe to dip her head under the hood and pointed out the battery. "You connect these two plugs right here and right here and that's it."

"Okay got it."

As they were raising their heads their eyes met. There was an invasive quality to his gaze. Like an x-ray operator she felt as if he could see right through her, pass the skin and sinew and down to the bone. Feeling as if she had lost her bra, she recovered herself and came from under the hood and he did the same.

Emma noticed the moment between them. She also recog-nized that if Alex were to make a choice, he would choose Zawe, as most men tended to do, however, this time she wouldn't begrudge her best friend, as Emma was beginning to believe a tryst with Alex maybe just what Zawe needed to get over her break up with Gavin. "Thanks again," she said to Alex.

"No problem. And you guys get home safe." Alex began walking back to his car.

"Hey, maybe you guys will run into each other again," Emma called after him.

"It's possible, we go to the same gym, and I'm always there in the mornings. Good night."

He got in his car and drove off.

"You are so stupid." Emma said to Zawe after he had left.

"No, I'm not. Believe me that man is trouble."

19

It was almost two in the morning when they got to Zawe's house. Given the hour they decided Emma would spend the night. The guest rooms hadn't been made up so Emma took the sofa downstairs. Zawe changed into her pajamas and slid under the covers. It had been six months still she hadn't gotten used to sleeping alone. A bed feels extra empty when you go back to sleeping alone. The dark is more haunting, the night sounds more foreboding, the pillows only smell like you and when you're used to the scent of someone else, enveloping you almost like an extra blanket, it made falling asleep all the more difficult.

She kept seeing Alex's face under the hood of the car and the look he gave her. It was a knowing look. As if he already knew something she didn't. What did he know? That she was attracted to him. Yes. He would be handsome if he wasn't so damn sure of himself. When a man approaches a woman for the first time that slight sense of awkwardness and vulnerability he has as he tries to put his words together can be very endearing. It showed that talking to you meant something to him and he'd risk embarrassment to do so. Alex didn't have that. He was just so disgustingly calm as if everything was a great plan and he had already read the blueprint. He was so full of it. Then again maybe he had because why was she still thinking about him.

20

It was 7:33. She had gotten up at six am to use the bathroom and hadn't been able to go back to sleep since. When you don't get to do it on weekdays sleeping in was one of the benefits of a Sunday morning. This was one of the reasons she disliked going out and coming in late. It did havoc to her circadian rhythm.

It was no use. She wasn't going back to sleep, not now anyway. So what should she do? Continuing to lay here looking up at the abstract patterns in the stucco ceiling seemed pointless and wasteful. This could, however, be a good time to get in a workout. Despite some of the ogling men, which honestly happened at every gym, she did like the new gym and the range of equipment and classes it had. Also finding time to work out during the week would be difficult. Yeah that was a plan. She should go to the gym—but wait—he might be there. Didn't he say he worked out in the mornings? Yes he did. But so what if he was there? It was a small world but a fairly large gym. If he was there she more than likely wouldn't run into him, and if she did who said she had to talk to him? Who said she wanted to?

21

Zawe sat alone on an exercise mat with her legs extended doing her stretches. She didn't bother trying to wake Emma and ask her to come along. She was fast asleep and Zawe had learned from experience Emma was prone to violence when roused prematurely. She tried to do that years ago and Emma gave her a back hand and a black eye for her efforts. Also it was better this way. Emma would have been a distraction. Every time she had gone to the gym with her, Emma always spent more time looking at men and talking than actually working out.

Now what would Zawe do today? She had worked on her legs yesterday so maybe today she'd do some light weight training. Zawe was planning out her routine in her mind when she caught a glimpse of Alex, about fifteen yards away, entering the gym. *So he did come every morning.* He walked with his head down while texting on his phone.

Shit. Zawe just realized he would have to pass her to get to the Men's Locker Room. If she kept her head down and he kept on texting maybe he would walk right by and wouldn't see her. But that was silly. Was she going to keep her head down for the entire time? By doing that she'd be allowing him to control her without even trying. She raised her head and stretched her neck just as he put away his phone. He looked genuinely surprised to see her. "Hello again," he said and she said . . . nothing. Why didn't she say anything? She didn't mean to be rude or cute. It was sort of a mental lapse. "Hey I swear I didn't plan this."

"I didn't say anything." And now she was being cute; perhaps too cute.

"Okay, well, have a good workout," he said and walked away. She was a bit surprised. She had expected him to say more, to flirt more, to do—she didn't know what exactly, and now she felt a little silly, catching herself watching him walk away and enter the locker room. "What are you doing?" she thought out loud.

An hour later Zawe finished her workout and walked to the exit happy she came. She had done a half hour on the treadmill, some upper body weight lifting and had finished off with some lower abdominal work. It was great and other than glimpsing Alex occasionally as he did his own workout the fact that he was there was completely irrelevant. For the most part she had forgotten about him until, "Have you eaten yet?" someone called to her from behind. She turned around and saw Alex behind her ready to leave as well.

"Excuse me," she said.

"Breakfast, did you have it before you came here?"

"I never eat before I work out."

"Me either. That's why I'm always hungry afterwards. Do you wanna get something?"

22

She agreed and it didn't take a lot of coaxing. He simply asked, she thought about it for a second and then said, "Okay." He told her about a diner six blocks away and they agreed to take their separate cars and meet there.

It was a fairly nice diner, owned by White people, patronized mostly by old people and staffed almost entirely by Mexicans. For the both of them it was their first time being here. Alex chose it because it was close by and he figured once you'd been to one diner you had basically been to them all. They sat across from each other at a booth by the window. The Waiter took their orders and left with their menus. Now what happened next? They hadn't said a word to each other since they agreed to come here. Was he waiting for her to say something first because if he was he would be waiting a long time?

"So what made you come to the gym today?" he asked ending the stalemate.

That was a weird question. "Because I felt like working out. And? What made you come?"

"Like I said, I always work out in the mornings."

"Even on weekdays? Doesn't that interfere with getting to work?"

"No," he replied flatly.

"I guess you don't have a regular nine to five? What do you do?"

"Why do people always ask that? I thought we were here to get to know each other."

"Is that what we're doing? I thought we were just having breakfast."

"If that's all you thought, then why did you ask?"

"Ummmm—well if we were doing more than that then why won't you answer?"

"Because I don't equate what we do with who we are, and who you are is what I'm trying to find out."

"Well I do, sort of, and the fact that you're dodging the question is kind of—dodgy."

"Okay, fine, but you first. What do you do?"

"I'm a CPA," she answered forthrightly.

"That's a nice, stable, well earning profession. Your parents must be proud."

"It is and they are. Now back to you, what do you do?" The fact that he was being so mysterious was very shady. Then again what did it even matter? After today she more than likely would never go out with him again. But was that what they were doing—going out? Was this a date?

"I'm happily unemployed," he answered and confirmed everything she needed to know about him.

"Okay. I'm beginning to see this was a mistake. Could you tell the Waiter to cancel my order," she said and readied herself to leave. But why was she leaving? Why did it matter to her that he was unemployed?

"Why are you fighting it so hard?" he asked.

"Excuse me? Fighting what?"

"Your attraction."

This got her attention and she eased back into her seat. "Woooow—you are arrogant."

"No I'm not. Why is it arrogance to state the obvious? We're attracted to each other. I'm willing to admit it, why are you denying it?"

"I'm not denying anything. I'm not attracted to you."

"So you just got up early on a Sunday and went to the gym knowing I'd be there because . . ."

The unmitigated gall of this man. "Is that what you think? I went to the gym this morning because that's when I felt like working out."

"And it never occurred to you that I might be there?"

"I could have given two shits if you were there. But from now on I'll make certain to avoid that time." He was really beginning to annoy her. He laughed, and now he was mocking her as well. "Okay, that's my cue to go."

"Alright, I'm sorry for laughing. I didn't mean to upset you."

"I'm not upset. You can't upset me." She felt the need to stress he had no power to manipulate her emotions.

"Oh I'm sure I could if I put my mind to it."

"So you're arrogant and obnoxious. And weren't you supposed to be some kind of Player, because you have like no game."

And there she may have revealed too much. "Who said that I was a Player?" Recognizing her gaffe she was silent. "And if I am a Player, wouldn't that mean I'd be trying to get you into bed right now?"

"Isn't that what you've been trying to do since yesterday?" she said, deciding to be done with the charade and have everything out in the open.

"I don't know, but obviously that's what you think, which makes you agreeing to have breakfast with me very telling, and a little hopeful."

"Oh please, don't flatter yourself."

"Alright, I'll flatter you instead."

"Don't do that either, believe me it won't get you anywhere."

"Actually everything I've gotten in this world I got through flattery."

"And where has that really gotten you—Mr. unemployed?"

"Here, having breakfast with a beautiful woman," *oh please,* "with the hope of taking her to bed," *oh hell no.*

"Well you can keep on hoping because that will never happen."

"Never say never," he said.

"Never," she reiterated emphatically.

"You wanna make a bet on that?"

"What?" she guffawed "No."

"Why not? Is it because you know you'll lose?"

"No, it's because it's a stupid bet and it's impossible for me to lose."

"Then make the bet."

This man was annoying beyond belief "This has to be the weirdest conversation I've ever had." Yet she couldn't get herself to just get up and leave. She had wanted to on two separate occasions yet still here she was. Somehow she believed if she left he would have gotten the better of her and she couldn't stand to have him think he had won some sort of victory. "How do you think you're going to win this bet?" she found herself asking.

"With you on top, screaming my name." She shook her head. Just when she thought he couldn't be any more obnoxious. "Or you could be on the bottom, and hell you could call someone else's name, it makes no difference to me."

"It makes no difference." That sounded a lot like 'it didn't mean anything,' which reminded her of Gavin and pissed her off even more. "Well if a place to stick your dick is all you're looking for I'm sure you can find a lot more willing receptacles."

"You're right. So then make the bet."

"Idiot, you can't win the bet. To win the bet you have to be around me, and I have no intention of seeing you again after today."

"Why not?"

"Because I don't particularly care for your company."

"Of course you do. If you didn't you wouldn't still be here."

There it was. He had seen right through her. She should have left already, however, to leave now would be completely reactionary as if she was doing it only because he had goaded her into doing so, as if it wasn't really her choice, and then he would have won. Then there was the issue of this bet. Of course it was a silly proposition and there was no way on earth he could win it, especially not after today. So then why not make a bet she was guaranteed to win. But what would she win?

"Just for the sake of argument, what would I even get for winning this bet? Money?" she asked.

"Wow, I've never heard of a man paying a woman for not having sex before. I don't think I want to start that precedent."

"Then what?"

"Something way more valuable."

"What?" Now she was intrigued.

"Honesty."

"What?" Now she was confused.

"You heard me."

"What the hell would I do with that?"

"Learn from it. Haven't there always been things about men you've wanted to know?"

"I already know everything I need to about men. You guys wanna fuck everything that walks."

"True enough. But it's a little more to it than that, and I think you know that as well." She was silent. He was right. There seemed an almost infinite amount of questions about men she didn't know. So many her mind was flooded trying to think up just one. These were questions that never truly bothered her before but after the breakup they had been the cause of many sleepless nights.

Men are never completely honest with women. This she learned the hard way. Even when she spoke to her brother, who she assumed had no reason to lie to her, she always got the sense he was weighing his words to make sure he said the right thing because he never wanted to appear diminished in her eyes. Of the little she knew of him she knew for certain that would not be a problem with Alex.

"And how would this even work? After you lose you start telling me everything I want to know?"

"Actually I'll start telling you everything you want right now."

"Really? So I've already won?"

"Sort of. The thing is we have to meet up for at least an hour every day for the duration of the bet."

That was an interesting element. How did he come up with all this so quickly? Had he done this before? "And how long is the bet for?" she asked.

"What do you think is fair?"

"Three months," she said.

She believed in the 90 day rule, meaning any man she dated had to wait at least 90 days before she even considered having sex with him, and if Alex could actually, miraculously, convince her to do so within 90 days then by all means he deserved to win.

Alex knew the rule as well and he knew it didn't apply to him. "You're too generous. I'll do it in one."

"One?" she was aghast. "You think I'm a slut?"

"Not at all. But I've never met a woman that it took me more than a week to get into bed. The other three weeks are just for you to get over your hang-ups about the bet."

He was so smug it was literally disgusting.

"Oh I'm so going to enjoy the look on your face when you lose."

"Not as much as I'll enjoy the look on yours when you come."

And so the bet was on.

23

Youth is beauty. All truly beautiful things are young. All young things are inherently beautiful. Youth is beauty in and of itself. Look at two men at the age of twenty, one average the other handsome. On the grounds of aesthetics alone at this age there is no comparison. Now keep the average man at twenty and age the handsome one to thirty. There is still no contest—handsome wins. At age forty, however, we begin to have a competition, and somewhere between forty-five and fifty average begins to take over. After fifty handsome would have to be exceptional to still be in the contest and by age sixty the race had been over a long time. At twenty even if you were hideous you would give an octogenarian a run for his money. Youth in and of itself is beauty. Ian believed that and that every second he aged was a second of beauty and youth he had lost.

Already he wasn't the man he was ten years ago. He looked at a picture of himself at age twenty-three. He was roughly the same; a bit less fat in the cheeks, and definitely the stomach, no lines by the nose and the jowls—but the eyes, the eyes were brighter. Those were the eyes of a man who had seen struggle but had a pervading hope in the future. Now he had the eyes of a man treading water deep at sea hoping to see the headlight of a boat. He looked at a picture of himself at sixteen and those eyes were the boat. They were brilliant. He was awestruck to look at them and almost ashamed. What a pale reflection he made. At sixteen he was beginning to tell jokes at thirty-three he was becoming one. Good thing he was still a comedian. There was no better comedy than self-deprecation.

24

He lived in a studio apartment in the basement of a brownstone in Bedford Stuyvesant, Brooklyn. It had wood paneled floors and in certain areas would scream bloody murder when stepped on. It had an old fashioned radiator that sounded like you were across from a construction site on cold winter nights and a toilet that ran for ten minutes after you flushed it. Beyond that it was adequate. It had adequate space for one man; adequate furniture, a queen sized bed, a futon, an entertainment unit with a forty inch flat screen and a desk with a computer. He sat by his desk and the only light was the light from his monitor. The rapper Souljah Boy's Booty Meat was playing and a fitting tribute to the song was on the screen.

It was a video clip of a Girl, who he imagined to be no older than nineteen though he couldn't be certain because he couldn't see her face, dancing in her underwear. It was something of a rage these days. Booty Dancing, or rather Twerking, was what they called it; young girls recording themselves dancing in varying degrees of undress and putting it on the internet.

Ian believed the internet was the greatest invention in human history if only for what it had done to revolutionize the distribution of porn. He remembered when he first started liking girls and how monumental and elusive a thing it was to see a naked woman. He remembered being in sixth grade and a friend of his brought a Playboy to school and how at lunch all the boys gathered round flipping through it. They all got a day in detention after a Teacher reported them—and it was worth it.

He remembered going into newsstands and having to sneak a glimpse of the magazines in the back, and if he was lucky the Arab working the counter would let him buy a copy, and hopefully there wouldn't be any women or girls in the store, because if there were they would look at him and whisper pervert under their breath.

These kids nowadays didn't know how lucky they had it. At any moment a naked woman was only a Google search and a mouse click away. He supposed he was lucky as well. How else would he be able to see this gorgeous creature dancing on his screen as if she was in his room performing just for him? "Ohh look at that. So firm, so perfectly round, and you're shaking it just for me, aren't you? Go ahead girl, shake it for Daddy."

Youth is beauty in and of itself.

His hand slid into his pants. The clip was ending and the Girl was finishing her dance. She had been dancing with her back to the camera, only now she began to motion as if she might turn around. "Oh, you're going to let me see you." Then she teased as if she might not. "Oh c'mon baby girl don't do me like that." But at the last second she did, "Yes, yes, come to—" and blew a kiss to the camera, and his pupils shrunk to dots.

25

Looking as if he got dressed in the dark, with his shirt buttoned out of order, Ian rushed up the steps of his basement apartment and got in his eleven year old Acura parked outside. As soon as he turned the ignition his feet hit the gas and the car sped off catching the beginning of a red light and almost causing an accident.

Thirty minutes later he screeched to a halt in front of a house in Jamaica, Queens. This neighborhood would be described as lower middle class but decent. It wasn't the projects. Your kids could feel relatively safe walking home from school and playing on the street but it certainly wasn't the suburbs. There weren't any drug dealers on this block but they were five blocks over and those five blocks made a difference.

Ian got out the car and hurried up the steps to the front door. He rang the bell three times in succession and when no one came after thirty seconds he started banging. A few seconds later the partial face of a nine year old girl peered through the curtain blocking the window. When Kyra saw that it was Ian she opened the door. "Hey—" she began but before she could say another word, Ian had entered, brushed by her and was on his way up the stairs to the second level. "Well hello to you too."

Ian approached a closed bedroom door and thought about knocking. Then he heard the Booty Meat song playing and an extra gear of anger came over him and he barged in. The music was too loud for them to notice he had entered the room, so Tyrone, a boy—no a man who looked to be in his early twenties— kept on videotaping and Tiana in her underwear with her back to the camera kept on dancing. "Yeah shake that ass, girl," Tyrone said. Ian became so incensed he rushed Tyrone and tackled him to the floor. "Yo, what the fuh—" Hearing the commotion Tiana stopped dancing and turned around.

"Oh my God."

Ian was on top of Tyrone trying to strangle him but Tyrone was the stronger of the two and he overpowered Ian, turned him around and got on top. "Yo, what the hell is wrong with you?" he shouted.

"I'm going to kill you," Ian strained to say. He tried to punch Tyrone but Tyrone blocked his blow and punched him. Tiana ran over and tried pulling Tyrone off.

"Tyrone, stop it. Get off of him."

Tyrone listened and backed off.

"Yo, what the hell is going on? Who the hell is this guy?"

Catching his breath, Ian propped himself on his elbow and looked directly at Tiana.

She was the same girl from the video clip.

"He's my Father."

26

Two hours later Ian sat with a black eye and his arms folded at the Kitchen table pissed as all hell. "So this is the type of shit you let go on around here?" he asked Lillian.

Lillian was Ian's ex-wife. Actually she was still his wife as they had not officially divorced. She was thirty-two but on occasion could be mistaken for forty. This was one of those times. She had just gotten home from work and was still wearing her scrubs. She worked as a Medical Assistant at the local Veteran's Affairs Hospital. After being on her feet for the better part of twelve hours the last thing she needed was to come home and deal with this.

"I told you I had no idea that this was going on," she said

while massaging her forehead. Suddenly the ache in her feet had just gone to her temples.

"You had no idea? You got a grown ass man up in your daughter's room shooting porn and you had no idea?"

"It wasn't porn," Tiana who also sat at the table said though no one paid attention.

"No I didn't, because I couldn't be here, because unlike some people I work for a living."

"What's that supposed to mean? What the hell do you think I do?"

"You tell jokes."

"You know what, I ain't gon' go there with you, not today. Not when this is clearly your fault."

"My fault?" Lillian's headache really began to throb. "And tell me why weren't you here to see what was going on?"

"What? Woman, I don't live here."

"And who's to blame for that?"

"Hold up—did I kick myself out?"

"No, but maybe if you were taking care of your responsibilities, I wouldn't have had to kick you out and you would have been here."

"You see Lilly, this is what I can't take with you. You always twist shit. Even when I don't do anything you turn shit around on me."

"Whatever, Ian. You never do anything."

"Whatever? Our daughter is shooting porn in your goddamn house and you're saying whatever."

"It wasn't porn," Tiana interjected.

"Tiana I think I know what I saw."

"Did you see me having sex?"

Ian had already seen too much and had almost done, *Oh God*, "Thank Jesus, no," he said.

"Exactly. It was just booty dancing. A lot of girls do it now, it's no big deal."

Ian was well aware of the twerking phenomenon, but it had always been the other man's sister, wife, auntie, cousin or even mother. Now it was his daughter, arguably the worst possible relation, and he didn't like it one bit. Seeing it had literally made him sick. His stomach churned and he could feel the buildup of saliva in his mouth, which was always a prelude to throwing up.

"You're dancing naked on the internet and it's no big deal," he said.

"No it's not. And how did you even know it was on the internet anyway?" Tiana asked.

There she had him stymied. "What?"

"Yes Ian, how did you know?" Lillian asked, fearing she already knew the answer.

Being a comedian made one adept at improvisation. "Alex—Alex saw it and he told me." That should work. Lillian knew Alex and how debauched he was. That was a credible answer.

Mmm-hmmm, Lillian hummed, sounding doubtful.

"And this is coming to an end right now. I don't care about the other girls, they're not my daughter."

"Yeah, whatever," Tiana said.

"Whatever. See, she gets that from you. And Tiana, you are not seeing that man again."

"What is this? You trying to play father all of a sudden. Nigga please."

Tiana got up from the table and started walking away. Her insult was directed at her father but it was an affront to both parents. He wanted to reprimand her but she was right. He hadn't been much of a father in the last five years so what could he do? She deserved a smack but she was too grown for that and surely it would only exacerbate matters.

"This is not finished get back here," Lillian said to her.

"I need to use the bathroom. Can I go?"

Neither Ian nor Lillian said anything and their silence was their acquiescence.

"You see that? This is all on you," Ian said after Tiana had left the room. "You disrespect me in front of them, so they have no respect for me. That's why this shit happened."

"Ian you disrespect yourself."

27

Alex and Ian sat at a table having drinks at a lounge in Soho. It was a trendy joint filled with attractive people, playing easy-listening hip-hop (more times than not something with Drake on it), set outside on the rooftop of a hotel. You could see the city all around you; all the buildings and the lights and the varying colors. It was beautiful but strangely lacking. Over ten years later and he still hadn't gotten used to looking up and not seeing it. There was like a perpetual vacuum in the sky. The Empire State Building looked so alone.

From time to time women would throw looks in their table's direction. Ian knew they were all for Alex, still every once in a while he'd like to believe that smile was meant for him. Alex was inspirational for all the wrong reasons. He made you want to live the life he lived. He made you believe if you just worked out a little more you too could sleep with a different beautiful woman every night. It was that kind of thinking that made Ian believe separating from his wife wouldn't be so bad that there was a whole world of free pussy out there just waiting to be had. There was only one problem. He wasn't Alex. The copper skinned Belizean three booths down boring a hole through Alex's skull as she looked right through Ian reminded him of that. Tonight, however, Alex wouldn't pay her any mind. He was here for his friend.

Ian had just told Alex everything that happened, and consequently if Lillian ever decided to do a little fact checking, Alex was supposed to cover for him, saying it was he who had first discovered the video clip and reported it to Ian. Alex was happy to do it. Lillian already believed he was a slut and if she thought he was into porn as well, which he was, there was no harm done. In this day and age most men would freely admit to watching pornography and those who wouldn't, watched it the most. But if all men watched porn and there were so many women (and the numbers were increasing daily) who were getting into porn and they all had fathers, the odds were there were more than a few Dads running into an unpleasant surprise.

"So what are you going to do?" Alex asked him.

"I don't know, but I gotta do something. I can't have my daughter going out like that." Frustrated Ian covered his eyes while rubbing his temples.

If you covered her eyes Tiana could be mistaken for a woman but she wasn't. Kids grow up so much faster these days but they matured just as slowly. She still needed a father. He hadn't been much of one since Lillian kicked him out and to be fair he hadn't been much better when he was living there. He had always been on the road performing in one city or the other, in small clubs and dive bars, places where they told you if they hadn't served enough drinks they couldn't afford to pay, and even if they did they'd still find some reason to stiff you, or pay you in checks that never cleared. When they did pay it was paltry—a couple hundred bucks here and there.

His highest achievement was a single appearance on BET's Comic View. That show fed him well for almost two years. The exposure led to a lot of bookings. He made the most money he ever made in his career during those two years. He used a bulk of that money to make the down payment on the house Lillian and the girls lived in. Ten years ago things were looking up. Then Lillian got pregnant again. That was another curveball he didn't see coming; compounded with his bookings drying up and losing his agent it gave him a concussion, which only recently seemed like it was beginning to clear.

"You know I've been getting a lot of traction with the new material we've been doing and I feel like a break is finally coming around," he said.

"I hope so," Alex said.

"I'm passed hope. I need it to . . . I need it to" he exhaled exhaustively. "But I'm tired of talking about this now. So what's up with this craziness you were telling me about this bet?"

"What about it?"

"You're really gonna tell this chick the truth . . . about everything?"

"Everything she asks, pretty much."

"You're going to give away all of our secrets, you can't do that."

The idea that women were essentially incapable of understanding how men really are was one of the first tenets of the Man Club. It wasn't written in a book or officially stated. It was more of an oral tradition that had been passed down through the generations whenever men sat around bloviating. Men made a habit of blanking out their women when they argued because they knew the more they spoke the more likely it was for them to accidentally spill one of these Man Club secrets. Now Alex was just going to give them away for free. But, "Don't worry about it. It won't make a difference," he said. "It's like telling a Christian, Jesus never existed. No matter what they won't believe you."

"What are you talking about, Jesus never existed?"

"You see. And plus I've never been completely honest with a woman before. I'm curious to see what happens."

"But why, when lying works so well? I mean, look around you, you can get a lot of other women with a lot less effort. What's so special about this chick?"

"That's the point. I'm getting bored with that. I need a challenge, something different. And it's not that she's special, it's just . . . sometimes it's fun to play with your food before you eat it."

"Yeah well, just make sure you don't choke."

28

"Why don't you just have sex with him and get it over with?" Emma asked as she and Zawe lifted the sofa.

"I don't wanna have sex with him," Zawe said as they put the sofa down.

Emma was helping Zawe put her house in order. They'd been unpacking boxes and arranging furniture all day. They had begun in Zawe's bedroom, then moved onto the kitchen and were now working on the living room. Things were coming around. All of the furniture was in place and there were only ten boxes left to unpack, which Zawe would take her time doing.

"So then why did you make the bet? You're just giving him the chance to be able to do it," Emma said exhaustively plopping herself down on the couch.

"No I'm not. I made the bet because he's arrogant and it's obvious he's used to other women just falling for him and I wanna show him that that'll never happen with me."

"Oookay, makes perfect sense."

"Also I already won the bet. He can't lie to me. Everything he tells me has to be the truth. So I'll get to know everything I've ever wanted to about men."

"But there's only one question you really want to know, right?"

Zawe smiled deviously.

29

It was the evening of the next day—day one of thirty. They sat opposing each other at a wooden table at a cafe in Dumbo. It was the kind of place that specialized in exotic teas, like peach-berry jasmine sutra green tea, and if you ordered something as simple as peppermint the Girl with the dragon tattoo behind the counter would look at you as if you were a right wing conservative. Alex could imagine her thinking, 'What? Do you believe in off shore drilling and getting rid of Planned Parenthood as well?' That's how she looked at Zawe who, coming from work in the city, looked like an ideal corporatist. Alex thought she looked sexy. He loved women in pants-suits and he loved the way hers fit her; well enough to show off her shape without distracting from her intelligence, and she thought she was so smart.

"Why do men cheat?" she asked as soon as they sat down, the steam still coming off her tea.

He smiled knowingly. "Ask me something else."

Zawe didn't appreciate his deflection. "No, that's what I wanna know."

"But you're not ready to hear the answer."

"You can't tell me what I'm ready for."

"Well then maybe I'm not ready to give it to you."

"Wait a minute, what is this? You promised you had to tell the truth no matter what I asked."

"Yes I did and I will. But I never said when I'd tell you."

"That's such bullshit."

"No it's not, we have a month what's the hurry? I thought women were into foreplay."

"Oh I see what this is. You won't answer that question because you know once you do I won't have any reason to continue this."

"Well you have to give me a fair shot at winning. Now ask me something else."

Zawe was disappointed in herself. She had been too obvious going in for the knockout on the first strike. She should have known he would have seen that coming. She needed to feint and work her jabs, then hit him with a right hook when least expected.

"Okay, why do men have such a hard time with commitment?"

She was pleased with that one. It was a subtle nevertheless aggressive move.

"That's kind of the same question isn't it, but I'll say this. The ones who have a hard time with commitment are the ones who have a hard time with cheating, because the ones who don't have a hard time with cheating don't give a fuck about commitment."

She looked nonplussed. "What the hell was that?"

"That was an answer."

"No it wasn't, it was a riddle. Is this your game? Is this how you're going to answer all the questions."

"I don't know, ask me something else and find out."

"Fine . . ." She exhaled through her nose. "Why do men leave the toilet seat up?"

"Are you for real? This really bothers ya'll to no end doesn't it?"

"Yes. Now answer the question."

"Okay. Because when we pee we do it standing and it's convenient."

"But why can't you just put it back down when you're done?"

"See this is the problem with women, you think everything should work to best suit you. Men have to pick the seat up before we use it why can't you put it down before you use it?"

"Because it's supposed to be down, leaving it up is just nasty."

"Only if you have a nasty toilet. And speaking of nasty why are ya'll always leaving big ole globs of toilet paper in the bowl? I swear you must use half a roll every time you pee because no matter how much you flush toilet paper is always bubbling back up."

She wanted to respond but had to bite her tongue. After all he was right. When she used to have guests over those were the ways she would tell if it was a man or a woman who had last used the bathroom. If the toilet seat had been left up it was a man and if there was excess paper floating in the bowl it was a woman. She always thought those globs of paper were nasty to look at as well—as long as they weren't hers of course.

"Hey I'm the one who's supposed to be asking questions," she said.

"Fine, ask another."

She thought for a good ten seconds before coming up with, "Why do you guys have such a hard time asking for directions?"

"What's with all these cliché questions?"

"Well you won't answer the real ones, so go ahead."

"I don't know, I don't care, I have a GPS." Fair enough she thought. Though it was something that annoyed her, given the prevalence of GPS's these days, she supposed it was an outdated question. She was going to let it go and ask another when he said, "But here's something for you to chew on. Men never have a problem asking for directions when they're driving alone." That struck her like stepping on a thumb tack barefoot, sending a sharp pain shooting to her brain's hippocampus.

Years ago Zawe and Gavin had flown down to Atlanta to attend her cousin's wedding. When they arrived Gavin decided they should rent a car for the weekend, though neither of them had ever been to Atlanta, had no idea how to get around Atlanta and she had family members there who were happy to take them wherever they needed to go. Gavin insisted on renting a car because being driven around made him feel like a child and they wouldn't be able to pick up and go whenever they wanted. She gave in because she hated having to wait on people as well. However, on the day of the wedding Zawe ran late (very unlike her) getting ready and the family member whose car they were supposed to follow to the Church left without them. What happened next was the worst two hours in a car she had ever experienced. She had forgotten the charger to her phone back in New York, her battery had died and her phone was the only one with her family's contact numbers. So all they had to go on was a small map printed on the back of the invitation. The map gave directions to the Church coming from three separate highways neither of which they knew nor knew how to get to. Gavin believed he knew how to get to one of the highways because it was the same one they took when they came from the airport. After a half hour it was readily apparent he had no idea where he was going but refused to ask for directions, believing they were better off figuring it out on their own. After an hour he gave in, but the first person Zawe asked gave her wrong directions, as did the second, which went to support Gavin's theory about not asking for directions. A heated argument ensued, which concluded with Gavin saying it was her fault why they were lost because she took too long getting ready and he didn't know why because it wasn't as if she was the one getting married. They drove around in silence after that. They finally did reach the Church but after the ceremony had ended. They followed the parade of cars to the reception and hardly spoke to each other for the rest of the trip.

"Listen, nothing matters more to a man than his manhood, and when he's with his woman he always has to prove it. Part of being a man is that you're strong and self-reliant. Now for some men to ask for directions is admitting he doesn't know something and he couldn't figure it out for himself, and then he more than likely has to ask another man for help, which makes him look weak."

"Are you kidding me? Are you freakin serious? That makes

him look weak? Well I think driving around aimlessly and getting lost because you don't wanna ask for simple directions makes you look stupid."

"Well for some men it's better to look stupid than to look weak. And you say all this now but you wouldn't want a man who wasn't able to do things for himself and figure things out on his own. And you're also missing the point. This is all for your benefit. He only looks weak because you're there watching him. He has no problem doing it when he's by himself."

"Looking weak in front of a woman means that much to a man?"

"Yes."

"Is that the same reason why you won't cry in front of us?"

"You don't want your man crying in front of you."

"Yes I do. I think it's so stupid you guys can't show your emotions."

"Yeah, and do you want us to squeal when we see rats and spiders as well?"

"That's taking it to the extreme."

"No it's not. Women always say you want your man to be more sensitive and open, and when he is, do you know what you tell him . . . that he's acting like a bitch."

30

After dinner, sushi take-out from the Japanese restaurant four blocks up, Zawe set about putting the rest of her living room together while some off-shoot of the Kardashians played on television. Zawe wasn't so much watching it as she just had it on to keep the house from being quiet and reminding her she was alone.

Emma had helped her put up the book shelf in the living room but it was still empty. Zawe had a large volume of encyclopedias her Uncle Benji had given her as a graduation gift after high school. They had never been opened. They were too heavy to take when she went away to school. Not to mention Cornell had rooms upon rooms of the stuff along with this new thing called the internet. Zawe always kept them, however, because they were beautifully bound and added a lot of character to whatever room they were in. She was putting a box of them away while speaking on the phone to Emma.

"So how did it go today?" Emma asked.

"Not very far. He won't answer the questions I really wanna know—not yet at least."

"He saw through you. He's smart."

"He sure likes to think he is."

"So what, are you gonna end the bet?"

As Zawe took the last encyclopedia out of the box she noticed something at the bottom. She picked it up and turned it over. It was a picture of her and Gavin. This was during year three when they had taken a cruise to the Caribbean. They were standing at the prow of the ship, off the coast of Nassau, the sun was setting behind them and one of the ship's photographers asked if he could take their picture. That was a wonderful trip. It seemed they made love the entire seven days. For some reason sex is always best on vacation. Seeing how happy they were then began to upset her. It was like watching a good movie that had a horrible ending. Everything that came before it was ruined and for what? She still didn't understand. But maybe Alex could help her with that.

"No . . . no," she said to Emma. "I have a month. I'll get them from him. Plus he is answering other questions, and it's kind of refreshing talking to a man and knowing he always has to tell you the truth. No, I'm gonna keep this going and I'm gonna bleed him for everything he knows." Zawe placed the photo back in the box face down.

31

The next day Zawe met Alex at the neighborhood smoothie and parfait shop. It was five blocks from the train station and she would have to walk twelve in the other direction to get home but she didn't mind. It was a beautiful evening; sixty-five degrees, and the sun was just beginning to set. She had come straight from work, admittedly excited to see him. Their meeting yesterday wasn't everything she had wanted but it was productive. He had cleared up an issue that had confounded her for so many years and she was hoping he could do it again.

Alex was excited to see her as well. It had been three days since they met and an hour hadn't gone by wherein he did not think of her at least once. Whenever he thought of women he thought of her and he thought of women often. He spent last night in the arms of another woman and thought of Zawe as he orgasmed. He woke up this morning with that antsy feeling in your diaphragm you get when you expect to have a good day.

She didn't wear a suit today, just slacks and a button-down shirt. The shirt was cut low enough to reveal a hint of cleavage while always remaining professional, and the pants were store bought but expertly cut, elucidating that arousingly cute ass of hers.

They sat at a table outside under a canopy. The sunset reflected on her skin: a tinge of orange on her bronze cheek, ochre in her brown eyes, a cherry highlight on her round nose and her lips were the color strawberry. He wondered which would taste better, the flesh or the fruit. Alex would prefer to relax and reflect on just being here with her. Zawe, however, got right to business.

"Okay now this always bothers me, why do men—"

"You look very nice today," he said.

"Um . . . thank you." She didn't like getting compliments from him. They felt cheap because she knew he gave them out so freely. "Now as I was saying, why do men—"

"Which is not to say you don't look good on other days, you do. You always look good. It's always sexy but sophisticated. I really like the way you carry yourself."

"Okay . . . thank you." He was trying to be charming and she wouldn't fall for it. She had business to get to. "Now again as I was trying to say, why do you—"

"You're wearing the new Dolce?" he asked inhaling the air.

"Yes," she said peeved at being interrupted yet again.

"It smells great on you."

"Doesn't it smell the same on everyone?"

"No, it doesn't," he said while looking intently in her eyes, which forced her to look intently into his. Like the tractor beam of a space ship he was trying to draw her in. Lesser women may have fallen for those engaging eyes, that disarming smile and kissable, very kissable lips (couldn't help wondering how they would taste, how they would feel between her teeth) but not her. She could see through his charade.

"I see what you're doing. You're avoiding the subject by trying to seduce me."

"Am I . . . seducing you?"

"No, I said trying to seduce, and not very well. You're so obvious." He laughed and his smile was golden and the image of them kissing reentered her thoughts. She quickly pushed the thought away and tried to get back on message.

"So what? Are you like not going to answer any of my questions today?"

"How about this? Every other day I answer your questions, and on the others we just talk."

"What? Hell no. That's not what we agreed on."

"Other than the bet we never really agreed to any particulars."

"But this whole getting to know you thing is not going to work," she said shaking her head vehemently.

"Your car is a stick shift isn't it?"

"Um, yeah—so? What does that have to do with anything?"

"I knew it. Stick shift drivers are all such control freaks. They always need to manipulate everything the car is doing just like they do in their own lives."

"Wait, are you calling me a control freak?" Alex didn't say anything. "Where do you get off? I am not a control freak."

"Okay, maybe you're not. I stand corrected. So then you can just let go and let things flow naturally?"

"Yes, I can."

"So then every other day we answer your questions works for you?"

She saw what he had done, how he had trapped her. If she refused she would prove him correct, and if she didn't he'd get what he wanted. Either way he would win. He was obviously a manipulator and a far better one than she was. He had planted a seed in her mind and it grew quickly until it was all she was thinking about.

32

Even as she got ready for bed it was still bothering her. "Do you know what he called me today?" she said to Emma during their nightly phone call. "A control freak; he called me a control. Can you believe that?" Emma didn't immediately answer. "You aren't saying anything? Why aren't you saying anything? What are you trying to say? You know what, to hell with both of you."

Emma eventually did speak and said she hadn't heard the

question because she had been distracted by something on television. She refuted Alex's claim but did say Zawe simply wanted things the way she wanted them but that didn't mean she was controlling.

Emma sounded more like she was equivocating than telling the truth. Still Zawe wouldn't press her to give the answer she wanted to hear. To try to argue Emma into believing she wasn't the type of person who always strived to have things the way she wanted would be to prove the contrary. And all of this wouldn't have bothered Zawe half as much if Gavin didn't used to tell her the same thing.

33

Tiana looked out her bedroom window at the black BMW M6 parked outside. Damn that was a beautiful car; an erotic car; it turned her on just looking at it. Cars are aphrodisiacs and people who think otherwise have only ridden in Hondas and Toyotas. Its shape was as sexy as a woman's body and you could see the entire world in its curvature.

She loved the way it smelled. She loved the way the leather felt on her skin. She loved the way the dashboard lit up, how the radio would always display whatever song was playing and who the artist was. She loved the way it felt inside when they were driving. It was always so smooth as if it hovered ever so slightly above the road. Her mother drove a ten year old Accord and that car made you feel every bump and pothole. In the M6 it was as if she felt nothing save for the thrust of its acceleration. It was like the thrust of a man going in and out of her. After she'd driven in the car once she had been spoiled. How could a boy her age talk to her when all he had to offer was a bus pass?

She remembered when Tyrone first pulled up to her, how the car gleamed in the summer night, how handsome he looked behind the wheel, which was not to say she fell for him because of his car but the car helped. She fell for him because of what the car represented. A man who could afford that car was a man of means, a man of purpose.

He was seven years older but that was okay. That wasn't too old. It wasn't as if he could be her father—and her Father, who was he? Some stand-up comedian who was always on the road and made so little her mother couldn't even bother suing him for child support. How could she tell her friends her father was a comedian that no one knew about? She preferred to tell them he had abandoned the family. That was a respectable excuse because it was such a common occurrence.

Tyrone was part of a gang and dealt drugs on the side. She knew this but so what? Who in this world making any kind of real money wasn't doing a bit of hustling? Look at Madoff, look at all those Wall Street bankers. That was real hustling. And as much as people bad mouthed them they were still doing what they were doing, making their money. Life was too short not to make money. She didn't want to become like her mother, straddled with two kids, a dead beat husband, working double shifts comparatively for pennies, with a bad back and corns on her feet. At sixteen she had no idea what she wanted to do with her life but Tiana knew she most assuredly didn't want to do that.

She was smart, at least she had been. She got good grades through grade school and the first two years of Junior High. Then at thirteen her ass began to develop and the attention from boys came with it. Then came the new friends, the other pretty girls the boys fawned over. Her breasts came along two years later and she became a trifecta—face, tits and ass—and if you got it why not flaunt it? Wasn't that what they always said? She had even heard her mother say that. And there were so many girls getting into it—dancing on the internet. It was becoming something of a competition. Who could get the most views and the most comments? And there was no shame in doing something if everyone was doing it. Well maybe not everyone, but enough so that you became something of a minor celebrity rather than a scandal. Yeah all the boys had seen you but that only made them want you more. Some of the girls called you slut behind your back but that was only because they were jealous. She had her looks and she had Tyrone and he had his car and they were both downstairs and he wanted to come up, but, "Things are kind of crazy here since what happened," she said over the phone. "I told you I don't really wanna do that . . . yes even if it's with a girl." There was a knock at her bedroom door. "Someone's at my door, I'll call you back . . . okay, I'll think about it." She hung up, walked over to the door and opened it. It was Ian.

"Hey Titi," he said.

"Hey. What do you want?" she replied listlessly annoyed.

"Nothing, just wanna talk for a bit."

"So . . . talk."

"Mind if I do it inside?"

"Fine."

She stepped aside and allowed him to enter. He didn't really know how to start and the way she was looking at him as if he was wasting her time didn't help matters.

"Look I know things have been hard these years without me being here."

"No, actually things have been fine."

"Tiana, things are not fine. What you're doing online is not fine, you seeing that man is not fine."

"Well it's fine for me."

"No it's not. Look, you think it's no big deal, but believe me, it maybe tomorrow, it maybe next week or even years from now, but eventually you're going to regret it."

"Well it's my life and if I'm gonna regret it let me regret it. Why do you care all of a sudden anyway?"

"Tiana I've always cared. I'm your father and I love you." She rolled her eyes. "I do. And as your father I can't allow you to see that man anymore."

"You can't allow me? That's real funny. You lost the right to tell me that a long time ago."

"Tiana—"

"And at least Tyrone is here. Where are you? Off doing your comedy. Well stay doing that, because honestly we're fine without you."

There wasn't much to say after that. How do you instill fatherly advice in someone who doesn't respect you as a father? He had lost her. She had aged from the girl he knew. If the little girl he knew were to grow up she'd look like her but she wasn't her. His Tiana had been bright and curious and a little cheeky but never outright disrespectful. This girl was patently impertinent and though she was still pretty her attitude made her quite unattractive. He couldn't talk to her. He left the room.

34

As he descended the stairs going to the first floor the per-vading thought in Ian's mind was, 'to hell with it.' If she didn't want to respect him as a father he could go right on and not acknowledge her as a daughter and she could continue whoring herself about. There was just so much a parent could do. Children are going to be their own adults.

He got downstairs and overheard Snooki and JWoww getting into a row. Kyra was watching the Jersey Shore in the living room but it was hard to tell if she was enjoying it as she just sat there silent and transfixed. There might be a joke in that he thought.

Seeing her put a smile on his face. He loved Kyra. Kyra was a product of good (well not altogether terrible) times. He wouldn't say she was planned but her pregnancy wasn't entirely unwanted. She came during the two years after he had been on Comic View. The world seemed so promising back then. When he looked at Kyra he was reminded of that promise. Then he saw Lillian standing at the doorway between the living room and the kitchen and was reminded of the present.

"Did you talk to her?" she asked.

"Yeah, I spoke to her."

"And?"

"And, she's like her Mother she doesn't listen to me." Ian turned to Kyra. "Kyra I'm leaving come give Daddy a hug." Kyra got off the sofa came to Ian and hugged him tightly. Though she only reached his pelvis it warmed his heart. "Thank you. You still love me right?"

"Yes."

"Good, at least I still have you. Alright go back and watch Jersey Shore." He let her go and looked up at the television as Snooki was cursing someone out at a night club. "That Snooki is crazy," he said forgetting for a moment his troubles with his elder daughter. Lillian must have read his mind as she looked at him admonishingly. "What?" he said.

"So you only have one daughter now?"

Ian walked over to the coat rack. "When did I say that?" he asked while putting on his jacket.

"I like your jacket by the way."

By the tone in her voice he knew she had already examined it and determined its market value. Lillian had a way of itemizing all of his possessions. "I got it from Alex, okay."

"I would hope so. I'd hope you didn't spend 3,000 dollars on a jacket when you have us here."

"Well I didn't. And look some things are in the works right now and pretty soon I'm gonna be able to help out a lot more around here."

"As opposed to the nothing you give now."

"Three hundred a month is not nothing."

"It's practically. And how is this different than all the other times things were in the works?"

"Why are you always so negative?"

"I'm just asking a question."

"Look, me and Alex have been working on some new material and I've—"

"Alex again," she huffed.

"Yes. And? What's the problem?"

"You're wearing his clothes Ian."

"It's Gucci, and he wore it like two times, and he offered it to me, otherwise he would have just given it away. I'd be an idiot not to take it."

"Or a man." That was a slap in the face. "And now he's writing your jokes. What is it, do you wanna fuck him or just be him?" And there went a knee to the groin.

A man's anger is a cocktail and his woman is his bartender. Lillian knew just the right balance of ingredients to mix together to truly piss him the fuck off.

But not this time.

He inhaled his rage and exhaled indifference—pained indifference.

"You know what, I'ma leave before this gets out of hand," he said and headed to the door.

"Yeah you do that," she said and closed the door behind him.

35

Time stands still for no man . . . unless of course he has a camera. Photography was a hobby of his. Then again since Alex didn't work everything he did could be considered a hobby. What he enjoyed most was the ability to steal time, to steal moments, natural moments, candid and unpretentious, with no red-eye correction. Nothing real ever happened when people knew they were on camera. Being on camera is like being on stage, and when people are on stage they tend to act, and when they don't know how to act, they tend to overact, which is why Alex had always felt Reality TV was such a farce. Reality can only be witnessed invisibly.

He caught a photo of a couple having a violent argument on the side of the street once. He called it True Love. He caught an extremely over weight woman sitting on a park bench reading a newspaper with the headline, Markets Brace For Double Dip Recession. He titled it Double Dip Obese. He had dozens of these captured images, all of them with these ironic labels. He went out with a woman once who worked at a Gallery who, between fellatios, swore she could get him an exhibition. He refused. He had no desire to have his work patronized or patronized. He didn't consider himself an artist. He didn't feel that self-important. He wasn't one of those people with dark rooms in their apartments either. Digital was perfectly fine with him. He took pictures for his own personal musings and whosoever he chose to share them with.

He was at Pier 1 of the Brooklyn Bridge Park. It was another one of the benefits of living in Dumbo. You had one of the best parks in the city as your backyard. He took pictures of the Brooklyn Bridge and the City behind it from the View Lawn. He captured images of the young children running around the playground, the exotic plants in the salt marsh, the people walking over the pedestrian bridge, and the women—oh yes the women. You look like a stalker if you go about taking pictures of women you don't know, unless you look like Alex and you're walking with a 6,000 dollar Nikon. The women who crossed his lens seemed more honored than suspicious. Most smiled pleasantly and kept on walking. Then there were those who were intrigued and came forward. They assumed he was a professional and he didn't see the need to correct them.

Alex asked Zawe to meet him by the bridge at six-thirty. She was happy he chose the park as a rendezvous. The park had been one of the selling points for buying the house and she had been meaning to go there. She hadn't yet because the park seemed to her to be a place for couples and families and going there by herself would remind her she was a part of neither. Now that she was here to meet Alex would that mean they were becoming a couple? *Ewww. Girl stop thinking so hard.*

She found him by the bridge, as he said he would be, talking to an attractive woman. They were flirting and right out in the open where he knew he and Zawe were supposed to meet. She didn't know why but she was a little peeved by this as well as feeling a tad disrespected. She contemplated walking away but decided to wait on the woman to leave before approaching. She wasn't able to do either, as Alex saw her and called to her with his eyes.

"So like I said I get to use you in my portfolio and you get a set of professional grade pictures," Alex said to the woman.

"Great. So when do we do the shoot?" she asked him.

"I'll call you," he said.

"You better," she said and walked away just as Zawe approached.

"Hey you."

"So you're a photographer now," Zawe said with a sardonic smile.

"It's one of my hobbies."

"Don't you mean hustles?"

"If you wanna call it that. How was your day?"

"Fine."

"Great. C'mon let's take a walk."

They strolled through the Harbor View Lawn. As the name suggested the harbor could be seen all around them. The sun had set and the park lights gave their walk a slightly romantic quality. Romance, however, was the furthest thing on Zawe's mind. She had questions to get to. "When men approach women on the street or at a bar or wherever, why do they act like such assholes when we turn them down?"

This was a question that had irked her for so many years

now, even more so after her run in with Dexter at the Comedy Club.

"For the same reason they use pick-up lines," Alex said.

"Okay." She looked at him to elaborate. "Why?"

"Because chatting up a woman you don't know is one of the hardest things for a man to do. Most men can't do it. A lot of men get panic attacks just thinking about it."

"For something that's so hard you guys seem to do it a lot."

"Because if you never put yourself out there you'll never get laid."

"And that's the most important thing, right?"

"No, but it is the most primal."

"But then why the fake lines, why can't you just be natural?"

"Because rejection is a bitch—and it's a bitch for everyone, women especially, which is why you guys so rarely initiate in any way shape or form. Men have to deal with rejection all the time and for some guys it's better to be rejected as a jerk than to open up and be yourself and then the rejection really hurts."

"Hmmm. I guess that makes sense. But still why are you cursing at me just because I turned you down?"

"Because if you're going to turn me down and make me feel stupid, I'm going to make you feel worse."

"That is so immature. Is that what you do?" she asked.

"No. But then again I don't know. I've never been rejected."

"You are so in love with yourself. Like you actually get every woman you talk to."

"I do, actually, for the simple reason that I don't approach women who don't want me to approach them. Every woman that I talk to has already invited me in with her words, her eyes or her body language. If she doesn't then I don't. That's why I never get rejected, and that's why I know we're going to have sex."

Her eyes opened wide when he said that.

"What are you trying to say that I invited you in?"

He simply looked at her.

"I did not. If I do recall I turned you down—three times."

"Yeah, and that's why we've been seeing each other every day for the last week."

36

Zawe worked at McAlpin Publishers. It was one of the seven major publishing houses in the country. It was amazing how they needed accountants in just about every field of business. People will always need someone else to count their money, her father said to her. Go into accounting and you'll always find work. Her official title was Senior Accounting Specialist (Payroll Analysis & Tax Reporting). Basically she oversaw the company's payroll and made sure all its taxes were in order. She liked what she did well enough. It wasn't sexy but it was more than sufficient. She never really looked at a job as being something that should be enjoyable. Fun is what you do on your own time. The main point of a job is that it is stable and well earning—and if it didn't make you want to slit your wrists when you got up in the morning all the better.

Alex would be in the city at around the time she would be getting off work so he suggested they meet at her job and then take the train back to Dumbo together. It was the only free time he would have as he'd be busy for the rest of the night. She agreed to take the train with him but wouldn't meet him at her job. She didn't want anyone she worked with seeing him and getting the wrong idea. She decided to meet him at a Starbucks an avenue and two blocks over.

Whenever she could help it Zawe always tried to get to wherever she was going early, at least by ten minutes. It was a habit her Father broke into her. He found the whole concept of Colored People's Time patently offensive. "Black People are already running a race with shackles on our feet," he would say. "How do we expect to compete at all if we start the race late as well?" She absolutely agreed. Also she felt being early gave her an upper hand. She was always in control and never harried and when dealing with Alex she'd take all the leverage she could get. She entered the cafe and looked around for a place to sit and wait. While scanning the room she spotted a man sitting at the counter by the window with his head down working on his tablet. Before recognizing him, her first thought was that he was handsome and well-dressed; the kind of guy she would go out with. Then he looked up and she saw it was Alex. A sickening feeling came over her as if she had just caught herself checking out her cousin. Alex smiled and she didn't want to smile back so she sort of scowled. He sort of laughed. She didn't like that. It was as if he could see through her again.

As always he complimented her on her appearance and as always she rolled her eyes. Before he put his tablet away she noticed it had been on the stock exchange. "Do you invest?" she asked him. "I gamble," he replied. He was being ambiguous and she decided not to pursue it further. She had only asked out of polite curiosity anyway.

They left Starbucks and headed toward the nearest subway station. As they walked she caught a glimpse of them in the reflection of a window display and had to admit if they were together they would have made a handsome couple. Apparently she wasn't the only one who thought so. People were looking at them, women especially—and they especially seemed to be looking at him—and he was looking back. He wasn't doing anything extravagant but he was flirting and right in front of her.

They were passing a newsstand and he asked her to stop for a moment as he wanted to buy a bottle of water. While he made his purchase she looked at the covers of some of the magazines on display. Her eye drew to the latest issue of KING. She didn't like KING and she never read it but she couldn't help looking at it. On the cover was a woman with a backside like a Buick wearing a bikini. *How disgusting.* And unfortunately this wasn't the only one. There were four other magazines, all geared towards Black Men, all showcasing some back-shot of a woman in a bikini, but the back was so big the bikini was barely visible. This was soft-core porn right next to Better Homes and Gardens.

"God I hate Black Men's Magazines," she said.

"Why? Do you prefer the White ones?" he asked as he paid for his water.

"I don't care for them either but at least their covers are classier."

Alex picked up a copy of MAXIM. There was a blonde with enormous boobs wearing a bikini on the cover. "Yeah, I can see the classiness," he said.

Zawe pointed to the cover of KING. "Well at least it's better than this. I'm so sick of it. I can't walk by a newsstand without being bombarded with big black ass all the time."

"What's wrong with that? You have a big black ass." She gave him a sour look. "You do, and it's beautiful."

She rolled her eyes and gave him a smile which was more like a grimace. "Thank you."

"You should be proud."

"Oh I am." They started walking again. "But that doesn't mean I want my ass to be my defining characteristic."

"You're right. I completely agree, it's not fair—I mean you have great tits as well."

With that she just had to smile. It was obvious his whole purpose was to get a rise out of her. Maybe it was a turn on for him. Gavin used to tell her she was her sexiest when she was angry. She turned and looked at him wondering if he might be looking at her now the way Gavin used to. He wasn't. He wasn't even looking at her at all.

Alex was looking at a woman who was walking by them. It had bothered her before but now it was beginning to really piss her off—given especially how this woman was now looking at Zawe, as if she was saying, 'you think you're hot shit but why is your man looking at me?' "Can you stop doing that," she said to him.

"Doing what?"

"Flirting or looking at every woman we come across. If your point was to show me that you can get other women, you've accomplished it, as if picking up skanks means anything."

"Wow, where's this coming from? Are you, are you jealous?"

"What? Are you insane? No."

"Okay, but we're not together, so then what's the problem?"

"No we're not together, but when we're walking like this to the rest of the world it appears as if we are, and when you look at other women it looks as if you're disrespecting me."

"But I'm not."

"But it looks that way and that's disrespectful, so can you stop."

"Okay."

"While we've been walking a lot of men have looked at me but do you see me pay them any mind?"

"You're right. I get it. You're all about appearances."

"You know what, forget it."

"No it's cool. But you know if you really want it to seem like we're together maybe we should kiss." She exhaled exasperatingly, walked away and descended into the subway station. "Can we at least hold hands?"

37

It had been a week into the bet. One whole week. Alex couldn't remember the last time he had seen a woman for a week and hadn't already slept with her, not to mention kissed her, touched her breasts, fingered her labia or even held her hand. He felt like he was sixteen again, like a virgin again— with her at least. He was still having sex (still had bills to pay) and in a manner he was having sex with Zawe as she was who he thought about when he was with his other women. When he touched them he imagined touching her. When he entered them he imagined it was Zawe's lips pulling on him ever so sweetly. When they came he imagined her face at crescendo; how her eyes would squint, how her legs would quiver, how sticky her juices would feel, or how wet. Could she be a squirter? This made the anticipation of sex with Zawe even sweeter and he would have sex with her. It was only a matter of time. So far he had been toying with her. She hadn't seen anything close to his real game. When he decided to fully turn it on he would have her. For now he was having too much fun simply talking. Who would have thought it? Still it was time to start raising the stakes in order to keep the game from getting stale.

"Hey you must live close by, how about we walk to your place?" he suggested as they stood outside the York street sub-way station.

"Very slick—no."

"Okay, I'm about ten blocks away, we'll walk to mine."

"Slick again. No."

"Zawe no one asked you to come upstairs. It's just a walk," he said and started without her.

She let out a harrumph but eventually followed. She figured he was up to something but it wouldn't make a difference. She knew for certain she wasn't going into his apartment no matter what he said, and by following him she would get to see where this mysterious unemployed man called home. As for now she had other questions that needed answering.

"Is it true that all men need to feel needed?" she asked him.

"Where did you get that from?"

"Read it in a magazine. It said that's the reason professional women have a hard time keeping a man because we make them feel like they're not needed."

"Sounds pretty needy."

"Yeah, it does. Soooo . . ."

"So it's not true—not exactly. What all men need is to feel powerful."

"Powerful?" That sounded intriguing. "How so?"

"All men have a fear of impotence, especially of the pocket and the penis."

"The pocket and the penis?"

"Those are the two things men are mostly defined by, and you'll find if a man is ever lacking in one, he'll always over compensate with the other. For instance, broke dudes are always fucking, they stay fucking. Most times it doesn't matter who they're fucking; big, fat, tall, skinny, ugly, they just have to do it, because it's the only way they can feel relevant. And rich old dudes who can't get it up anymore, love spending money, especially on beautiful young women. They like telling themselves things like, 'it ain't trickin' if you got it', but that's only to trick themselves into forgetting that spending the money is the only real way they can please her."

"Okay that makes sense. But what does that have to do with us?"

"If you're not giving him any or enough sex, you're essentially making your man impotent and he'll go somewhere else where he can feel powerful, because remember sex for a man is not just about pleasure, it's also a power game. That's why when you tell him this is his pussy it's such a turn on. And now if you're lauding the fact that you make more money than him, bossing him around, telling him what to do, treating him like a child, you're making him feel impotent again and he'll go to someone who doesn't. So it's not that he needs to feel like you need him. Most modern men are happy to have a woman who is independent and can take care of herself financially and isn't nagging him all the time for dumb shit, like taking care of your hair. But don't use your independence as a way to dis-empower his manhood."

Don't use your independence to dis-empower his manhood. That line stood out to her. Had she done that to Gavin, dis-empowered his manhood? Is that why he had his affair? The pocket or the penis, which one had driven him to another woman's bed?

They were both doing fairly well for themselves and were making roughly the same amount of money, so she couldn't imagine the pocket had anything to do with it. So it must have been the penis. Maybe she didn't give him enough sex. There were nights he went to bed disappointed. But was she just supposed to lie on her back spread eagle whenever he wanted, regardless of her own desires or lack thereof? She wasn't a machine. Was that what men wanted, a veritable Bangbot who was always ready and willing to please. Was that how the other woman was? Did she make him feel powerful? She was confused. Maybe Alex had the answer but for him to answer those questions she would have to reveal so much more about herself. Was she willing to do that? And if she did, what would Alex do with that information? Remember he was trying to fuck her not help her.

38

They arrived at Alex's building. "This is me," Alex said and Zawe took a moment to look it over. It was a gorgeous sixteen story complex with the East River as its backdrop. She knew this kind of building. She had been in many like it and could already imagine Alex's layout in her mind. This was too much for someone who was supposed to be unemployed.

"You know I said I wasn't going to ask but now I really have to know. I know this area, and looking at this building and your view, your rent must be at least two thousand dollars and that's just for a studio."

"It's a one bedroom, and it's 3,400."

"Exactly. And you drive a 150,000 dollar car."

"I prefer to think of it as a 2,000 dollar lease."

"And you don't have a job," she reiterated.

"No."

"So how do you afford your lifestyle?"

"Don't you know it's not polite to ask someone about their income?"

"I'm not asking how much you make. I'm asking how you eat."

"The truth?"

"That is what you promised me."

"I live off the kindness of women."

"Oh my God. You're a whore." She knew it. She had always known he was a slut, now she had confirmation.

"No. I don't get paid to have sex with women," he corrected her.

"Then what's this kindness?"

"I go out with women, and from time to time they give me money."

What? What kind of bullshit was he trying to pull? "Wait a minute that's the same thing you're still taking their money."

"Borrowing their money. Whatever they give me I always give it back . . . after a certain period of time."

"And what are you doing with the money when you have it?"

"I invest it."

"In what?"

"Stocks primarily. I day-trade now and again."

"Do you tell these women what you're doing with the money?"

"No, I just tell them that I'm cashed strapped, my money is tied up in investments and that I'll pay them back, which I always do."

"And they just give it to you?"

"They see the car I drive and the clothes I wear. People are always willing to give money to people they think already have it."

"And to people who they think care about them. God, the more I learn about you the more turned off I am."

"Yeah, keep telling yourself that."

Alex leaned forward as if to give her a kiss. She assumed he was going for the lips and even though her brain was telling her to move or at least turn her cheek, she didn't, she froze and he kissed her just above the brow. "Have a good night Zawe," he said then turned away. She stood there for a moment and watched him enter his building. There was a woman exiting as he was going in and he immediately sparked up a conversation. He had her from hello, and seeing this all Zawe could think was, women are so stupid.

39

To live off the kindness of women necessitated that one also be kind to women. It usually began with a kind word.

"Wow, you look great," he said to her, and Tamra looked up bemused. It's not every day a stranger on line at a Subways compliments you out the blue while ordering your turkey on honey oats sandwich with extra sweet peppers—and he had said it as if he knew her, as if they were already friends, which made it more significant than if they really were.

A compliment can go a long way. It can make someone's day and it can sometimes last them a lifetime. It can be a pleasant memory that cheers them up whenever they are down and when they are already feeling gay it can make them feel even better. Tamra had been feeling good about herself today when she got dressed in her favorite blouse and slacks combination and wore her hair down, but to have this handsome man confirm it was very . . . confirming.

"Um . . . thank you," she replied flatly though secretly she beamed.

"And I like your hair. That cut suits you, and the color really brings out your skin."

He said things she wished her boyfriend would or rather had. She didn't have one at the moment and when she did they rarely said it. Few men had figured out the trick that a woman wanted to feel noticed every day and not only on special occasions.

"Um, thank you . . . again," she said.

"You're welcome," he said. Then they were silent and it was a bit awkward but not at all unpleasant, and she began wondering if he was waiting for her to say something when he said,

"You don't have to you know."

"Excuse me. Don't have to what?"

"Usually when people give us compliments, we feel like we have to give one back, and I'm telling you, you don't have to."

"Are you waiting for me to give you a compliment?"

"No. Because you don't have to."

"Okay," she said and couldn't help laughing.

He laughed as well, "Hi, I'm Alex," and extended his hand. She shook it. "Tamra."

Tamra was just shy of thirty-five, just shy of five-seven, just shy of having c-cups that were just beginning to sag, juxtaposed with an ass a lot firmer than a lot of women ten years her junior. Her face had just enough details to let you know she was no longer a girl without detracting from her verve. Unmarried and unfettered she made for a perfect Game.

There were two types of women Alex went out with, what he called Fun and Games. Games tended to be older (ranging anywhere from their early-thirties to their early-forties) well earning professional women with ample disposable income. He called them Games because of the games he played with them.

He told them he was a Photographer and worked for an obscure European magazine they never heard of nor could they disprove. The subterfuge was a necessary one. A woman may let you explore the depths of her vulva after a night or two but to get into her purse required a little more time and finesse. After a week of some of the best sex Tamra had ever had Alex asked her for a favor.

"Can you loan me ten thousand dollars?" It was the figure he asked of all his Games. "I hate to ask but I get paid quarterly, some unexpected expenses came up, my next check doesn't come in for another month and the rest of my money is tied up investments." Asking ten thousand dollars from someone you barely knew would seem an absurdly extravagant request, but here was a curious thing he had learned: if you ask for a grand or less you look like a bum, if you ask for less than five you may look suspicious but if you ask for ten you look like a businessman and the women were more inclined to believe your story and that they would be repaid.

While thinking over Alex's request Tamra itemized his attire. The PRPS jeans he wore were roughly three hundred dollars, the Bruno Magii boots were just over four, the Burberry button down was two, the John Varvatos leather jacket was another two (thousand) and to top it off he wore a Jaeger-LeCoultre watch worth at least twenty. She was sold by his presentation. She felt comfortable loaning ten thousand dollars to someone who was wearing at any moment what a lot of people made in a year.

She hardly saw him again after she wrote the check. Saying he was on location doing a shoot in some far off country was always an excellent excuse for why they couldn't meet. Within a month they went from seeing each other, to calling each other to texting to nothing and just as she began to believe she had been conned, ten thousand dollars was deposited in her bank account along with an email memorializing the end of their relationship.

Dear Tamra as promised I deposited the ten thousand you lent me back into your account today. I want to thank you again for helping me out as you did. Your generosity saw me through a dire time and I will be forever grateful. You are a truly beautiful person inside and out and I am better for having met you. Unfortunately I believe this is where our paths separate. I know you said you were fine with the way things were and you wanted nothing more from me than the special friendship we held. But you and I both know deep down you wanted more and I know you deserve more, you deserve better, a better man than me, and it would be selfish of me to waste your time and keep you from finding him—and you will find him. Your beauty and your goodness will draw him out. And when you do I will be happy, for I know that you will have found the happiness you truly deserve. Sincerely Yours. Alex.

He wrote roughly the same letter to all of his Games and they were all disappointed when they read it but not angry. He had promised them nothing and taken nothing from them. Whatever he borrowed he returned and the time they spent together in some minute way had enriched their lives. It was a story to tell their girlfriends and something to masturbate to on a restless night; and on the occasion they ran into him on the street it was all hugs and kisses, and they were often inclined to lend money to him again. Only fools break hearts and burn bridges.

40

Then there were the women he saw purely for fun. Fun Girls were mostly in their twenties, never younger, and preferably between twenty-five and thirty. These were women who hadn't fully matured mentally or financially but physically were in their prime. With them there was no subterfuge or subtext. To them he was a Philosopher, this enigma that seemed to inhabit the world but not be a part of it.

One of Alex's Games had invited him to a movie premiere at the Ziegfeld but at the last minute business called her to the West Coast and she left him with both tickets and the passes to the after party. Alex was a loner but he didn't like being alone. He wanted a date. He supposed there would be women at the premiere he could meet but while riding the train an idea came to him.

"What are you doing tonight?" he asked her, having to speak above the noise of the A train.

"Excuse me?"

"Tonight? What are you doing?"

"Um. I'm going home," she said a little apprehensive at being questioned by this strange man who had taken the seat across from her.

"Do you have to go home?"

"Um . . . since that's where I live, yes."

"Do you think maybe I could persuade you to put that off for a few hours?"

"Going home?"

"Yes."

"No . . . why?"

"I'm going to this movie premiere at the Ziegfeld," he held up his two passes, "and I don't have a date."

"Okay," the woman replied. "And you—are you asking me to go with you?"

"Only if you say yes."

"Ah, no."

"Why not? May I ask?"

"Ah, for one, I don't know you."

"That's okay. We never know anyone until we get to know them."

"Yeah, and usually people talk first, get a phone number, email address, Facebook, whatever."

"I don't have time for all that. The event starts in a little over an hour."

"And you figured you would just get on the train and find some strange woman to go with?"

"I don't think you're that strange."

"Are you crazy?"

"Only in the best way."

They both had to laugh at the ridiculousness of this whole scene and it had become a scene as nearby passengers listened in.

"What's for two?" Alex asked her.

"Excuse me," she said coming out of her laughter.

"When you said, no, you said 'for one I don't know you,' which meant you also had another reason for saying no. What was it?"

"Um," though she had said for one, she really didn't have a for two, so she improvised. "I'm coming home from work, and if I was gonna go to a movie premiere, which I'm not, I wouldn't go looking like this."

"I think you look beautiful." If said with enough sincerity it's amazing how effectively that word always worked on a woman. From the look in her eyes he could feel her defenses beginning to crack. "But if you like we can stop off at Bloomingdales and get you something for the night . . . my treat of course."

She looked utterly gobsmacked.

"You are crazy."

And this was one of the weirdest and concurrently most exciting experiences of her young life. But would she end it here?

"Believe me I get it. This is a crazy world, and there are a lot of sick and dangerous people out there," he said and she nodded emphatically. "But this is also a beautiful world, and life is short but it can be filled with amazing experiences. This could be one of those experiences."

After that she was a little speechless, which caused someone else to speak up for her. "Girl if you don't go, I'll go," said a woman in her mid-forties who sat adjacent to Alex. Everyone nearby broke out laughing, Alex and the pretty Girl included. "A movie premiere and free clothes, you don't have to ask me twice."

The pretty girl furrowed her brow, squinted her eyes, bared her teeth and eked out a yes. The spectators applauded. She justified her answer by thinking if Alex had approached normally she would have given him her number, and if he had called her and asked her out she would have went, so why not cut through the minutiae.

At the next stop he held out his hand and she took it and they exited together. As they left, it occurred to her. "Hey I don't even know your name."

"It's Alex," he said.

"Aissa."

Alex took Aissa straight to Bloomingdales and spent almost a thousand dollars on a new outfit, shoes included. She couldn't help feeling a little like Cinderella. When they got to the premiere it was as if she was at the ball, and though she saw a lot of movie stars for her no one shined brighter than Alex. He made her laugh and feel completely comfortable in a room filled with people who she didn't know. The paparazzi even took their pictures. They assumed they were famous or people on the inside who were very important.

The after party was at the lounge of the Millennium hotel. Two hours into the party Alex asked if she'd like to go upstairs and she said yes. For her, they made love and it was one of her best experiences. She went to bed thinking she was dreaming. When she woke up she realized she had been. Alex was gone and he hadn't left a card, a number or even a note. He did, however, leave her with the clothes and a story she would be telling for years.

41

Emma lived in a one bedroom flat on the eighth floor of an apartment building in Fort Greene, Brooklyn. Fort Green was a lot like Dumbo but more artsy, less expensive and more Black— however that was changing day by day (becoming less Black that is).

Emma's apartment was organically disheveled. Those were Emma's words for describing what Zawe called a mess, which didn't exactly mean it was dirty. There was never any food lying around or dishes in the sink (not for more than two days anyway). Emma was clean she just wasn't organized. She had a futon and a sofa set. She had the futon first and when she got the sofas she couldn't stand throwing the futon away so she kept it. That was the same reason why she had two coffee tables piled high with magazines (mostly back issues of Sophisticate's Black

Hair and Essence), a bean bag and a bunch of framed paintings stacked in a corner because she couldn't find any more space on her walls to put them.

Her apartment was cluttered in a very homely way. It was a great place for a party. She often had friends over. When you entered Zawe's place you instinctually wanted to take your shoes off and walk quietly because the place looked so clean and well-kept and you wanted it to stay that way. Emma's place made you want to relax and talk loud and put your feet up in the sofa. That's how Zawe and Emma were seated now. Tired of being in her own head Zawe had come over for a visit and as was becoming a custom she was talking about Alex.

"He lives off the kindness of women. Can you believe that shit? It astounds me that some women can be that dumb." This wasn't so astounding to Emma. She knew a lot of women who were financing broke men who had a lot less going for them than Alex. If he had asked her for money she would have given it to him (if she had it, damn near broke as she was) and if he always paid them back, where was the harm? Emma was far more intrigued with where he was living.

"And he said he's paying 3,400 for rent. Shoot I could get him a house or a condo in that area and he'd be paying less. Hey why don't you—"

Zawe already saw where Emma was going and decided to cut her off. "No. Definitely not."

Emma had been doing real estate for the last seven years. A friend got her into the business during the whole sub-prime craze. She made a lot of money during those years before the bottom fell out, utterly and abruptly. She had been surviving the Obama years through her savings and by renting apartments, mostly subsidized housing for people with Section 8 and Work Advantage. Every once in a while she was able to close on a house but they were few and far between. Though the truth was if you had the cash now was the best time to buy, and that was something Alex seemed to have on hand.

"Zawe, you know how rough the market is right now. And

you owe me after you didn't use me to get your house."

"Oh my God, you're never gonna get over that are you? I told you, you didn't have the listing."

"Whatever, like you just had to get that big ass house by yourself. And all I'm asking you to do is just mention it to him."

42

Zawe and Alex were riding the F Train to Dumbo. This was their third time riding the train together and it was beginning to feel not unlike a boyfriend picking her up from work. She would never say it but she enjoyed riding home with him. Beyond having someone to talk to (or in spite of as he at times really got under her skin) he made her feel protected.

An attractive woman riding the subway alone can get a lot of attention from male passengers. Most will periodically shoot you a glance hoping you'll look back giving them some kind of signal it'd be okay to approach you. For the most part they were harmless but you had to be careful you didn't inadvertently look at an ad in some guy's direction for more than a second and he get the wrong idea.

Then there were the men who would sit on the opposite side and stare at you nonstop the entire trip. They didn't care if you looked back and you could even give them the stink-eye and they'd still stare. Did they do this because somewhere in their deluded mind they thought this was a turn-on, or were they actively trying to creep you out? Zawe leaned towards the latter believing no one could be that deluded. Either way when Alex was there it didn't happen. They weren't a couple but, as she had pointed out to him, to the rest of the world they appeared to be. There were still a few glances here and there but for the most part the other men were respectful as was Alex. Since the day she spoke to him about looking at other women he hadn't done it again. He looked at her now as if she was the only girl in the world—not like some lovesick school boy, just very attentive and respectful and she appreciated that.

"So if you don't work, why do you come to the city in the day?" she asked him.

"I go shopping sometimes."

She looked down and reminded herself he wasn't carrying any bags.

"I guess you didn't see anything you liked."

"No, I did."

She rolled her eyes. "Then where are your bags?"

"I had the store deliver them to my apartment."

"Aren't you special?"

"No. I just never like walking around with bags."

"Speaking of apartments," she said, happy he had brought it up as she had been trying to find a natural way to ask, "Have you ever thought about buying a house?"

He looked at her with a sardonic smile. "Don't you think we should have sex before we buy a house together?"

"God I knew this was a bad idea."

"What was?"

"Nothing. I'm just saying . . . it doesn't make sense to spend so much on rent and have nothing to show for it."

"Sure it does. I only plan on staying there for six months."

"Why? Don't you like it?"

"Oh I like it well enough. But I never live anywhere for more than six months at a time."

"And why the hell not?"

"I don't know. I just start feeling claustrophobic and stifled and I have to move."

"So you're moving like at least twice every year."

"Just about."

"That's the dumbest thing I've ever heard." Alex smiled. "I'm serious. Moving is one of the most tiring things you can do. I know, I just did it. Why would you want to go through that twice every year?"

Just the thought of going through all of that again anytime soon made her heart contract.

"Look, moving is a chore for you because you probably have a lot of stuff, and it's a bitch to pack everything up, move it and then unpack it again. If I had to go through that it would be a pain for me as well, but I don't have that problem because I don't own anything."

"What do you mean you don't own anything?"

"I mean at any time I have a certain amount of clothes in my closet and the laptop and phone I'm using, but beyond that everything else I rent."

Alex had already said a lot of very unusual things to her about the way he lived his life, living off the kindness of women being at the forefront, but this was about to take the cake.

"What are you part of some silly new age religion? Why don't you want to own anything?"

"Because when you own something it also owns you, and I don't want to be owned."

She thought about that for a second.

When you own something it also owns you.

It sounded profound and would probably look good on a t-shirt but it was really bullshit. It was the kind of pabulum he fed himself because he so desperately wanted to be different and avant garde.

"Also I'm addicted to newness," he said.

"You're addicted to what-ness?"

"Newness. And I think we all are to some degree."

"Newness . . . no—don't think so."

"Sure you are. Don't you love buying new clothes, new shoes? Don't you love the way they smell, the way they feel when you put them on?"

"I do love buying shoes, but I don't love the feel of them when I first get them. It usually takes three wears before they become comfortable."

"See I make sure they're comfortable before I buy them and after three wears I don't wear them anymore."

"Then what do you do with them?"

"I give them away."

"You just give away new shoes?"

"Fairly new. Yes."

"What about your clothes?"

"Same thing."

"Don't you ever have a pair of pants, or a shirt you really like?"

"Yeah, and when that happens I buy more than one pair."

"You have got to be the strangest person I have ever met."

"I take that as a compliment."

43

"He's certifiable," Zawe said to Emma as they perused through the racks of clothes in Nordstrom. Emma had a date that night and (being the type of person who bought new clothes because she would forget what was already in her closet and was too lazy to look) swore she didn't have anything to wear. She had asked Zawe to help her pick something out. Zawe came along though she had no idea why Emma was going to all this trouble for some guy she met on Facebook; some friend of a friend who friended her and had been chatting her up for the last week. Emma knew why? He was a doctor and potentially her future ex-husband. Emma had never walked down the aisle before but knew to her bone she had at least three trips in her before she turned fifty.

"That's so interesting," she said.

"What's so interesting?"

"His life. Wouldn't you love to be free to move around and wear new shit all the time?"

"No I wouldn't. I like calling something my own. And oh yeah, you can forget about him buying a house."

That was one good thing that came out of her talk with Alex. She could get Emma off her back.

"Yeah unfortunately he isn't the only one who isn't buying houses now. Hey can you tell him to use me when he's renting his next place." Zawe shook her head and walked away. "What?"

44

The next day they met at a deli in Dumbo. It was one of those upscale delicatessens that charged fifteen dollars for a tuna fish sandwich and sold a small bag of chips for two. Alex hadn't gone into the city so there was no after work pick up today. Zawe had to suffer the train ride home alone. The ride wasn't as bad as the wait. She'd been worked up ever since their last meeting as she kept thinking about, "This newness thing, does it apply to relationships as well?" He gave her a wry smile. "Of course it does."

"Oh come on, you love the beginning of a new relationship just as much. You know when you just meet someone and all you have to do is touch them and it sends shock waves through your body, you think about them all the time and you feel this intense longing when you're not with them. That feeling is what I live for. Unfortunately it always fades away. Sometimes it fades away after a night, the longest was seven weeks—"

"Seven weeks? You can't learn anything more than what's superficial about a person in seven weeks."

"What's wrong with superficial?"

"It's superficial. In the beginning it's all pretense everyone pretends like neither of them farts."

"That's what I love. In the beginning you get the best of the person."

"You get the best of what that person is trying to be, but it's not real."

"Reality is overrated, and once you start farting in front of each other the relationship is over, you just don't know it yet."

As was often the case something Alex said made Zawe reflect on her relationship with Gavin. She had never farted (or as her Mother liked to say: eased her bottom) in Gavin's company—at least not audibly; and the few times she did he had never noticed it—at least she hoped he hadn't. However she had used the bathroom. She had to, they lived together there was no avoiding it, though there was a way to disguise it. She always locked the door and stayed in there a good ten minutes after she finished, giving the smell time to dissipate as well as take a quick shower. When she left, the bathroom smelled like lavender body wash and no one could tell for certain that showering wasn't the only thing she had done.

There was one time, however, when she couldn't shower her way out of her shit. Unless you grew up in the culture or your stomach happened to be lined with titanium as a habit one should never experiment with Indian food. The restaurant had been Emma's suggestion and it was one of the things Zawe had never forgiven her for. Thirty minutes after finishing her meal she knew something was grossly wrong and told Gavin she was feeling sick and to take her home.

They could not have gotten home fast enough. She was in deep meditation on the drive back and every bump and pothole was a test of the resolve of her bowels. When they finally got in she made a beeline for the loo almost knocking him over in the process.

She could hear his laughter through the door as he could hear her evacuation. It was that loud. All of her games and gimmicks were dashed in one night. Was that the beginning of the end? Gavin had laughed but maybe his laughter had been masking his disgust. Men can piss, fart and shit with impunity because they are 'men', while women, whether real or perceived, are held to these unnatural standards of gentility. Men say they didn't care and wanted you to be 'real' around them but deep down what were they really thinking? Alex just told her. No wonder women were so much more constipated.

"And you have to admit sex is always best in the beginning," Alex said.

Zawe had to get her mind off shit and back on sex.

"No way. There's nothing like when you're with someone and they really know your body. They know just where to touch you and where not to."

"But where's the discovery? That's what makes it intense and exciting."

"It's already been discovered that's what makes it beautiful."

Alex remembered the first time he touched a woman intimately and the sensation it sent through his body. How good it felt just to hug her, how she felt firm and soft concurrently; how good she smelled, how her lips and tongue tasted. It was as if all of his pleasure centers were excited at once. But invariably with each subsequent touch through the course of a relationship the sensation diminished. Then the woman became just a body and her vagina a sleeve. It was better than masturbating but just barely and sometimes not even. It was not that he had relationships just for the sex but if the desire for sex was gone why not just be friends.

For Zawe sex was good but never great off the bat. This had nothing to do with her partner's skills as a lover. Their first time together Gavin was already experienced, however, he was not experienced with her. In the beginning it would take him twenty minutes to make her come once. By the end she could have four orgasms in that time. Like a well-tuned guitar he had learned the chords to make her body sing. Making love is both a physical and mental act but they are not always conjoined. Your body can be one place and your mind can be at work, at the park, on the television show you watched earlier or on someone else. You experience a sort of synesthesia when all of your senses mental, emotional and physical are going off simultaneously. You can't achieve that in the beginning: that takes love and love takes time.

All this talk about sex and Alex's addictions brought Zawe to an inevitable conclusion. He had been with a lot of women. She always knew he was a whore, now she was curious just how big of a whore he was.

"How many women have you been with?" she asked.

"I was wondering when you were going to get to that?"

"Well wonder no more. Now go ahead and answer."

"Fine. But Ladies first and don't lie, because I'll know if you do."

"Four. One in high school, two in college and Gavin," she said forthrightly.

"That's a respectable number."

"Thank you. Now go ahead, list yours."

"Ah, I don't know about listing. That might take a while."

"It's that much isn't it?"

"I don't know. What do you consider a lot?"

"Well why don't you tell me your number and then I'll tell you."

"I don't really have an exact number."

"Why? Is it because you don't count or you stopped counting."

"A little of both."

"Then just give me an approximation."

"Okay then, I'd say it's more than a hundred . . ."

"Oh my God I knew it, I knew it. You're such a whore."

"and less than a thousand."

"What the fuck?" She blurted, her voice rising sharply and drawing attention to the table.

This was the first time he had ever heard her so excited.

"Zawe calm down."

Realizing she had gotten outside of herself she lowered her voice. "Are you serious? Please tell me you're joking—less than a thousand?"

"Exactly, it's less than a thousand. It could be a hundred and fifty, or two hundred."

"Bullshit. No one says less than a thousand unless it's pretty high up in the hundreds." Alex couldn't help laughing. "And you're laughing about it. Honestly, you're so gross. You're like a walking body of disease. And you thought you were actually going to win this bet. Oh you should have never told me that."

"Why? Was I beginning to wear you down?"

"Hell—no," she said emphatically.

"And you don't have to worry. I don't have any diseases. I always wear a condom."

"Yeah right. For a thousand times. I really believe that. And even if you did condoms aren't a hundred percent."

"Yeah well, you'd be surprised just how effective ninety-seven percent can be. Also I get tested regularly. I'm probably the cleanest healthiest person you know."

"Whatever," she sighed and rolled her eyes. "No wonder you don't have a job. You can't find time to do anything other than have sex. To get that number you must be having sex with some-one new every day."

"Zawe, I'm thirty-two years old and I've been having sex since I was seventeen. Following your math I would have hit that number by the time I was 20."

He was right but it didn't matter. Less than a thousand could have very well been less than a million. It was an astronomi-cal number—it was an offensive number. Any man who could be with that many women couldn't have very much respect for them.

"I have to go. You just turned my stomach."

Zawe got up and left Alex alone at the table and for the first time he began thinking maybe he was taking this honesty thing too far. He hadn't needed to tell her the truth. He had never done it before when other women asked that question. Sixty was his usual number. Whenever women met him they always assumed he had already been with a lot of women so sixty was a number he felt was large enough for them to accept but still digest. Zawe just threw his real number up in his face.

45

Still what was his real number exactly? He honestly didn't know. There are a lot of women walking around in the world and if you were decent looking and made a habit of talking to a few you'd sleep with your fair share. He wasn't with someone new everyday but on average once a week. Then there were the times he had been to Europe and Brazil and the Caribbean. Then there were the orgies and the network of underground sex clubs in the city. He got put on to those by one of their promoters.

She was a very chic looking woman; blonde and bosom heavy; a bit too made up for his tastes but the mildly attractive tend to be that way. He had assumed she was a Madam trying to get him to join her stable. He had been approached by Madams before and always turned them down. He lived off the kindness of women but didn't feel right openly charging them. Borrowing their money seemed more dignified.

Still he was wrong about her—in a sense. She wasn't a Madam but she was a purveyor of sex. She saw him on the train and eye-fucked him the entire ride. When she got off she slipped him a card with an address and a password. Seeing the card Alex instinctively knew what he was getting into and dived in head first. At those parties you didn't so much have sex with one person as you sampled many. It was quite possible to be with more than ten women in one night—and he had had a lot of those nights.

He hadn't been to one of those parties in some time, because after you've been to your umpteenth orgy it all gets pretty boring. After you've slept with almost your thousandth woman it can get fairly quotidian as well. These last two weeks meeting up with Zawe was the most fun he'd had in at least a year, and they hadn't even had sex. Maybe he was having fun because they hadn't had sex. By that logic maybe they shouldn't have sex. No. The game was fun because it had a goal and a purpose. Without that it would become boring as well. No. The bet must stand and he was going to win it. To do that, however, he would need to placate Zawe's sensibilities.

46

The next day they met at the Park by a bench overlooking the harbor and the city and he brought her a present. "What's this?" she asked looking at the manila envelope he handed her.

"Open it," he said.

It was the results of an AIDS test and other STDs. It was an official document proving he was disease free—at least as of two weeks ago.

"This is two weeks old," she said.

"And?"

"Are you telling me you haven't had sex since you took these tests?"

"I haven't done anything different than what I did before I took those tests."

"Well, I'm not sure why you showed this to me. It doesn't matter to me. It's not like I'm going to have sex with you."

"Keep saying that to yourself and you just might begin to believe it."

"I could say the same thing about you. Maybe you're still trying to psych yourself into thinking you can win. I mean it's been over two weeks and you haven't gotten anywhere yet."

"Don't worry about that. I'm a fourth quarter performer. I'll win the game when it counts."

"You know, I know you, I know your type. You play around now, and you talk all this shit, but in a few years you'll settle down and get some kids, you'll see."

"Not likely."

"Yes likely. Eventually you're gonna wanna get married."

"Never."

"Never say never."

"Never."

"You wanna make a bet on that."

"You'll lose that one too."

"Whatever. And what about children?"

"Didn't I just say I never want to get married?"

"They're not tied together."

"Yeah, children are worse. You can annul a marriage, but you can't annul a child. It's always there binding you to that person like a perpetual chain."

Whenever Alex spoke there was always some double meaning or a hint of sarcasm in what he said—but not now. As he talked about his disdain for having children he had never sounded more emphatic and convicted.

47

Children can be a beautiful thing . . . when they're not yours. There was nothing better than playing with a child and then handing them back to their parent when they needed to be fed.

"Go ahead Brian. We got him. Do it," Seychelle shouted, wrapping her wiry seven year old body around Alex's torso and blindfolding him with her hands.

"Oh, you guys are cheating," Alex said, speaking of the three youngsters he had to contend with.

While Seychelle jockey-rode his back, her four year old sister Tasha turned her body into a boot and locked it around his left leg. The two girls did this for their ten year old brother's benefit. Brian used the distraction to drive by Alex and lay the ball in the basket in a brand new professional grade hoop and backboard. Alex squinted through Seychelle's fingers and watched the ball go in. "I won," Brian said, grinning from ear to ear.

"Oh you wanna cheat. Let me show you what happens to cheaters. C'mere." Alex pulled Seychelle off his back and began tickling her. She laughed furiously.

"Let her go," Tasha said, wanting to protect her big sister, and began pulling on Alex's leg.

"Oh you want some too."

Alex switched the older sister for the younger, held Tasha in the air and began blowing into her tiny pot belly. The child looked like she was having a seizure from laughing.

"Come on, let's get him," Seychelle said to Brian. They both attacked Alex and the combined might of all three brought him to the pavement. From the ground he watched a car pull into the driveway as the kids continued to pile on. "Hello Alex. You still in there?" Adriana asked after Alex's head had disappeared from view for a good half minute. Adriana was thirty-five and looked every bit her age. She had been through three pregnancies and one divorce and had gained seven pounds for each adventure; still pretty but a bit faded.

"Hey Adriana," Alex said peeking his head out.

"Having fun?"

"Having a ball."

"I can see. And speaking of balls, why is there a big ass basketball hoop in my driveway?"

"Alex bought it for my birthday. Isn't it cool?" Brian said.

"And very big and expensive looking." And it was. It was the same quality hoop and backboard they used in the NBA and it cost Alex roughly 5,000 dollars for the purchase, setup and delivery.

"Well you know it's my job to spoil them," Alex said.

Still Alex wouldn't only be spoiling Brian he'd be spoiling all of the kids in the neighborhood. When word got out Brian had a professional hoop in his backyard kids from all over town would be coming over. Merrick, Long Island was for the most part a safe middle class community but that didn't mean Adriana wanted her house becoming its basketball epicenter. This thing would draw too much attention to her house and that was never good. She would let the kids play with it tonight but she'd tell Alex to return it tomorrow. Brian would be upset but if Alex bought him a new PlayStation or something comparable he should get over it.

"Is she upstairs?" Alex asked Adriana.

"Yeah. She should be in her room."

48

Katherine sat at her vanity table in her bedroom fixing her wig—an auburn hairpiece with side swept bangs and layered sides that framed her face and extended to her clavicle covering most of her neck. This was important as her neck showed her age more than any other part of her body. Katherine was fifty-three but because of her illness looked ten years older and her neck alone made her look seventy. In her mind she kept seeing a chicken when she spoke and it bothered her to no end, more than her near-bald head, her detumesced bosom and her diminished complexion. She had taken up wearing silk scarves in the past few months and would wear one tonight on her date with Alex. He took her out to dinner every Wednesday and it had become the highlight of her week. She loved him (a mother couldn't have loved a son more) and since her marriage had long since ended no other man's opinion mattered as much to her.

"So how do I look?" she turned and asked.

"Beautiful," he said, and to him she still was; a bit more ravaged than ravishing but still regal, still alive and that was what mattered most.

She looked a bit disappointed. "I was hoping you'd say hot."

"Oh you're that too."

"Hot enough to be a MILF?"

"Most definitely." Alex chuckled at Katherine calling herself a MILF though he was not surprised. Katherine always had a bawdy disposition. Even when he was a child and the other adults would cover the children's ears when their talk turned untoward she never did. She always spoke her mind uncensored.

That was one of the things he loved most about her. Her daughters, Adriana and Bree, did not share his opinion. They spent a lot of family gatherings apologizing for their mother's behavior. Subsequently both daughters were fairly chaste in public; Adriana especially, who rarely cursed if ever.

Katherine once told her to, "take the stick out of your ass and put a dick in it," at a family reunion in front of practically everyone. The two of them didn't speak to each other for almost six months after that one, and that's difficult to do when you own a house together. That was all pre-illness however. Ever since the diagnosis they had been exceedingly close. Cancer had a way of making you realize what's important.

"Then again because I'm a grandmother I guess I'd be a GILF," Katherine mused.

"Aunt Kate that's disgusting." Alex looked as if he had re-swallowed his own sputum. "How do you even know that expression?"

"Well I went on David's computer the other day and I was doing a search for gift cards and a very disturbing website came up." David was Adriana's second husband.

"Interesting." Alex could only hope for Adriana's sake David had come across those GILF sites by accident.

"And speaking of grandmothers, you're not twenty-five anymore, when are you going to stop all this foolishness and get married and have some kids of your own?"

"I'm fine with Adriana's."

"And what about your Mother? What about what she would have wanted? Don't you think she would have wanted some grand kids?" For Alex mentioning his mother was like touching the soft spot on a baby's head that hadn't hardened and for him likely never would. Katherine knew this and should have known better. Alex didn't say anything but his silence spoke volumes. "Okay, okay. I'm sorry," she said. Now they were both silent and it was a little awkward and Katherine was searching for a way to change subjects when an interesting rumor came to mind. "Have you heard about Lincoln?"

"Is he dead?" Alex asked with a complete an utter lack of emotion or deference.

"Hardly. I heard he knocked out another one."

Alex shook his head. "I guess that's what keeps him going."

"Who knows? What's that bring the count to now . . . twelve?"

"Thirteen."

"Wow."

"Whatever." He exhaled. "I stopped being wowed by Lincoln a long time ago."

"Bree's wedding is next Saturday," she said changing subjects again. "You are coming right?"

"Isn't that like inviting the Devil to a christening?" She gave him a disapproving look. "Yes I'll be there."

Katherine reached out and held his hand. Her grip was thin (he could feel every bone under her shifting skin) yet still strong, still alive and that's what mattered most.

"I just want you to be happy," she said to him.

"Believe me I am."

49

Zawe stood outside the entrance of the High Street sub-way station where she and Alex had agreed to meet. This would mark their seventeenth meeting. Less than two weeks to go and the closest Alex came to getting her in bed was kissing her forehead. There was no doubt in Zawe's mind now she would win the bet—not that there ever was.

"But you promised," she said to Emma over the phone as Alex approached coming from across the street. She held up her finger, saying give me a minute. Alex obliged and stepped aside. "You know I've been needing your help putting up these curtains," she continued. "No I won't ask him," she said under her breath. "Whatever. Thanks for nothing." She hung up and turned to Alex. "Hey."

"Hey. Is everything alright?" he asked seeing her look a little dismayed.

"Yeah, everything's great."

"Cool. So how about we walk to your house this time?"

"No, that's okay," she said smiling at how smoothly he'd made the suggestion.

"God, you are so uptight," he said.

Calling her uptight stuck under her craw. It was similar to calling her a control freak and she hated that so much she had allowed him to manipulate her into agreeing to these getting to know each other days, which today happened to be one of.

"Fine. It's this way," she said conceding, but because it was practical and not due to his conniving. It was a chilly late October evening. Day Light Savings had passed over the weekend and at the moment six pm looked no different than midnight. It had been a long day, Zawe was looking forward to getting home and if they went somewhere else she'd have a longer walk back to her house. Also as a rule, as a woman, whenever you can get an escort to your doorstep you should take it. You just had to be certain your escort wasn't who you should be watching out for.

"So tell me about your family. You have any brothers and sisters?" he asked as they crossed the intersection.

"I have one brother."

"Older, younger?"

"Younger."

"Are you guys close?"

"As close as brothers and sisters normally get. He can be a knucklehead at times but yeah I guess I love him."

"How about your parents, are they still together?"

"Not for seven years."

"Any of them remarried?"

"My Dad did five years ago and has two kids with his new wife."

"I thought you said it was only you and your brother?"

"It is. My Mom maybe a pain in my ass but unless you came out of her womb you're no sibling of mine." Alex smiled at that. They had more in common than she knew. "And hell no I'm gonna acknowledge that woman's children."

"What's with the hate for Step Mom?"

"You mean besides the fact she's my age yet tries to act like my Mother." Her Father's new wife wasn't exactly her age but thirty-five was close enough. It wasn't as bad as her being in her twenties but the fact that her father at fifty-five could easily be his new wife's father turned Zawe's stomach. "Then again I think I'm more upset with my Dad for that—and oh yes this is something that's always irked me. What the hell is this attraction to younger women?"

"You mean besides the obvious."

"You know, It's really disturbing that a woman's most important attribute is always her body. Sex isn't everything, you know."

"No. But it's everything else," he said and she fought the urge to smack him.

When Zawe was a child she saw every adult as being old. When she was seven and her mother was twenty-nine, her mother could have been one hundred, the gap between them seemed so wide. Now that she was the age her mother had been she realized just how young her mother really was. Even at fifty she was still a relatively young woman. Still she wasn't twenty-five anymore and neither was her daughter, and Zawe found herself sympathizing more with fifty than twenty-five because twenty-five was her past and fifty was her future. She didn't want the same thing that happened to her mother to happen to her.

"Answer me this: what would you have in common with a woman that young? You have little if anything to talk about."

"True, but you also have little if anything to argue about. And after being with women his age for years and going through the litany of arguments he has, he probably wants someone he can just chill with."

"You mean someone who he can control, who won't talk back."

"Believe me, young or old, all women talk back. And with all these Cougars going around let's not even act as if Men are the only ones going after someone younger."

"Hey women are only doing that now because of what men have been doing for years."

"And I'm all for it. What's good for the gander is good for the goose."

Zawe stopped walking.

They had arrived at her house.

"This is you?" he asked looking the brownstone over.

"Yes, and thank you for walking me."

"No problem. Now go ahead and invite me up."

"What? Boy, you are not getting into my house."

"Why not?"

"Because I-don't-know-you."

"Zawe we've met up every day for more than two weeks. You know me a lot better than you knew the moving men and you let them in."

"That's different. They had a reason for being in my house; you don't—besides what you're thinking."

"Actually I was thinking about your curtains. You said you needed help putting them up right?"

50

Twenty minutes she kept repeating in her head. She would allow him in for twenty minutes and no longer. She'd let him set up the curtains in the living room but not the ones in her bedroom (didn't dare having him anywhere near her bed) and then she'd kick him out. She cursed Emma in her mind. She'd been asking her for help with the curtains for the last two weeks but Emma kept putting her off. Now Zawe was forced to let this man into her house but only for twenty minutes.

"So here are the curtains," she said cradling the drapes in her arms and leading him to one of the living room windows.

"This is a nice place," Alex said as he surveyed the room.

The way you keep your house can speak more to your character than the way you keep yourself. Everyone will put on a good face when they go out but the way they keep their house tells you the type of person they really are. On more than one occasion Alex escorted a woman home, who by all appearances was clean and well-kept, only to discover she lived in a sty. This was a more common occurrence with younger women. The younger they were, the less likely they adhered to the mores about being a lady, and the more likely he was to find a dirty bra sticking out of the cushions in her couch and wet panties hanging from the shower rod in the bathroom with the musty funk of having been used to clean certain nether regions. This would always be a turn off if he had intended anything more than a night with this woman. Fortunately with Zawe the carpet matched the drapes.

Now back to the drapes.

"Now you know you have to put up the sheers first," she said wanting to keep his mind focused on the task at hand.

"And you decorated it yourself?" he asked speaking of the house and completely ignoring what she had just said.

"Well I'm not finished, but yes."

"You did a really good job."

"Thank you. Now about the sheers—"

"And the entire house is all you?"

"Yes. Why? Do you think it's too big for me?" she asked defensively.

"Do you think it's too big for you?"

"No. I mean yes, it's a four bedroom house and I'm a single woman. But I'm not going to be single forever, right?"

He wasn't sure if that was a question and if he should answer, but "Right," he did anyway.

"Exactly. And I got a really good deal on it. It was going for twice what I paid just six years ago, and when the market turns . . ."

"It'll be a great investment."

"Exactly." She looked at him and remembered they were alone in her house and were wasting time. He was only supposed to be in here for twenty minutes and she had already spent three talking. "Yeah, so, the curtains."

51

Thirty minutes later Alex had installed the hooks, the rods, the inner sheers and the curtains for all four windows in the living room. They both stood back to take in the full effect.

"Wow, those look great," she said.

"Yeah they really help to bring out the room."

"You really think so? You're not just saying that are you?"

"No, they do," he said and seemed genuinely sincere.

"Great. You know my ex, he never got it with curtains, he never saw what the big deal wah—ow."

"What is it?"

"Nothing. I think I have a cramp or pulled something in my ham—ow."

"Okay, well lay down and I'll rub it out for you."

"What? I am not letting you touch me."

"What's the big deal? You have a cramp I'm just rubbing it out."

It came out of nowhere. One moment she was fine and the next she took a small step forward and a sharp pain, like an electric grip, rode up her inner right thigh. She'd had her share of leg cramps before. They weren't excruciating but were awfully annoying and if they weren't treated could nag the hell out of you the entire night. A massage would help but that would require him touching her.

Besides the handshake when they first met at the gym and the time he kissed her forehead outside his building they hadn't touched each other and she'd like to keep it that way. Still what was she worried about? Like he said it was just a massage. If she went to the spa the masseuse would touch her, so how was he any different from Alex? Namely the masseuse wasn't trying to fuck her, at least not at the spas she went to. But she didn't want to have sex with Alex so the massage could only work to her benefit unless of course Alex was a rapist but if he was a rapist she was already damned the moment she let him through the door.

"Fine. But watch your hands," she said as she hobbled over to the sofa and sat up with her back braced against the arm rest.

He looked at her quizzically. "Zawe?"

"Yeah?"

"It's your hamstrings."

"And?"

"So—face down ass up."

"What?"

"Just lie on your stomach." She gave him a dirty look. "I

need to be able to get to the back of your thigh." She kept giving him that look as she reluctantly turned over. He then knelt beside the sofa and began rubbing her feet.

"Hey. That's not where my hamstrings are."

"Relax, I'll get to it. And trust me, it'll feel good."

"That's what I'm worried about," she whispered.

"What?"

"Nothing."

Alex started on the back of her left foot, one hand kneading the heel while the other worked the pressure out through the Achilles tendon. She still had on her socks. A fact she was both regretful and thankful for. Alex worked with a professional's pace and precision. It felt good and would feel even better barefoot but like having sex without a condom she didn't dare risk it, lest it felt too good and when the moment arrived pulling out becomes unbearable.

He would have to bear with the socks as well; wouldn't risk asking her to take them off; best to take things slowly with her. If he moved too fast she'd likely tighten up and this opportunity would be lost. The socks were a hindrance but he could still feel her and even through the cotton finally touching her felt good. He moved down to her instep making certain to apply enough pressure to avoid being ticklish. Afterward he went to the ball of her foot and then the toes, giving each digit its own personal massage.

He did all this for the left foot first and then the right. Zawe hadn't realized how badly she needed a foot massage until he started. He worked out a couple days' worth of stress and work related aggravation.

"So I have another question for you," she said beginning to let herself go now.

"Shoot."

"Why aren't men more romantic?"

"Why is the burden of being romantic always placed on the man?" He left her feet and moved onto her left calf.

"You can't do that!" she shouted inadvertently. She had

meant to say what she said just without all that vigor. Recognizing her voice had risen she simmered down. "You can't answer a question with a question?" Her outburst had more to do with him moving onto her calf than what he said. It surprised her and her body tensed up.

"Well if you answered my question you'd get the answer to yours," he said, taking it even slower now, trying to work the added tension out of her body.

"Your question makes no sense. Women are already naturally romantic."

"No, women are naturally expecting. Whenever it comes to romance it's always about what the man is doing for you, never what you're doing for your man."

"What? We already do a lot for you."

"Like what?"

She thought for a moment and the best she could come up with was, "We cook for you."

"Really, a modern woman? Sometimes you get offended if we even look at you and the kitchen in the same glance."

She chuckled and the tension in her body eased a bit. His touching her calf began to feel more natural. "That's not true. I cook. I can cook," she said.

No one would mistake her for a chef but she knew how to fry chicken, how to make rice, store bought pasta and an omelet, and in this day and age living by yourself what more did you need.

"Yeah but do you do it well? Because if you don't, it doesn't count. We'll just end up eating take-out anyway."

She laughed internally. She did eat a lot of take-out. Then she began thinking about what other ways women were romantic? It surprised her she was having such a hard time coming up with an example. Women were all about romance so she should have ample examples of women being romantic to men. Then why wasn't anything coming to her?

"We wear lingerie for you," she said finally, because thinking about romance made her think about Valentine's Day and

Valentine's Day made her think about Victoria's Secret.

"No you don't, you wear that stuff for yourselves."

"Are you kidding me?" she retorted almost turning around. "Have you ever worn a thong?" He had. "It is one of the most uncomfortable things ever created." He would have to agree, which is why he had only worn it once. "Trust me when I tell you no woman wears that for herself." But he would disagree as to why women continued to suffer through it.

"No, you wear it because you don't want to show a panty line. And you don't have to wear thongs, I much prefer boy shorts, and they don't have to be lingerie."

He left her calf and moved up to her thigh. It was a more gradual transition than it had been going from her feet to her calves. She didn't even realize it until he was there. It was like a dissolve in a movie. One second they were in one scene and the next his hand was between her legs. "What is this? I thought men were supposed to like lingerie."

"We do. But what's the first thing we do when we see you in it?"

"You take it off," she said, thinking about taking her pants off, imagining how much better his hands would feel on her bare skin.

"After you spent all that time picking it out, which you did for yourselves, because we don't care whether your bra and panties match? You'd get the same reaction in a t-shirt and a pair of cotton briefs, or even better no briefs."

His hands moved up higher, deeper and her legs opened ever so slightly letting them in. He was rubbing the cramp out of her. He braced himself against the base of the sofa not wanting her to see his growing erection. It was taking a good deal of restraint not to rip her clothes off.

"So all that talk about getting lingerie to spice up your relationship is all crap?"

"When your man wants you, you could be wearing a clown suit and you'd still be sexy to him. Now that doesn't mean we want you wearing granny drawers, but the fact that you've chosen to wear granny drawers means you've settled in and decided to be comfortable in your relationship," he said in a calm measured voice belying the hunger gnawing at him inside.

"What's . . . comfortable?" Likewise it had become increasingly difficult for her not to show any signs of pleasure.

"Stop working out, letting yourself go, stop thinking being sexy is important, stop . . . having sex." And there he touched her and they both knew what he had found. They took a moment to appreciate the significance of what just happened and to think about how to proceed.

"You're very good at this," she said.

"I'm experienced," he said. He should have said something else or nothing at all. Mentioning his experience made her think of, 'less than a thousand' and just where in that approximation she would fall if she were to let him leave his hand where it was.

"Maybe a little too experienced," she said, then turned around, he pulled his hand away and sat up. They were facing each other now. "I think it's time for you to go."

"Are you sure?" he asked.

". . . Yes."

They both knew she was lying. He knew what he had felt and she felt him feel it. Her doubt reflected in her irises. He was so close he could see himself, so close he could kiss her but he wouldn't. Having her initiate would make winning the bet so much sweeter. She wouldn't do that tonight however. She was hungry but she wasn't starving and this was a woman that needed to be starving before she would get on her knees. That would be a wonderful sight; Zawe genuflect and supplicant— but not tonight.

She walked him to the door.

"Well thank you again for the curtains, and the massage," she said.

"It was my pleasure," he said. "And yours too, I think."

"Oh please. You wish."

She slammed the door in his face and proved to herself she

was still in control for all the good that made her feel now. She hadn't climaxed but she had been on the precipice. His hand touched her perineum; through her pants, but it was close enough, and too close to other parts and the other parts were connected to parts of her brain, the pituitary, the hypothalamus. The endorphins shot through her; her mouth watered, her teeth bared. His hands were the ideal balance of strength and gentility. They felt so natural on her body it was as if they were her hands. No man had ever made her feel that way before. Not even Gavin had touched her and made her feel as if she was touching herself. For the first time it crossed her mind she might lose this game. "I need a shower—a cold one. No. A bath. Definitely a bath," where she would finish what began on the sofa and for the first time think of someone other than Gavin as she did so.

52

She walked away from the foyer and was half way up the stairs when there was a knock at the door.

Shit.

He was back.

Shit.

But why?

Did he leave something? She surveyed the living room from where she stood. She didn't see anything of his. So why was he back at her door? Silly rabbit. Stupid question. For the same reason he had made the bet. For the same thing she was thinking about right now. She returned to the front door but "No matter what, don't let him in. Be strong, be—" She put her eye to the peephole and was a bit taken aback as she opened the door for, "Mom! What are you doing here?" Andrea was her daughter plus twenty years. One glance and you knew they were related. You saw it in the face, the build and even the demeanor. The differences were in the details. Zawe was a line drawing while Andrea was shaded in and cross-hatched. Her face had more lines, more character, more history; her body was just as slim but less shapely, less firm, less spry; her eyes were more circumspect and her smile more cynical. The elegance was there as well but Andrea's was a little less enchanting.

"Well hello to you too," she said, and then waited . . . and waited. "Can I come in?"

Zawe was so surprised to see her she had forgotten her manners. "I'm sorry, of course."

Andrea entered and began looking the house over. She hadn't seen the house since a month before Zawe closed and Zawe knew her Mother was analyzing the placement of every piece of furniture, every painting on the wall, every fixture, vase or figurine, looking for something, anything that wasn't just right. "The house is really coming along." She said a compliment but now wait for it . . . wait for it, "If still too big for one person." She never failed and Zawe had learned a while ago to nip this in the bud otherwise she'd be hearing snide remarks all night.

"Mom, I moved out of your house a long time ago so I wouldn't have to deal with your judgments. It's really not fair that you bring them to my house as well."

"Who's judging you, I just said one thing."

"Okay, fine—no fighting. But really, why are you here?"

They walked together into the living room.

"What is this? I can't just come by and visit my daughter?"

"Mom, c'mon, really why are you here?"

Andrea paused a bit for dramatic effect. "Gavin called me."

"Gavin called you? Are you serious?"

"Yes, and are you serious? There are so many women out there looking for good men and you have one and you're letting him get away."

"He's so good that's why he fucked some hood rat."

"I know and he's sorry about that."

The fact that Gavin called her Mother was uninspired but not all that surprising. They always had a special relationship—a little too special as Zawe saw it. Andrea always gave Gavin a hug and a kiss on the cheek when she saw him (and she didn't even do that for her own son) and whenever they came over to visit she would prepare his favorite meal and wear her good blouse and earrings. A small part of Zawe believed her Mother had a tiny crush on Gavin.

"So you're his messenger now?" Zawe asked.

"Well if you would take his calls I wouldn't have to be."

"Well then you can go to him and tell him that I don't want anything else to do with him and he's free to fuck all the hood-rats he wants."

"When did you become so unforgiving?"

"I'm not, I'm just not stupid."

"He made one little mistake."

"He cheated on me for three months. That's not a little mistake."

"And you don't think your father cheated on me? You don't think he had his affairs?"

Zawe wanted to say, just because you didn't respect yourself enough and put up with that shit for years doesn't mean that I should. Instead she said, "And that's why you guys are not together."

"I didn't break up with your father because he cheated on me. I broke up with him because he was an asshole."

"And so is Gavin."

"Well he's a handsome asshole."

Zawe huffed. "That's not enough." *And why are you paying so much attention to how handsome he is?*

"And he has a great job and can take care of you and provide for you."

Sometimes Zawe wondered what era her Mother was living in. "I have a great job and I can take care and provide for myself."

"And he loves you. Can you do that for yourself as well?"

"That's what I'm doing," Zawe said, this time with less conviction however.

"Maybe, but you can't love yourself the way that a man can, believe me."

"Well that love broke my heart. Love like that I don't need."

"Zawe you have to learn to bend sometimes. It keeps you from breaking."

Yeah, but maybe I'm already broken.

53

Alex and Zawe met at a sports bar after eleven the following night. It was a local bar but no less extravagant than one you'd find in Midtown with its rich dark-chocolate leather booths, wood-grained floors, mirrored walls and over forty, forty inch flat panel TVs. At capacity the venue could hold three hundred people. About two hundred and fifty were there that night. The Yankees were hosting the Red Sox in the ALCS and Zawe could have honestly given two shits. She came here to talk and had no interests in sports especially baseball. Alex suggested the sports bar because it was the only venue still open where you could sit down and talk as she wasn't about to invite him to her place again or go over to his.

Besides the comedy club this would mark only their second time meeting in the night and their first doing so on purpose. Having a prior engagement (a date with a Game) Alex couldn't meet after work as they normally would. That left them either meeting in the night or skipping a day. Zawe didn't want that. She needed to see him. Not him in particular she told herself. She just needed someone to talk to. She had her share of friends; a little over 200 by last count on Facebook. But Facebook friends aren't real friends are they. Other than Emma there was no one she felt really comfortable talking to (not about this) and she didn't want to speak to Emma this time because she already knew what Emma would say.

"He cheats on me. I break up with him and everyone makes it seem like I'm the villain."

"Who's everyone?"

"My mother, Emma"

"And you care that much what they think?"

"No, yes. I just don't see why it's no big deal, that I should expect it. I don't accept that. I deserve better," she said and waited for confirmation. Alex just looked at her and she rolled her eyes at her own naiveté. "Why would I expect you to say anything different?"

"How long were you guys together?"

"Six years. We were supposed to get married this past June."

"Did you love him?"

"I just told you I was going to marry him."

"That's not what I asked you."

"Yes I loved him."

"Was he good to you, did he treat you well, was he non-abusive?"

"Yes."

"Was he a good friend, did you feel like he had your back?"

"Mostly."

"And the sex?"

"None of your business."

"I'll take that to mean it was at least adequate, and in that case I think you should forgive him."

"Typical. Why? Because it was just sex and it was no big deal, right?"

"No, it's obviously a big deal to you. But when you add up his plus and minuses he comes out on top." Alex knew this wasn't what she wanted to hear and would seem incongruous with his own intentions. However, he was trying to win a bet—and he would—but her life going forward was a bigger issue, and from everything he had heard, this Gavin sounded like an okay-guy. "And if you're going to leave him to find some other guy who's guaranteed to never cheat on you, well—good luck with that."

"What are you saying then, all men cheat so just accept it?"

"No. And let's get this straight, women cheat just as much as men and you guys do it worse, you make it personal. But what I am saying is, it's more important that your man is respectful than that he's faithful."

"What?" Zawe's neck jerked back as if she had smelled something foul. "That makes absolutely no sense. How can he be unfaithful and be respectful? Being unfaithful is the ultimate disrespect."

"Not if you don't know. And if he's really respectful, you never will."

The stench of what he was saying was so acrid it made her eyes water. "Whether I know or not it's still disrespect, and I refuse to accept this ignorance is bliss bullshit."

"And that's why you're so happy right now."

"Well I'd rather be unhappy with the truth than happy with a lie."

"I take happiness however it comes."

Was it a woman's lot in life to endure pain? Was this the extension of Eve's curse, not only to suffer the pangs of childbirth but to endure the indignity of man's hypocrisy as well? A man could never go through childbirth and he would never turn a blind-eye to his woman's infidelity. Some men go into a rage at the mere suggestion. These men tend to be the biggest philanderers. In some countries a husband can sleep with as many women he wanted but if his wife cheated on him just once he had the right, both legal and moral, to chop her head off. The United States did not advocate spousal decapitation but the principle was more or less the same. Boys will be boys. What's most important is not that your mate be honest but that he is respectful in his dishonesty.

Alex knew this would be a hard pill for her to swallow, nevertheless it was the truth and it wasn't even his truth. It was his mother's. A lot of what Alex understood about women he had learned from his mother. She always told him to respect women (she also told him never to trust them, but that was another matter). She told him that was the true key to a woman's heart and more importantly her loyalty.

She told him she never knew any woman who left her man because he had been unfaithful. It was never the cheating that really upset them. It was finding out about the cheating. It was finding phone numbers, used condom wrappers. It was when the other women would call your house, telling you they had fucked your man. The infidelity hurt the disrespect burned. Even Zawe had to admit what burned the most about Gavin's affair was who he had it with.

"Okay, let's say I buy what you're saying, which I don't, but let's say I buy it. Did he have to cheat on me with some low life skank?"

Her name was Sophia and she was one of those women who were full of pride and had no shame. She dressed trashy, dyed her hair bright red (which unless you were Rihanna you should never do), wore high heels when it wasn't called for and swayed her hips more than needed when she walked to give them extra emphasis. She had at best graduated high school, if that, Zawe surmised from her diction, as she seemed incapable of speaking anything beyond, what's the word . . . ghetto.

While working through her suspicions Zawe had an opportunity to observe Sophia in her natural habitat. She worked as a hair dresser at a hair and nail salon in downtown Brooklyn, which happened to be adjacent to the Barbershop Gavin always went to. That's how they met. Zawe went in to get a manicure and kept a sidelong glance of Sophia the entire time. She wasn't very pretty in the face (not by Zawe's estimation); she however had a decent body and more butt than Zawe. This Zawe attributed to the junk food Sophia ate (Popeye's chicken from across the street) and so she did not begrudge her, her lone windfall.

After all Zawe was trying to look good for the long run. Sophia would look like a train wreck after her twenties. What did Gavin see in her? Besides being the same race and gender she was everything Zawe wasn't. It was almost as if Gavin was trying to make a statement. Was she Zawe's referendum? "Would it have been better if she was more like you?" Alex asked.

"No, it wouldn't have been better but at least I would have understood. But to do it with her, it was like he cheated on me and then he slapped me in my face at the same time."

"I think you're looking at it the wrong way."

"What other way can I look at it?"

"Let's think of women as cars."

"Cars? Really now?"

"Believe me for a man, there are a lot of similarities. Now like cars you have many different classes of women. And let's say that you're a Porsche. Now a Porsche is an impressive car and it's a car you use to impress people. This is the car you take with you when you want people to see you. You give it the best gas, you make sure it's always washed and tuned up, you never push it too hard and you avoid potholes with a vengeance. This car is your baby and you put it up on a pedestal. Unfortunately this isn't a good everyday car, and sometimes you need a car that you can drive hard, like a Honda. This car never gives you any problems, it's ready to ride whenever you are, it's less costly to maintain and you don't care too much about it. You drive this car over all kinds of shit, feed it regular gas and don't worry about where you park it."

"So are you trying to say that I'm high maintenance?"

"No, I'm saying your high quality, but unfortunately most times those two things come together."

"Okay, and for one she was not a Honda, I used to drive a Honda, Hondas are good cars. If anything she was more like a Pinto."

"They don't make Pintos anymore."

"I know. And do you always have to talk in riddles can't you just talk plain?"

"Okay, plain and simple. Be the Porsche that you are and let him have his Pintos because you don't wanna be driven over potholes."

"What?"

"You'll get it when you get home."

54

You'll get it when you get home? Zawe thought about that all night. It troubled her before she went to bed, after which she had a dream about Gavin having sex with Sophia in a Porsche. She woke up agitated, went to work frustrated and by the time she saw Alex again at the park the next evening she was more confused than she had ever been.

"I still don't get it. How can you say you love me and then make love to another woman?"

"That's where you have it wrong. He never made love to another woman."

"Oh yeah, he just had sex with her, but made love to me," Zawe said facetiously.

"No he never made love to you either."

"What the hell are you talking about now?"

"He never made love to you because there's no such thing as making love."

"There's no such thing? Then what were we doing for all those years we were together?"

"You were having intercourse, coitus, coupling but you weren't making love because there's no such thing, because making love is nothing more than a euphemism poets came up with to trick women into forgetting that they were getting fucked."

That one hit her like a slap in the face but it was her insides that turned red rather than her cheeks. Alex had said many things she found offensive: the fact he made his living by conning women, the less than a thousand of them he had been with, the fact he saw no problem comparing them to cars and now this. This one offended the most. The true offense came in the insinuation that what Gavin had with that woman wasn't any different than what he'd had with her. "I hate you, you know that. I don't even know why I thought talking to you would make me feel better."

"I told you I'd tell you the truth, you may not always like it." She walked away from him with forty minutes still to go in the hour. She would have to reimburse him for the time another day. That's if there would be another day. She looked so angry he wouldn't have been surprised if she ended the bet right then and there, and even if she didn't the days remaining in his month were dwindling.

55

His name was Jeff and Jeff was a gastroenterologist, which in Emma's mind was an ostentatious way of saying Jeff dealt with a lot of shit. Jeff was the friend of a Facebook friend Emma had gone on a date with the night before.

Finding a Black doctor with no wife and no children seemed to her like she may have hit the jackpot. Then she started wondering how was it at thirty-five this never been in jail, highly educated, well earning man—and straight at that—had not already been snatched up. Granted he wasn't handsome (but not ugly by any means) but that shouldn't have been an outright deal breaker.

Once you've hit your late twenties for a woman looks stop having as much sway as they once did. They were still important and preferable just not paramount. He was a fixer-upper but there was nothing a woman loved more than transforming a man into her own image of what a man should be. So what was his deal?

Within twenty minutes at dinner Emma found out. Jeff was an asshole, an old school bona fide jerk, who obviously loved being a doctor because he mentioned it fifteen times for the night. He believed his intelligence was his greatest asset and like a woman with a great rack loved showing it off.

Snarky and condescending he just about corrected everything she said, and had the gumption to tell her to get out of real estate, as if she needed him to tell her how rough the market was. She knew it. She lived it every day and was getting by. He must have believed he was turning her on with all his bloviating and he had good reason to as she invited him back to her place after dinner.

She kept telling herself he was a doctor, that he had a solid foundation and just needed to be worked on. By the end of the night she thought the foundation should be razed. He had sex (well at least attempted to) like a man who was used to paying for it.

He gave commands and expected them to be followed. When she didn't, he couldn't get it up, blamed her for his flaccidity and suggested she help him out with her mouth. That's when she'd had enough and kicked him out but not before he called her a fucking cunt.

Zawe listened with feigned interest only she wasn't feigning very well. They sat in Emma's living room and Emma had just told her about her night with shit-man. After what Emma went through she thought at the very least she had a great story to tell her friend—apparently not. Zawe looked as riveted as a cockroach—not very.

"What are you talking about? I heard every word. He was a doctor and an asshole but you let him fuck you anyway."

"He didn't fuck anything. I told you he couldn't get it up."

"But if he had been able to you would have let him."

"Well I'm sorry we all can't make love all the time like you do."

"Oh no I don't. Because apparently none of us are making love, we're all just getting fucked."

Without fail another one of their conversations had centered back on Alex. This had been cute for the first week or so but now at the close of week three for Emma it had gotten . . . well . . . *fucking annoying*. "Honestly, if you're gonna fuck him, do it already, if not just stop seeing him and end this charade," Emma said with a twinge of rancor.

"Fuck him? Are you not hearing me?"

"Oh I hear you. I've been hearing you for about three weeks." *Funny how I've listened to all of your stories but you can't give me the respect to listen to one of mine.* "And it boils down to either you're going to do it or you're not."

"I'm not."

"Good. Then can I call him?"

"What?" Zawe was flabbergasted. "Why would you want to?"

"Why would I want to? So I can do the same thing you want to but keep fighting."

"I'm not fighting anything."

"Yeah, whatever."

56

Ian thought so hard his head hurt. His head was begin-ning to feel like his ass and he was straining to defecate an idea, a joke, a bit, a punch-line . . . a bit of anything but nothing was forthcoming, nothing he hadn't already said a thousand times in a thousand different ways.

It seemed he had been telling the same joke all of his life. Still he couldn't fault himself too much. He was a product of his environment. It was the same joke most Black comedians told. What was the difference between Black and White people? Which usually boiled down to, Black people were cool and White people were corny? Black people were ghetto and White people were haughty.

"White folks always wanna do shit like go camping in the woods. Only people who ain't scared of losing their shit think going out and building a tent and sleeping on the hard ass ground playing like they homeless is fun. Niggas don't go camping—nah uh. That's cause most Niggas is just a couple pay checks away from really camping—on the street.

"Do you know what the major difference between Black and White people are? It's not the skin color, or the hair, or the nose, or the lips—it's the calves. It's the fucking calves man. White people got some big ass calves. I mean, White people, goddamn, where ya'll get them big ass calves from? I mean some of them be some tree trunk looking like motherfuckers. Have you ever seen a white person with skinny calves? If you do, report them to National Geographic because that motherfucker be the missing link."

Years ago Ian got a good deal of traction with those bits. His best routine, however, and the one that landed him on BET's Comic View was his spoof on Black theatre. "Our plays always got something to do with somebody's Mama and Jesus. Don't they? Be some shit called, 'Lord, Mama Done Stole Ma Man So I Shot Them Both.' Starring a buncha Black actors who can't get another job so they forced to do this shit. Like that big Black chick from Amen, and Cockroach from the Cosby Show, and Thelma from Good Times playing Mama and starring Vivica Fox as the Daughter. And Vivica be saying some shit like, 'Lawd, I know you said to honor your Mother and Father, but you ain't neva said nothing about if your Mama was a hoe.'"

That bit fed him for two years. That bit bought him a house. But inevitably like all things it got old and there was a nothing an audience hated more than a stale joke.

He used to have a series of jokes about the impossibility of there ever being a Black president. He used to pay his rent on those jokes and then 2008 came. It had been a rough four years. His lowest point came in talking about the difference between White people dogs and Black people dogs, and how well behaved they were as opposed to 'Nigga' dogs. When Alex came to him with new material they were like a life line for a drowning man.

"You ever be buying jeans at the mall and you find a pair you really like, I mean it's the right color, the perfect fade, it got the right amount of rips in it, so people know you bought it in a store and just pretending to look like a bum instead of really being one, and it's your size too—and then you look at the cut and it say some shit like super skinny. Super fucking skinny. Who the fuck can wear super skinny jeans? Only women should ever wear super skinny jeans. Because you can't have balls and wear super skinny jeans. The only way you can wear super skinny jeans is if you put your balls between your legs and walk like this. I did that once when I was a kid, and my father saw me and he beat the shit out of me. Now, I know what you all are thinking. That's so terrible your father was so homophobic. Yes he was but so was everyone else in here up until ten minutes ago. Also

I think the term homophobic is a misnomer. I do. I don't think anyone is really homophobic. A phobia is an irrational fear. You ever seen people with phobias? They are as crazy as fuck. Like my Auntie, she has a fear of teddy bears. Hey don't ask, don't tell. But you put a fucking teddy bear, big small whatever, next to her and that woman will lose her fucking mind. She'll break out in hives; she'll start sweating and will literally get a panic attack and run from the room if you force that teddy bear on her. Now I ain't never seen nobody break out in hives and run clear out of a room because they seen a drag queen. People are not homophobic. What the people who don't like Gay people are, are homo-intolerant. Now that's not me. I believe in Gay rights, I believe in Gay marriage, I believe Gays should serve openly in the military. Hey if they wanna go to Afghanistan and get blown up so that Exxon Mobil can get tax breaks more power to them because I know I ain't fucking doing it. And for all those people talking about the sanctity of marriage ask them if they willing to vote for a law that outlaws divorce and see how quick they shut the fuck up. There ain't no sanctity of marriage once you can get divorced. Goddamn Kim Kardashian was married for 72 days. Sanctity of marriage my ass. I believe Gay people have the right to be miserable like everyone else. Now what I might be though is a little homo-uncomfortable, homo-I don't wanna see that shit. I ain't gon' lie, I'm trying to get over it, but when I see two Gay guys together, holding hands, making kissy-kiss, it turns my stomach. I'm all for coming out the closet but can you keep it in the bedroom. Hey I'm sorry, and like said I'm trying to get over it. Hey I tried watching Brokeback Mountain. I really did, but once they got into that tent I was like that's it honey put Batman on, I like Joker better as a psychopath."

Alex's bits were like a breath of fresh air. They were riskier but because of that they paid off even more. Ian used to joke about race but he would never get political and he'd talk about sex but never really got into the complexity of relationships. Alex opened him up to an entirely new avenue and audience. Ian had been swimming in a lake. Alex brought him to an ocean.

Now Ian was trying to swim on his own again but the best he could do was tread. Nothing was coming to mind, nothing that wasn't already put there by Alex. Was he really, like Lillian said, less of a man for having Alex write his jokes? He had never thought about it that way before. He began to question himself? Was it true? Did he want to be Alex? He wore his clothes and he told his jokes. It seemed everywhere he looked he saw the man. So it was fitting that he would now be on his caller ID. Ian answered his phone.

"Yo Ian."

"What's good?"

"I have an idea for a new bit."

Did he want it? Would he take it? Of course he would. What did Lillian know? She didn't know comedy. Ian wouldn't be the first comedian to have a writing partner. She didn't know what the hell she was talking about. She didn't know shit. Fuck Lillian. "Let's do this."

57

"The difference in the way men and women see sex is like the difference in how we take a piss." Ian was performing on stage at the Laughing Stock. "Yes for a man it's nice to piss in a clean toilet but it don't mean all that much. We'll piss on the street, we'll piss in a bush, we'll piss in a back alley next to a crack head. Hell we might piss in a motherfuckin crack head. We don't give a fuck, we just whip it out and whip it back in. And that's how we see sex, it feels good and it's no big deal. A Woman now, she ain't gon' drop her drawers and piss just any-where. She has to feel comfortable. Women have a hard time using restrooms. If it's too wet in there, she ain't using it. If it don't smell just right she ain't using it. Hell it could be perfect in there, she still ain't gon' sit, she gon' squat." He pantomimed a woman pulling down her underwear and squatting to take a pee. The audience laughed heartily. "Sometimes that's not even good enough and she'll hold it until she gets home. Fellas you ever try to talk to a woman on the street and she speed walks right pass you. Hey beautiful how you—" He walked like a woman trying desperately to hold in her urine. "Well goddamn bitch I was just trying to say hello. Fellas don't get offended. It's not you. It's cause she's rushing home to take a piss, because that's where she feels comfortable. And once a woman finds a toilet that she's comfortable with, she's holding onto it. She wants a commitment from that motherfucker because she knows just how nasty all those other toilets outside are."

There was no greater high than killing. The sensation you feel to have a room filled with people riveted by your every word and pouncing on every punch-line was like having the best sex but only better. This orgasm lasted longer.

As usual Alex stood to the back in the dark of the room. Ian walked over and they greeted each other with a pound. "How was it?" Ian asked, already knowing the answer but just wanting to hear Alex confirm, "You killed it."

"Yeah. It felt damn good out there." Just then he saw Troy Dixon the owner of the Laughing Stock walking over with a beaming smile. That was because walking just behind him was Jamie Murphy. Jamie Murphy was the preeminent Black comedian of the day. He was in his early forties but had already had two comedy specials on HBO, been in multiple movies, three of which he starred in, and had had his own television series, which ran for four seasons and was now syndicated. He was what every comedian wanted to be. He looked and smelled like money. Alex dressed like money but Jamie smelled like money and there was a difference. He was dark complexioned but he glowed and seemed to light up the entire room.

"Ian Washington," Troy began, "I'd like to introduce you to—"

Ian didn't need him to finish. "Jamie Murphy, What's up man?" They gave each other a pound. He even felt like money. Everything about him was rich.

"What's up is you. I caught your set. You got some real funny shit," Jamie said.

"Thank you man. Coming from you that means a lot."

"Sex and pissing, I liked how you put them together."

How Alex put them together but that didn't matter. He and Alex were a team. "Wait till you hear my next one on love and shitting."

"Can't wait. But let me get your info. I got a few things in the works. I might be able to use you."

"Well use me motherfucker. Use me the fuck up."

Was this it? Was this finally the moment Ian would break through? It certainly seemed that way. He remained cool but deep inside his heart was beating with a kind of excitement that only a child and a dreamer can have.

58

Alex entered from the door adjacent to the driveway. As soon as he stepped inside he was reminded this was a house with children. Even when he didn't see them he smelled their youth and heard their tiny footsteps and faint laughter in the distance. Adriana's house was what a home should be, warm and welcoming with character and history; a stark contrast to his apartment. Where he lived had no personality, and if it did it would be that of the interior decorator—post-modern and very staid. Alex never stayed in any one place long enough for his presence to inhabit it; no photos on the walls, nothing magnetized to the fridge. He liked it that way. When you inhabit a place for too long things start to feel familiar, and when things start to feel familiar, you start to get attached and when that happens the inevitable detachment becomes less detachable. Adriana was by the kitchen counter preparing dinner. "Is she upstairs?" he asked her.

"Yeah, she is," Adriana answered.

Alex nodded and started for upstairs but before he could leave the room, "Bree's wedding is Saturday," Adriana called to him.

"I know. I got your invite, your email and your post on my wall."

If there was something to be said of Adriana she was conscientious. She loved that word. She saw it on her report card when she was seven and asked her mother what it meant. Katherine told her it meant she was thorough and careful. Adriana liked that. She liked it so much, like a self-fulfilling prophesy, she had endeavored to be even more conscientious ever since.

"Good. I want you to bring a date," she said to him.

"Um—Why?"

"Because I don't want a repeat of what happened at my first wedding, you hitting on all the single women, and two of them getting into a fight."

Alex couldn't remember their names or what had caused the kerfuffle. Adriana did. When you've been planning your wedding since you were six you tend to remember the things that ruin it. Alex flirted with two women that night. One of them was her cousin (but not his) Jennifer who had never heard a snide remark she didn't challenge. The offhand comment came from Macie (Adriana's ex-husband's sister) who, after a brief chat-up, had taken a territorial liking to Alex, and was miffed at him concurrently courting, "the chick in the red hoochie dress," she said under her breath but not out of earshot. Jennifer took offense and the low road, which devolved into brief fisticuffs (well slap-ti-cuffs) while the bride and groom were cutting the cake. "Oh yeah, that was fun," Alex recalled after Adriana jogged his memory.

"Actually no it wasn't." Thankfully for Adriana, Alex was in Europe during her second wedding but he would be coming to this one, "And I figure if you bring a date it won't happen again. So think of someone."

59

Come the next day he was still mulling it over. Alex knew a lot of women. Correction. He knew of a lot of women. To know of and to know are two different things. He'd never given himself the time to really get to know any of them, not on purpose but you can't feign desire. And now which one of these intimate acquaintances would he want to take to a family wedding? Would it be a Fun or a Game? Neither were very appealing options and his pervading thought was to say 'fuck it' and go alone as originally planned, but he knew Adriana had worked hard on the wedding and he did not want to upset her. Though right now upsetting Adriana was the least of his concerns. The Dow Jones Industrial Average closed down 225 points, the Nasdaq was down 50 and the Standard and Poor's 500 was down 27, which all added up to Alex being down a little over 50 grand.

Despite a popular myth most Day Traders are losers. On average, only 18 percent of them make money and the majority of people who get into the racket won't survive long enough to make it into that lofty 18 percent, and if they do, that majority will just be getting by (on a median annual income of 65,000) not getting rich—though some did. Alex wasn't rich (by any means—not by modern standards) however on most trading days he closed better than he started. On the days he didn't, like today, he didn't fret a margin call because Alex didn't borrow on margin, he borrowed on kindness. A kindness he would now have a little more trouble repaying.

Zawe entered the Dumbo Lounge and found Alex at the bar nursing a glass of wine. As she approached him, "Have a drink with me," he said and gestured to the Bartender to get Zawe a glass.

"Why, what's the occasion?"

"We're celebrating."

"Celebrating. Celebrating what?"

"Losing fifty grand."

"Who lost fifty grand?" He took a sip of his wine. "You lost fifty grand?"

The Bartender brought Zawe her drink and Alex clanked his glass to hers.

"Drink up."

"Oh my God. I'm so sorry." She looked genuinely concerned.

"Don't worry about it. It wasn't like it was my money."

His cavalier attitude reminded her just how he came by his income and whatever sympathy she felt quickly dissipated. "Oh well. It's your own fault. Day trading is stupid. You'd make more if you held onto your stocks and it would be a lot less stressful."

"Yeah but I don't like owning things, remember."

"Oh I remember. And what were you doing to lose fifty thousand in one day? How do you pick your stocks anyway?"

"Seriously?"

"I didn't know we were joking."

"Eenie meenie miney moe."

"You're kidding me, right?"

"Well not exactly but, pretty close." She shook her head and looked at him as if he was an utter moron. "Hey the people who think they can actually figure out the market are the ones really kidding themselves."

"Well seen as how you just lost fifty thousand in one day, I think I'll follow the advice of the professionals."

"Yeah, but I also made over a hundred last week."

She looked doubtful but could tell he was telling the truth.

It wasn't in his nature to try to impress you by lying. He would feel it was beneath him.

Alex was like a monkey picking stocks by throwing darts at a board, and he didn't even trade every day, just on the days he felt like making money, and unlike other day traders he didn't spend his hours on his computer anxiously watching his picks, buying and selling and reselling; subsequently paying all that commission tax. He simply bought stocks at 9:45, sold them all before 4:15 and accepted whatever the outcome was—more times than not he came out ahead, if only barely.

Zawe couldn't help thinking now about how much money he possibly had. If he made a hundred grand last week and lost fifty today, he should have at least another fifty in the bank. This was to say nothing of what he may have made or lost on previous days or what he got from those imbecilic women he talked to.

It just occurred to her Alex may not just be getting by, but actually doing very well and possibly better than she was. This she found offensive—not because she was competitive (though she was) but because she worked hard for everything she had and to think Alex could have more for doing nothing was an affront.

She was busy being offended in her mind when he kind of sort of blurted "By the way, my cousin is getting married, the weddings Saturday. Do you wanna come?" Zawe's wine went down the wrong tube and she began coughing to keep herself from choking. "Are you alright?"

"Yeah . . . yeah—no."

"No, you're not alright?"

"No I won't go to your cousin's wedding." She regained herself. "Are you crazy?"

"Why is that crazy?"

"You're even crazier for not knowing why that's crazy. Weddings are major dates, where you invite people you're serious about to meet your family."

"Nah, people invite friends to weddings all the time. And we're friends aren't we?"

That's what he settled on. He figured bringing a Fun or a

Game might complicate things and may also (being aware, as Zawe said, that Women take weddings seriously) give off the wrong idea. And frankly he didn't want any of them knowing that much about him or his family knowing that much about them. So he decided to take a friend, but outside of Ian he really didn't have any friends (they're hard to keep when you move about as often as he does) and he didn't think Ian was what Adriana had in mind—unless he wanted to give his family something very interesting to think about. Then he saw Zawe and thought if seeing someone every day for the last three weeks didn't constitute a friendship he didn't know what did. Granted this was a friend he had made a bet to have sex with but beggars can't be choosers.

60

They don't put price tags on items in the Louis Vuitton store and it's considered gauche to ask. It's assumed if you have to ask then you really can't afford what you're looking at and by extension should not be in the staore. Emma found their policy both bourgeois and ill-conceived. No matter how expensive something was it was always best for the consumer to know what they were getting into before they plunked down their credit. It also didn't make any sense. A new car cost exponentially more than anything the store sold and car dealers advertised their prices all the time. There was no logic behind the policy other than blatant elitism—nonetheless Emma gave them her 1,500 dollars without protest. There was a yellow tote bag she convinced herself she just had to have. "God this bag is hot. I am getting this," she said to Zawe.

"Yeah it's nice you should."

Zawe had accompanied Emma to the boutique having already gotten pass their argument from a few days prior. Ever since freshman year at Cornell they had never been able to stay mad with each other for too long.

The bag would be Emma's present to herself for selling a house. She closed on it yesterday, which was something of a minor miracle. She had worked diligently on the property for four months when there was a snafu on the bank's end and the deal was halted. After five months elapsed with no forward movement Emma thought the deal had been killed completely until two days ago when she got the green light and a closing date. That 30,000 dollar commission was like found money, and there was nothing better than found money—well except for a good hard dick. No thirty grand was better but a good dick was a close second. It was funny how making money made you so horny. She had dick on her mind as she glanced over at the male clerk at the register; tall, lean built and handsome—actually it was more like pretty with his flaxen hair and delicate features. White Boys weren't usually her thing but if pretty-boy asked her the right way he could get it.

"Forget it. He's gay." Zawe whispered.

"Yeah?"

"Yeah, just look at him."

Emma watched him with another customer, his mannerisms and his gestures. He was admittedly a fop, a metrosexual at the least. "But that doesn't mean he's gay. He might just be a little feminine. There are straight men like that."

"Oh please, that's a myth. There are no feminine acting straight men."

Emma looked again. He wasn't overtly flamboyant so it was hard to tell but then he told a customer her bag looked fabulous and that sold it. "Yeah you're right. Only Gay guys ever use the word fabulous." she said, her mouth in a moue, and they both laughed.

"Hey, he invited me to a wedding." Zawe said, figuring this a good a time as any to bring it up.

"What? He who? Alex?" Zawe nodded. "Did I miss something? Did you already lose the bet and you guys are planning on moving in together?"

"Hell no. That's why I don't get it either."

"So what did you tell him?"

"No, of course. I'm just confused why he would even think to ask."

Emma thought for a moment then an idea came to her. "I got it. He knows how women get at weddings, you know, emotional, vulnerable, and then there'll be free liquor and only a few days left to the bet. Yep, he's trying to do it that night, girl."

Zawe hadn't thought about it that way but now that Emma said it, it made sense. "You're right. That asshole. Now I'm definitely not going."

"We're you actually considering it?'

"No . . . no."

Another idea came to Emma. "You know what, you should go."

"Wait, but you just said—"

"Yeah but now you know, so you'll be prepared, you'll see him coming. Plus this is a great way to prove to him that he can't win, right?"

Zawe hadn't thought about it that way either. "Right."

"Good. Now you just have to remember to not get emotional."

61

Don't get emotional.

Zawe felt that had been a silly thing for Emma to say. Zawe had never been the type to get maudlin at weddings. She'd been to seven before, been a bridesmaid in three, and never shed a tear at any of them, and believed the women who did so did it more as a result of envy than empathy. She was, however, forgetting one important point. This was the first wedding she'd be attending since the dissolution of her own. Sitting in the pews she felt like a woman who had miscarried looking at a mother with a newborn. You're happy for the mother but seeing her reminds you of what you've lost and it burns, it burns deep.

It was a beautiful ceremony as was the church it was held in; Gothic and appropriately gauche. It sat five hundred and roughly two hundred of those seats were taken. The attendants were all well dressed and respectful, the Pastor spoke wisely and to the point, the Bride and Groom were very handsome and their vows were even more so.

"Bree, you are my moon and stars, my lighthouse in the storm. I promise to love you for now and ever after," the Groom said and Zawe couldn't help but see Gavin in his place. He would have looked so handsome in his tuxedo. "Jason, you are my sun and earth, my lighthouse in the storm. I promise to love you for now and ever after," Briana said. Imagining herself as the bride was a bit too much for Zawe however. It poked at her heart all the way to her back and she felt something akin to gas pain in her scapula.

Don't get emotional. Don't get emotional. Zawe couldn't help it. Tears began to line the corners of her eyes. She tried to fight it. Like holding in her pee she resisted crying outright, and was dabbing the water with the back of her finger when she felt a hand reach over and hold hers. It was Alex's hand. For the first time they were holding hands. It surprised her that he did it, that he knew to do it at that moment and more so that it felt so good. She held his hand back.

62

To Alex, Zawe was always beautiful but on that day she was what the French call éblouissant—dazzling. She wore her hair up, swept over to the left and slicked back into a bun, showing off her brow, and her face, and her neck, and her dress (steel green and slinky fit without being too scandalous, cut above the knees with a crowl neck and fluttery sleeves), had a delicate décolletage showing just the mouth of her cleavage. He wanted to put his mouth on it and kiss it.

At the church was the first time he saw her. She chose to take a cab and meet him at the wedding. She didn't want him picking her up. That would make this seem too much like a date—and this assuredly was not a date. It was a proclamation of . . . something that would never be. Also it was a reason for her to get dolled up.

Sometimes the best part of going out is getting dressed. She had bought this dress a year ago and loved it but so far never found an occasion to wear it. As soon as she put it on she was happy she agreed to go. It's not conceit or arrogance to acknowledge your own attractiveness. Zawe didn't go around saying it but she knew she was a beautiful woman. Nevertheless it was always nice to be reaffirmed. This dress was that reaffirmation. "You look good girl," she said to herself—and it felt good to look good—and damn if he didn't look good as well.

He met her as her car pulled up and like a gentleman opened the door. Zawe must admit on the ride over she was excited for him to see her, in this dress and these shoes (four inch black Manolos) and with this hair-do. How would he look at her, what would he say? He had never seen her all dressed up before nor had she ever seen him. That was something she hadn't considered though she should have. Even in jeans and sneakers Alex was always well dressed, so she should have imagined he would look good in his suit as well. However, imagining and seeing are two different things.

He wore a black Dolce and Gabana with a white shirt and a light blue-silver tie. It was simple and elegant and he looked absolutely gorgeous in it. He had the perfect build for a suit, just the right amount of muscles to fill it out without distracting from the cut. It was just cloth but there was something about a man in a suit that did something for her. This was to say nothing of the Patek Philippe time-piece he wore, which gave him a sense of other worldly class.

Wow, she thought and, "Wow," he said as he helped her out the car. "You clean up good."

"You too."

They said nothing else but their eyes elaborated. There were exclamation points in his pupils and ellipses in hers . . . she was a little speechless—and they didn't hold hands going into the church and though they did briefly sitting in the pews, they didn't hold hands going into the reception.

63

The reception was held in the grand ballroom of the Long Island Marriot. Zawe's reception would have been held at her Uncle Benji's house in Jersey. His house was something of a minor mansion and his backyard, an acre of verdant lawn and stately oak trees, made for an ideal wedding space. Hosting the reception would have been his gift to his favorite niece. As Zawe and Alex passed through the white rose arches leading into the ballroom she was reminded of the floral-pergola-covered stone path her guests would have walked to her reception.

The hotel ballroom was decorated in a classic black and white motif. The tables had champagne-colored linens, glowing candles as well as white hydrangeas and ivory roses arranged on gold pedestals. Zawe's would have featured garden cherubs surrounded by flowers in varying shades of purple, and her floral arrangement was to be made of peonies, garden roses, ranunculi and hydrangeas. Zawe didn't want to but she couldn't help comparing everything that was to everything that could have been. Both versions were beautiful but hers was also melancholy.

Don't get emotional. That had been Emma's caveat. It was more like Emma's curse as every time Zawe thought about not getting emotional she got emotional. She fought hard to hold it back and again felt Alex holding her hand. How did he know to give his hand just when she seemed to need it most?

"Thanks again for coming," he said.

"No problem. I'm happy I came."

"So, I guess this is what being in a relationship is about huh, having someone to go to weddings with."

She thought about that for a moment before saying, rather soberly, "No, it's not. It's about having someone to go to funerals with."

That took him aback. "That's kind of dark," and from Zawe so unexpected.

"Maybe, but it's true."

They approached Katherine and Adriana who were toward the front of the ballroom greeting guests as they entered. Katherine looked jovial and especially vibrant today, not showing any signs of her illness, none at least that Zawe who was seeing her for the first time could notice. She wore an amber wig that extended to her shoulders, complimented with a pearl colored silk scarf artfully tied around her neck, and a lavender full length Halston gown. Katherine had been happy before but she absolutely beamed when she saw Alex with this elegant woman by his side.

"Aunt Kate, Adriana, I'd like to introduce you to Zawe."

"Hi, it's nice to meet you. Thanks for coming," Adriana said extending her hand to Zawe.

Zawe politely shook it. "Thanks for having me. Everything is all so beautiful."

"As are you," Katherine said straight and to the point. Zawe was about to accept her compliment when Katherine continued, "and you have a good spirit too."

That pleasantly took Zawe aback.

"Really? Thank you. How, how can you tell?"

"Oh I can. It's a little gift of mine." Katherine had always claimed clairvoyance when it came to knowing people. More times than not she was correct. She had warned Adriana about her first husband and her second. Adriana hadn't listened to her on either account. "Alex don't lose this one. If you do, you'll regret it forever." Alex and Zawe laughed uncomfortably. "I love my nephew but he has all these crazy ideas. He thinks he's smarter than everyone."

"Yes he does," Zawe enthusiastically concurred.

"He's too smart for his own good is the problem. He probably hasn't said it but he likes you a lot."

"Does he?"

Had Katherine divulged one of Alex's intimations? If she had Alex didn't seem to mind. "Yes. And you like him too don't you?" Katherine said.

"Mom, please," Adriana interposed.

"What? I'm menopausal and I'm sick, I can say whatever I want."

"Yes you can. And you look hot," Alex said to her as he leaned in and kissed her cheek.

"Thank you. And I'm serious, don't lose her," Katherine said only to him.

Alex looked at Zawe and how stunning she was in her dress. "Not tonight, I won't."

64

When you reach a certain age and you don't have children every child you see becomes a reminder of the child you don't have. Sometimes it was a pleasant reminder. Zawe would call a friend and wouldn't be able to have a decent talk because all they did was scream at their kids in the background, and Zawe would say to herself thank God I don't have to deal with that; the sleepless nights, the cost of day-care, the lack of freedom, the overall knowledge that your life was no longer your own. Then there were the times she saw a child and they were well mannered and so loving and so full of life, and she looked at them and she wondered how her face would look on theirs, how would it be to have that face greet her as she came home every day, to tell her that they loved her. A child's love that was the purest kind. It was a love that would never betray you.

Alex said he didn't want children but he sure loved playing with other people's kids. Tasha, Adriana's four-year-old, held her breath like Dizzie Gillespie trying to outdo her much older cousin. She gave it all she had for a half minute then smashed Alex's cheeks causing him to exhale. "I win she declared," to Zawe's applause and Alex's mock chagrin.

"Oh, you're such a cheater," Alex protested and took his revenge on her tiny torso, tickling her till she cried from laughter. Zawe admired the absolute joy on Tasha's face. She had forgotten what joy looked like and how a simple thing like tickling could provoke it. For a moment she wished he was tickling her and thought, "Why don't you pick on someone your own size," out loud.

Alex turned and looked at her and they both realized she had said something she didn't intend. She sort of winced. He sort of smiled. She playfully punched him in the shoulder and smiled as well. Just then Seychelle, Adriana's seven year old, walked over to their table. Her chest heaved and she looked as if she was about to cry.

"Hey Sehseh, what's wrong?" Alex asked.

Holding back her tears, "One of Jason's cousin's pushed me. And I didn't even do anything to him," Seychelle said.

Seychelle didn't have Zawe's face but she could see herself in her because the exact same thing had happened to Zawe at that age. "Oh sweetie, don't worry. He did it because he likes you, okay." Seychelle looked at her as if she was crazy. "I know it never made sense to me either."

"It's because he doesn't know how to tell you he likes you, so he pushed you to get your attention," Alex tried to explain.

Strangely what Alex just said elucidated a lot of things for Zawe. Men hurt you because they don't know how to talk to you. It was that simple.

Seychelle looked confounded. "Boys are so stupid."

"Yes they are. And unfortunately they won't get any smart-er."

Alex smiled at the both of them. "You want me to beat him up for you?" He asked Seychelle.

"Yes."

"Alright, but give me a hug first." Seychelle happily obliged. As they hugged Zawe looked on and began to see something very different in Alex, and began to think that if he wasn't who he was he could be something special.

65

The Bride and Groom danced their first dance to Clair de Lune by Claude Debussy. Zawe found their choice very fitting and in keeping with the overall elegance of the reception. She wondered also if they had taken ballroom dance lessons beforehand as they waltzed so beautifully.

After they finished the DJ invited the guests to take the floor and started off by playing Michael Jackson's Human Nature.

"God, I love this song," Zawe said as soon as the opening melody began.

"Yeah, me too. I'm surprised that they'd play it here though."

To Zawe that seemed to be a very strange thing to say. "Why wouldn't they play it here?"

"Well the song is about not being satisfied with one woman. It seems kinda inappropriate for a wedding."

Given this was one of her all-time favorite songs Zawe took offense. "Where the hell did you get that from?"

"From the lyrics."

"Where in the lyrics?"

"Have you ever really listened to Human Nature?" he asked her.

"I've heard it a thousand times."

"Yes, but have you ever really listened to it?" She looked confused. "Go ahead, really listen."

As Human Nature played Zawe listened, perhaps for the first time, to the entire song, its lyrics and their context—and as she listened she watched the other couples as they joined the Bride and Groom on the dance floor. She watched the children running around playing tag. An eight year old boy pushed Seychelle and ran off, and she looked back at Alex and Zawe and threw up her hands. Zawe looked at her, shrugged her shoulders and smiled. Zawe then looked at the Elders sitting off to the side watching and smiling themselves.

When the song ended Zawe felt as if she had arrived at a new plane of understanding and was seeing the world in a different way, like someone who had just learned to read and could finally make out street signs.

"You're right. I've always been so enchanted with his voice and the music that I never really listened to what he was saying."

"See I told you."

"But it's not about him not being satisfied with one woman. It's about him feeling suffocated by the pressure that fame brought him and wanting to get away from it and see the city."

"Okay, for one, Michael Jackson didn't write that song, Steve Porcaro and John Bettis did, so it couldn't have been talking about Michael's experiences and desires. Also it says it pretty clearly in the song. In the first verse he's drawn to the night life in the city. The city winks a sleepless eye. Hear her voice, sweet seducing sighs. Now In the second verse he finds a girl, she knows I'm watching, she likes the way I stare. In the third verse he wakes up in bed with her. I touch her shoulder but already I'm dreaming of the street. And if they say, why, why? Tell 'em that it's human nature. Why, why? Why, does he do me that way? Because I like living this way. I like loving this way."

Zawe hated to say it, and she wouldn't, but Alex's analysis made sense and, after hearing it, she couldn't imagine interpreting the song another way, which sucked. She felt as if she had gotten a tattoo of Chinese characters on her heart believing they stood for love and just found out they meant 'I give free blowjobs.' She felt a little betrayed, but she wouldn't give Alex the pleasure of knowing it.

"Whatever, I don't buy it. It's a beautiful song and I'm not going to let you ruin it for me."

"Dance with me," he said—unexpectedly for the both of them.

"What? No. Especially not after what you just said."

"Zawe, you look absolutely beautiful and I'd be hurt if we went through this whole night and I never got a chance to dance with you. Please. Just one dance."

He extended his hand. She looked at it with a smirk and then looked in his eyes. For the first time she saw something new—vulnerability and an earnest desire—as if he really wanted her to dance with him and would be genuinely disappointed if she didn't.

66

Just one dance, she kept saying to herself; one song, maybe two, depending on how much she liked the song, then no more. Also she would keep her distance. Just because they were dancing together it didn't mean they had to touch each other. That would be a bit difficult at the moment as the music selection just went from R&B to Reggae."Hold up, changed my mind, I'm not doing this," Zawe declared.

"What's wrong now?"

She looked at him as if it wasn't already obvious, as if they had planned to go to a picnic and he didn't see that it had started raining outside. "I'm not dancing Reggae with you."

"What's wrong with Reggae?"

"Nothing, but it's not dancing. It's more like having sex standing up with your clothes on."

This he knew to be true. Reggae dancing was famously licentious. If you didn't get a bit of a rise while doing it you probably weren't doing it right. But still, "Zee, c'mon. It's a wedding. It's a family gathering. No one is going to be dancing like that."

"Oh really." She motioned for him to turn around. There were three couples behind them doing things that made dirty dancing look tame.

"Damn . . . and they're cousins." He turned back to Zawe. "Okay, what if I promise to stay at least a foot away from you at all times."

"You promise?"

"Yes. And you know I have to tell you the truth."

That's what he said but had he always told her the truth? She wasn't sure or if he would keep his promise now. She would have to do something she so very rarely did with Alex. She would have to trust him. Outside of letting him in her house she had never done that before and she remembered how well that turned out. That just reminded her of the bet and just how dangerous this man could be. Still she was being silly. What could he possibly do here, with a foot separating them, in the span of one, maybe two, maybe three songs?

The DJ played John Holt's A Love I can Feel. It was an old school slow tempo reggae jam. Alex held her hand making sure to keep the distance between them.

"See nice and easy," he said.

"Just make sure it stays that way," she said.

He two stepped and she followed his lead. He watched the way her hips swayed from one side to the other, how the sway moved delicately, intimately through her torso, her shoulders, her neck, her smile—she wasn't smiling. He had to laugh. She was always trying so hard to reign herself in. Relax girl, let yourself go, let the demon out, he wanted to say, but he wouldn't, because it wouldn't have worked. Zawe wasn't the kind of woman to initiate. If you wanted to see her demon you'd have to pull him out of her . . . slowly. So he took his time and kept his distance. The song changed. The DJ was in a John Holt mood as he faded from A Love I can Feel to Ali Baba. Ali Baba was a fanciful tale blending fairy tales and other children's stories with a roots rock reggae beat. The song didn't take itself seriously and neither did Alex. He danced like an old man, doing moves that had been obsolete for decades. It was funny and she appreciated that he didn't mind making a fool of himself as long as he didn't make a fool of her while he did it. Zawe enjoyed dancing but she was never the center of the floor kind of girl; didn't like having all those eyes on her. They had that in common. When Alex danced he always preferred to stay off to the side. For him dancing was the prologue not the plot. The trick was to seamlessly segue from one to the other.

The DJ moved onto song three. It was still reggae but more up tempo. Alex picked up the pace, and began to pace around, suavely two-stepping while seductively looking her over. Snaking her neck she mocked his expression and pushed him off. He came at her again and again she pushed him, but this time he caught her, and held her hand, and placed his other hand on her hip cutting three inches into the distance that separated them. Now they were dancing together. There was an almost commanding look in his eye and she acquiesced and followed his lead, and when the song ended she didn't want it to, not to mention that had been her third song. She wasn't quite sure what to do now.

"Do you want something to drink?" he asked.

After a moment she replied, "Yeah."

Alex left and went to the bar to get their drinks.

What should she do now? Should she stay here and wait for him or wait at their table? It looked odd to stay on a dance floor if you weren't dancing. She was about to head back to the table when, "Oh my God that's my song," (Bob Marley's Could You Be Loved started playing) she said to herself. She didn't want to go but felt she would draw too much attention to herself dancing alone. Fortunately, for the both of them, Brian, Adriana's ten year old, approached her and asked if she'd like to dance.

Across the room at the bar Alex watched her while he ordered their drinks. She looked stunning, absolutely stunning, as if there was a light shining just on her. Nothing as gaudy as a spotlight, it was more like what they'd call star lighting in the movies. She seemed brighter than everyone else. He felt proud that he was with her. Though it appeared now he may have some competition.

He returned to Zawe, drinks in hand, who didn't seem to notice because she was having such a dandy time dancing with Brian.

"May I cut in," Alex asked.

And Brian looked up and said, "That's okay."

Zawe had to laugh.

Alex laughed as well but not so much. Even at ten a man is a man and men never take kindly to other men encroaching on their women.

"That's okay? Funny, very funny," Alex said. "Now Brian, I wanna thank you for keeping my girl company, but I'm back now, so why don't you go find a girl of your own."

"Nah, I'm okay with her."

Zawe guffawed so hard her neck snapped back.

"You think this is funny?" Alex asked her.

"Extremely," she replied.

Playfully annoyed Alex bent over and spoke directly to Brian's ear.

"Look, get out of here now and I'll get you a new Xbox."

"You already got me an Xbox."

"Exactly, see how good I am to you? And now I'll get you the next one as well if you get out of here."

"Hmm, let me see. New Xbox, dance with pretty lady, new Xbox, dance with pretty lady . . . new Xbox. Sorry," he said to Zawe.

"Wow, I lost out to a video game," Zawe said with a sigh and a roll of her eyes.

"I know, and you're a really great lady and I hope that someday you can get over me. But really it wouldn't have worked out between us. Sorry."

With that Brian departed and now Alex was the one laughing.

"Oh, you think that was funny?" Zawe said.

"Extremely." He offered her, her drink. "Drink."

She took it and a sip. "I can't believe you bribed a ten year old."

"I know and I feel terrible about it."

"You should pick on people your own size."

This was the second time she had said this to him. He wouldn't let this one lie. "Oh I intend to." They both understood the implications behind those words and welcomed them.

The songs kept changing (going from roots reggae, to dance hall, to hip-hop, to R&B), and they kept dancing and drinking; and as she danced and drank she became more and more relaxed. The space between them steadily dissolved, until there was none, until they had completely forgotten that they had come up with such a silly addendum. Zawe hadn't danced like this in years and maybe never. Gavin was a lot like her. Neither of them really enjoyed the attention that came from dancing. Without someone to pull the other out it wasn't unusual for them to sit through parties. Alex taught her something that night. When you are truly dancing and you're in that zone, you don't pay attention to anyone but your partner. How he smelled, how he smiled, how he felt, how she felt being held by him. She couldn't deny it anymore, "You're very handsome."

"What?" he said, acting as if he hadn't heard because he liked the way it sounded coming from her lips and wanted to hear it again.

"Nothing," she said and took another sip of her drink. Her drink was finished.

"I'll get you another," he said.

"Okay."

He left her again to go to the bar. This time she didn't feel awkward being alone. She closed her eyes and kept dancing and imagined he was still dancing with her and before she knew it he was. He came to her from behind and matched her rhythm as if he had never left. She opened her eyes, turned and faced him and she imagined it wouldn't be so bad waking up to that face in the morning. She was so happy that she came. This was the most fun she'd had in a long time. By meeting his family she had learned a good deal about him as well. Yet there was something very glaring about his family she just realized.

"Hey, I don't see anyone else here for you. Where's your Dad, where's your Mom?"

Her question took him out of the moment for a bit before saying, "I never really knew my father and my Mother died when I was fourteen."

She'd thought the absence of his inner family at the wedding was strange but that was not at all what she expected to hear. A profound sadness came over her and she fought hard not to break down and cry. "Oh, Alex, I'm so—" she began.

"Don't worry about it," he said and continued dancing. But she wanted to hug him more than dance with him, and as they continued dancing she decided to do both. After two songs she forgot about why she started hugging him but knew she didn't want to stop. They were like lovers dancing together, and as the songs changed she could feel him and he could feel her and things grew more hard and more wet, until just how hard and how wet thing things were, were all that they were thinking about.

"This is a hotel, right?" Zawe said in his ear.

"Yes it is."

"Then we should get a room."

"Yes we should."

67

It was a four star hotel and the room was up to that high standard and price. It cost Alex three hundred dollars for the night and it was well worth it. But it wasn't because of the amenities. They didn't even notice them. The room had a bed and four walls and a closed door and that was all that mattered. It was worth it because they were finally alone together.

Zawe walked over to the dresser and put down her bag. She caught her reflection in the mirror and closed her eyes. Was she really going to do this? She wanted to so badly. But if she did what would happen afterwards? How would she feel in the end? A few minutes of pleasure wouldn't be worth the days of regret, she was telling herself when she felt him come from behind, his hard body pressed into hers, his erection at the cleft of her ass, pushing through his pants, his hands slipping through her dress touching her breasts—finally touching her breasts, and they were beautiful breasts, pear shaped and firm, b-cups but felt deceptively bigger; her nipples in his palms, she felt them harden as well as her resolve. This felt too good to stop. Stop being the good girl for once. She leaned her head back exposing her neck; he came in closer; he inhaled her; he kissed her—finally he kissed her. Her lips were full and sweet from the wine. Their tongues were entities all their own; spoke their own language. It was a contradictory tongue as they concurrently wanted to caress and devour each other. She thought she could have stayed kissing him for an hour. Yet just as that thought came to mind it went away. She wanted more. She turned around and faced him and began leading him backwards. He directed them to the bed but no, "The floor," she said. He happily obliged and went down. She got on top and straddled him. He threw off his blazer and began unbuttoning his shirt, but "No, let me," she said," and he obliged again. She unbuttoned it but didn't take it off, but it was enough to see his chest and abs. His abs were so defined they could have been a musical instrument. She played with them with her fingers while his hands went behind her and found her ass—finally—and it was bountiful and beautiful. How many times had he watched her from behind and imagined gripping it as he was now; firm, round, smooth and with a slight chill, which made him so incredibly hot, and hard, so very very hard. He went to his pants so that he could free himself and go from one enclosure to the next, but again she stopped him and chose to do it herself. She unbelted and unzipped his pants but just enough to expose his erection beneath it. She hiked up her dress and began to grind him. This felt incredibly good to the both of them. Zawe especially as she dry humped unabashed. Yet as good as this felt Alex knew it would feel infinitely better without clothes. "Okay, Zee, let me put my pants down," he said but she didn't hear him. "Zee, let me—" he attempted to continue but she kissed him. He tried to reach for his pants but she pinned his arms down and continued grinding, harder, faster, wetter. This was beginning to drive Alex insane and Zawe . . . to an orgasm—an audible one. She moaned like a baby wolf that slowly turned into a cat then collapsed on his chest completely spent.

68

"Can I pull my pants down now?" Alex asked ready to experience a climax of his own.

"Sure . . . I'm done," she said.

He didn't like the way that sounded. It sounded very final.

"What do you mean you're done?"

"I mean I came."

"I know, I saw. Now let me make you come again."

"That's okay, I'm good," she said and started rising to her feet.

"What are you doing?"

"I'm tired. I'm gonna go home now." She began fixing her dress.

"Go home? You're not serious . . . you're not serious." She began touching up her hair. "Are you fucking serious? Zawe," he shouted.

"Alex I'm tired and I wanna go home. Can you do me a favor and tell your family I got sick and I had to go."

"Are you really serious? Are you really going to leave me like this?" He got to his feet. "Look at this," he directed her to look down at his erection, which was stretching the elastic lining of his boxers. "I'm so hard I could fuck through a wall." She couldn't help but laugh. "Oh this is funny to you. Oh well, you know what, you lost the bet."

"If that's your idea of sex you go right ahead and believe that," she said, then picked her bag up from the dresser, turned and exited the room leaving Alex both flummoxed and pissed.

"Oh you bitch, you bitch, you bitch, you—beautiful fucking bitch. You sexy ass bitch. Oh I was so close, so close—and now I'm so hard. Why am I still so hard?"

69

Twenty minutes later Alex's erection hadn't gone down nor was it giving any indication that it intended to do so. Every erection he had ever had, going all the way back to age three, no matter how hard had always detumesced within five minutes and would only last that long if he simultaneously needed to pee. "It's not going down? What the hell? Wait. A cold shower. They say cold showers are supposed to help."

Alex stripped down, got into the shower and turned the lever to C. The cold water hit him like a volt of electricity and he jumped back as if he had literally been shocked. He then slowly eased himself under the downpour one appendage at a time. It took him two minutes before he could stand directly under the shower head. The cold water made his entire body tense. All of his muscles contracted save for the one he intended. He looked down shivering and dismayed as the cold water bounced off his erection having no effect. He tried to bend it down but it sprung back up and hurt as it did. "Oww. It's so hard it hurts. Why does it hurt? What the hell is going on?"

70

Scientist may have learned a lot of things about the hu-man brain but they knew shit about the mind. No one can explain to you why each person's mind works the way it does, why it makes you see the things you see, things that you don't want to see. As Ian sat by his computer in his apartment he was wondering just that. Why was it making him see these horrible things? He didn't want to see these things. How could he make it stop?

His mobile began ringing. He picked it up and saw that it was Alex calling. He let it ring three times before answering not sure if he wanted to talk to anyone but eventually giving in.

"Yeah, what's up?" he said sounding forlorn.

"Ian, I have a problem."

"Yeah, well you and me both."

This wasn't what Alex wanted to hear. He had problems of his own and didn't have time for anyone else's. Still it would be bad form to ignore his friend and Ian might withhold his help if he didn't get some quid pro quo.

"Yeah, what's wrong with you?" Alex asked. Ian wasn't quick to answer. "Ian!" Alex shouted.

"Remember when I told you I found my daughter on the internet."

"Oh shit, did you find another one?"

"No . . . but . . . I keep seeing her."

"You keep seeing her? How? Where?'

Ian let out a big exhale. "Every time I watch porn."

"What?"

"Every time I watch porn all the chicks in it keep turning into my daughter and it's fucking with me." Onanism much like intercourse is as much mental as it is physical. One's mind needs to be stimulated the right way in order to bring one's self to orgasm, and there was no greater turn off than the sight of one's progeny dallying about in your head.

"Is that your problem? I'm dealing with some real serious shit right now and you're telling me about this psychological bullshit," Alex said.

"Hey, it's not bullshit. Do you know how fucked up it is not being able to jerk off because you keep seeing your daughter? It's not cool alright. Now what's your problem?" Alex didn't know how to begin. "Well are you gonna tell me or what?"

With great trepidation, "My dick won't go down."

"What happened? You took Viagra?"

"No. I never take that stuff."

"Aren't you special? Well then were you messing with some chick and didn't get to do anything?'

"Yeah, that's it."

"Then you got blue balls."

"Blue balls? That shit's real?"

"Hell yeah it's real."

"I always thought it was just some shit dudes joked about, like an urban myth. Are you sure that's what it is?"

"Well, what does it feel like?"

"It feels like I got kicked in the nuts and the pain won't go away."

"Yeah that's blue balls."

"Well what am I supposed to do?"

"Just lie down, try to relax and the swelling should go down in like . . . two hours."

"Two hours! Oh that bitch, that bitch, that bitch, that bitch."

71

It was the first cold day of the season; a thirty-eight degree mix of sleet and freezing rain. Very nasty business and what Zawe could only imagine would be a nightmare to drive in. It was the type of weather you caught a cold in. She felt rheumy just thinking about it. What a difference a day made?

Yesterday had been sunny and in the mid-fifties and absolutely gorgeous. Autumn days didn't get more perfect. Thank God the wedding had been yesterday. Things easily could have gone sideways if it had been held a day later. Open toe Manolos wouldn't look cute wading through all that slush and mire. No. This was a day to be at home and to be happy you had a home to be in—a home with heat.

Zawe turned the heat on in her house for the first time. This was an old house but thankfully the previous owners had installed central heating. Zawe hated those old wrought iron radiators and how noisy they could get on days like this. The sound of pipes clanking as steam passed through them used to scare her at night as a child. When she'd go to her father frightened he used to tell her he enjoyed the noise and she should as well. The noise signified you had heat in your house and that was a blessing especially when so many people didn't. He'd spent his share of cold winter nights in an unheated apartment, wrapped in blankets, scared to move an inch lest he broke the seal of warmth his own body heat had created.

Remembering those times reminded Zawe of how much she'd loved her father. She'd loved him—past tense. No. That's not right. She still loved him but she didn't like him very much anymore. He had been unfaithful to her mother but even worse he had been unfaithful to her, to the image she had of him. He was the paragon of what a man should be; he was strong, learned and handsome. He could fix the plumbing as well as help with her calculus. He was the reason she had such a love for math. He gave her, her name and a lot of her character. He taught her how to drive. He said once he learned to drive stick he could never go back to automatic. It felt too limited and lazy and Zawe agreed. She always agreed with everything he said and she always took his side when her parents argued, until she couldn't, until she found out about his affairs, and his two other children and that they came before her parent's divorce. It's always terrible when your heroes become human. You never truly heal from the disappointment. Yet in spite of it all she couldn't unlearn the things he had taught her or take his voice out of her head.

She had the thermostat cranked to seventy-five. She loved the heat and never liked wearing a lot of clothes at home. Wearing sweats inside felt too confining and irritated her skin. At the moment she was wearing what she always did, cotton shorts and a tank top, as she walked about her living room recounting yesterday's adventure in detail to Emma over the phone.

Zawe was a stickler for chronology and wouldn't spoil the best parts by jumping ahead. Emma had to first hear about how Zawe chose her outfit and her shoes, then how badly the cab driver smelled on the ride to the church, then the vows (they were so beautiful), then Alex's Aunt Katherine (she was so nice), then dancing with Brian (he was a laugh), then dancing with Alex, getting tipsy with Alex and finally getting to the hotel room. It had taken a while to get there but all and all the climax was worth the wait.

"Damn girl, just from that?" Emma said.

"Yes, it was so . . . oh my god . . . it felt so good."

"Then why didn't you go all the way?"

"Believe me I wanted to but I had to be strong. I couldn't let him win."

That sounded very silly to Emma. She couldn't let him win? Win what? What would he win that she wouldn't win as well?

It was a problem with most women, Emma believed, that they thought fucking was unilateral. They were always the ones getting fucked and never mutually participating. If the bet was what mattered to Zawe, arguably by having great sex with Alex she'd be the bigger winner. She had already won. He'd already been answering her questions. What else would she gain by lasting the thirty days? Bragging rights? That seemed very short sighted. Emma would take a great lay over bragging rights any day of the week. If it had been that good with their clothes on how much better would it have been with their clothes off? Emma was getting tipsy just thinking about it.

Zawe's doorbell rang and she went to answer it. She stood by the front door and put her eye to the peephole. It was Alex standing there in six point perspective.

"Oh shit. He's here," she said.

"Yeah. Are you gonna let him in?"

"I don't know. Should I?"

"Yes. Do it, and put the phone on speaker so I can hear."

"No. I'll call you back."

"Oh God, you suh—"

Zawe hung up and stood debating whether or not to open the door. She knew what she would be inviting if she did. To open the door would be to make a decision to finish what they started in the hotel, what she had continued last night in bed and this morning in the shower. It may have been what she wanted but was she ready for it? She looked through the peephole again. It was cold and rainy outside and he looked especially handsome when wet. She had to let him in. It would be unchristian to do otherwise. At the very least she should find out what brought him to her doorstep in such inclimate weather. Maybe it had nothing to do with the obvious.

"Hey? What, what are you doing here?" she asked after opening the door . . . partially.

"Can I come in?" he asked.

"Um—why?"

"Zawe, just let me in."

She did let him in but only because he was getting wet and the open door was letting the heat out, but she wouldn't let him beyond the foyer. She would keep him there by staying there herself. He would say what he came to say and then leave.

"Okay, so—what's up?"

"I think we have some unfinished business."

"Annnnnd—what would that be?"

He began backing her down against the wall. Alex, usually so devil-may-care, seemed much more convicted and of a single purpose today. There was no dallying or witty banter. He hadn't come here to ask or answer questions. He had spent two hours on a hotel room bed supine and spread eagle, his cock skyward and his balls so inflamed they felt like they might rupture a vein if he moved the wrong way.

To say the least it was a painful night and now he was of the mind to dish out a little pain of his own. He would fuck her until it hurt—in a good way. She would enjoy it but she would also feel it.

"Why are you so close to me?" he dipped his head and kissed her neck. "What are you doing?" He moved up to her mouth. "Why . . . are you . . . kissing me?" Her lips were inquisitive but her body was accepting. He held her by the waist and unintentionally she began to grind with him. "We—shouldn't be . . . doing this. We really shouldn't—" He kissed the talk out of her. She gave in and kissed him back, kissed him fully; his tongue, his lips; he bit her chin and she came back to herself. "No . . . no. We're not doing this," she said and pulled away. She walked to the living room and like a predator he followed her. "Look I know what happened last night but it shouldn't have and I'm sorry, but we're friends and we can't keep doing this."

He backed her in against the back of the sofa, put his hands on her shirt and ran them over her breasts. "We're not friends," he said to her.

"We're not? So this was just all about the bet?'

"Zawe," he put his hands to the collar of her shirt, "fuck the bet," and in one motion ripped it open and exposed her bra.

"Oh my God," was all she could muster.

He spun her around, slipped his hands under her bra and bit at her neck ravenously. "I wanna fuck you so bad."

"You wanna fuck me? Yeah . . . yes."

He pulled down her shorts, exposed her panties and that fine round ass, which he had been thinking about all night. Bet or no bet this was going to happen right here, right now. But, "No . . . no." Zawe attempted to pull herself from the brink. However, Alex continued, touching her, kissing her, grinding. "No . . . Alex, I'm saying no."

"Are you sure? Because your other lips are saying something else." He put his hands in her panties and touched the difference for himself, and though he had discovered the truth he had gone too far uninvited.

"Alex, stop," she shouted and pushed him off and he fell to the floor. She pulled her shorts up and readjusted her bra. "What's wrong with you? No means no."

"What's wrong with me?" He shook his head. "You know what?" He got to his feet so incensed . . . he became indifferent. "I don't do this shit. This is bullshit. This is too much trouble." He recomposed himself and started for the door. Seeing him about to leave she realized she didn't want him to go but couldn't say that. Instead she said, "So you're giving up on the bet."

"You already won remember. Let's see how happy that makes you."

He walked out and slammed the door behind him.

72

It had been almost four weeks and there were still three days left to the bet.

73

Three . . . very . . . long . . . days.

74

They felt unnaturally similar to the days following her break up with Gavin. They were not that bad. There was no crying involved. The pain was not so great that she felt like cutting herself just to distract from it. Alex was not Gavin, but he had become a friend and at the very least someone she spoke to. That was what hurt the most, not being able to talk to him. She had spoken to him and looked forward to doing so every day for the last four weeks.

For human beings having someone to speak to is essential. She still had Emma of course, but losing Alex reminded her just how insufficient and imbalanced having Emma alone had been. She missed him and there was no denying it. She could always call him but she could never bring herself to do that. She had too much pride for that. She had missed Gavin as well and if she wouldn't stoop to call her ex-fiancée, she wouldn't do it for some guy who had tried to con himself into her pants.

75

It was 11:59 on the thirtieth day and Zawe laid in bed under her covers counting down in her mind as if it were New Year's Eve. The screen on her alarm clock turned one two colon zero zero and she declared, "I won," to no one but herself.

Now why did she feel as if she was the one who had really lost? She had lost out on an experience. She had lost out on knowing instead of fantasizing. Why didn't she do it when she wanted to so badly? When her mouth salivated just thinking about it? She had never been a fan of or proficient at felatio but she couldn't help thinking what his dick would feel like inside of her mouth. She wanted to give him pleasure. He had given her so much pleasure in the hotel room and she wanted to reciprocate, and reiterate and reiterate. She felt sorry now leaving him the way she did.

So then why didn't she do it?

Because sex meant something to her and as hard as she tried she couldn't make it mean something less. Also she would have proven that she was no different than the less than a thousand women he had already been with. And it wasn't that she felt she was better than those women (okay maybe she did), she just wanted more. She wanted more . . . she fell asleep.

It was two colon zero seven when her mobile started ringing.

Groggily she reached over, picked it up from her bedside dresser and answered it without looking at the caller ID. "Hello—Alex . . . No, no it's okay . . . oh my God—I'm so . . . yeah . . . yeah . . . I'll be right there."

76

"I had been living in Europe three years when we got the word she had ovarian cancer and it was basically terminal. I came back to be with her and she's been going two years longer than they said she would," Alex said as he and Zawe stood outside the entrance of the Intensive Care Unit of Long Island Jewish Hospital at three am on a cold November morning.

"Wow. She's a very strong woman."

"She is."

But Katherine was also human and cancer was humanity's greatest killer, and it had a stranglehold on her now, having spread to eighty percent of her body, including her lungs and brain. She had been sick up to and through the wedding but she'd kept it in, kept it secret, because she didn't want to spoil the day. The morning after the wedding she simply walked into the kitchen and told Adriana, "I think you need to take me to the hospital now." Looking into her eyes Adriana knew the moment they had put off for so long had finally arrived.

There were few people Alex loved in this world and of those he did he loved Katherine the most. He would gladly trade places with her if he could. He was younger and supposedly had more to live for, but what was he living for? More fun and games? It all seemed so trivial now. Life was best lived by those who cared about it.

"After my Mom died, she took me in and raised me like one

of her own." He was fourteen when he came to live with Katherine and her two daughters and her husband. Still even while Corrine was alive, Kate always treated her boy more like a son than a nephew. She was there when he was born and they had a bond from birth. He was the son she never had and she was a second mother to him. He'd always appreciated that fact until this moment. Losing one mother had been bad enough but to slowly watch a second one day was twice cruel.

"I'm sorry for calling so late," he said. "It's just I didn't have anyone else I wanted to talk to."

"Maybe it's because you go through friends like you go through shoes."

He had to smile at that one. "Maybe." He breathed and it was as if she could read his thoughts in the cold trail of his breath. They were heavy and burdened. He looked so sad and wounded and yet so handsome. His vulnerability was very sexy. This wasn't the time but she had never found him more attractive.

The feeling was mutual. He called her at two am and even though she had work in the morning she came; she came because she cared, and he liked that she cared. He wanted her to care, and that was something he would have to take ownership of. He reached over and held her hand and looked her squarely in the eye.

"I can see why your Boyfriend fell in love with you," he said.

"Can you see why he cheated on me as well?"

"No. Right now, no I can't."

77

Alex woke up the next day feeling rested and calm as if it was any other morning. Then he remembered Katherine was in the hospital and he suddenly felt saturnine, like a dark cloud coming over a sunny day. Then he remembered how beautifully the night ended and it did a lot to raise his spirits. He looked over to the other side of the bed but it was empty. He heard shuffling and looked up. They were in his bedroom and Zawe was dressed and getting ready to sneak out. "Like a thief in the night, huh," he said.

"I figured I'd beat you to it."

"It would be pretty hard to sneak out of my own place."

"Not really. You don't own anything, remember, you can pack up and leave at any time."

"Yeah I guess so."

"Well . . . see ya." She turned to leave.

"Zawe . . . have dinner with me?"

She turned and faced him.

"Maybe."

78

Manhattan was the only light in the room and it reflected on their bodies—bare bodies, barely distinguishable to the eye and to the touch. He sat Native style and she sat on top with her legs around his waist and her arms around his neck, his neck nuzzled over her shoulder. He was so deep inside of her he couldn't tell where he ended and she began. They were more than having intercourse they were interconnected. They barely moved; every breath was a stroke, every centimeter a sensation, anything more would be excessive. They were learning each other's bodies and what they learned was that their bodies liked each other. They fit like an asexual organism that had been split in two and had now been recombined. "What are we doing?" "Isn't it obvious?" "But you already won the bet." "No I didn't. It was passed a month." "That's a technicality. When you say never . . . it's supposed to . . . mean something." "This stopped being about the bet a long time ago." "So then why are we doing this?" "Because it feels good." "And what happens . . . when it stops . . . feeling so good?" "We'll deal with that then," But—" "—Zawe . . . just let it feel good." "Okay."

79

Post-coitus:

They sat facing each other.

The city was still their only source of light but with the drapes drawn it was more than sufficient. They could see everything they needed to and a bit more. He noticed her eyes had fixed on his pelvis. There was only one thing down there of any real interest.

"Are you looking at my dick?" he asked.

She chuckled realizing what she had intended to be a glance had turned into a stare. "I'm sorry, I didn't mean to, but it's just that it's so, amazing," he smiled, "how small it gets."

"What?"

"Oh c'mon, you were just inside of me. I know how big you are. You're more than—adequate."

"Okay," he said though he didn't care for the word adequate. It sounded too . . . adequate.

"But still, it's just fascinating how it can get so small. I mean look at it, it's so compact, it's adorable."

"Adorable? Adorable? Look puppies are adorable, babies are adorable, my dick is not adorable alright."

"Well it's kind of like a baby right now and it's so cute. Can I kiss it?"

"You do that and it won't stay a baby for long."

"I know."

She leaned over and before she put her lips on it, it had grown into an adolescent, and by the time she had it in her mouth it was a full grown man. It was like a large lollipop made of meat; meat that breathed, concurrently saline and alkaline, firm and seemingly edible; had to tell herself not to bite down (too much teeth is never good). It rode her tongue from her lips to her uvula; not enough to gag. This was about pleasure not masochism, and it was pleasurable for the both of them. She really put her head into it, and her mouth became her vagina, and it was as if he was penetrating that orifice instead, and that gave her pleasure, but what was even more gratifying was the pleasure she was giving him. He really seemed to be enjoying it and she took pride in that more so than if he was entering her vaginally. The vagina seemed to be its own entity with the ability to perform astounding feats all on its own. This was solely her doing and it felt good to know that she was good at it.

80

Post post-coitus:

They took a bath sitting at opposite ends of the tub.

His bathroom had a separate tub and shower. He had never used the tub before because, as he saw it, baths were an inefficient way of getting clean. The few times he had ever done it he always felt less sanitary than when he first went in. The only people who took baths were women in movies.

Apparently Zawe had seen her share as taking the bath was her suggestion. He agreed without an argument. After all they weren't doing this to get clean but to get close and they were closer now than Zawe ever thought they would have been. During the bet she had contemplated the possibility that during a moment of weakness she would give into temptation and they might have sex once. However, now they had done it three times, each time successively better, and counting, and she wanted to keep counting. It had been so good if this were a video game she'd want the high score. Yet it wasn't just about gameplay. This game had a story. It was a bit of a mystery but she wanted to keep playing and find out where it went.

"How did your Mother die?" she thought out loud. She had been doing that a lot with him lately, inadvertently speaking her mind. He was caught off guard while playing this little piggy with her big toe. "I'm sorry. You don't have to—"

"No, no, it's okay. She ah . . . she had a heart attack."

"Really?"

Zawe had anticipated a tragedy (all deaths are) but a heart attack was unexpected—especially for a young woman. After hearing about Katherine's illness she assumed his mother had likewise battled with cancer, but it was her heart that did her in.

"She had a sudden cardiac arrest. She was in the kitchen of our apartment and her heart just gave out on her. No prior history of heart problems or anything."

"Wow. And where were you when it happened?'

"I was there, I saw it."

81

She was the same age then as Alex was now, which brought it home just how young she was when she passed, or perhaps how old he had gotten, and passed was an appropriate way to describe the way she died. She simply passed. One moment she was alive and the next she was gone.

They lived in a two bedroom flat on the second level of a private house in Canarsie, Brooklyn. He was an only child and she was his only parent—the only one that cared about him anyway. It was a Wednesday and as usual they had finished the Sunday dinner left-overs. His mother always cooked on Wednesdays, something quick and cheap: usually corned beef and green peas with white rice, or canned pink salmon and green peas with white rice, and if she felt up to it, curry chicken with green peas and white rice. No matter the entree it was always green peas and white rice. Alex had no beef with the rice but he began to detest Green Giant sweet peas like Buckley's cough syrup. But Mom said they had to eat them since they rarely ate any other greens, because she had never been very good at preparing them, because she didn't much care for vegetables herself.

Wednesday's dinner would last them to the weekend when they would get take-out, usually Chinese or Pizza. Besides not having to go to school that was another reason to look forward to the weekends; so it came as a surprise to Alex when his Mother said she was going to order Pizza on a Wednesday. She said she felt a bit worn down and wasn't up to standing over a stove. For Alex, this was like Christmas coming early.

She ordered the pie and sat at the kitchen table. She complained of neck and back pain and asked Alex for a massage. For pizza on a Wednesday he told her he'd gladly throw in a foot rub as well. She smiled and said she would take him up on his offer but first the neck and back. At fourteen Alex was already an expert masseuse. He had been giving his mother massages since he was nine. It was usually the feet—most women had problems with their feet. It was the consequence of wearing high-heels and she wore high-heels to work.

She was a paralegal and worked for one of those law firms that ran ads on television you saw while watching Jerry Springer. She had always wanted to be a lawyer herself—but Man plans and God plans and so on and so on—and as smart as she was she would have become one too if she hadn't been blessed to have run across the wrong man, blessed only because he enabled her to give birth to the right one.

She loved her son; perhaps a little too much. She loved him so much she didn't want to have any other children. For one because it hurt like bloody hell pushing him out and she promised she'd never go through that kind of pain, voluntarily, ever again, and two because she didn't want to divide her love.

Parents lie. That was a sad reality she had to learn. They lie and break promises yet expect children to do the opposite. A common lie parents told was that they loved all their children equally. It's impossible to love two things equally. It's like apples and oranges. They're both fruits but they're very different and you're going to take to one over the other.

Her parents had three children: Katherine, Corrine and Kevin. Katherine was the oldest, which made her Daddy's Girl— and you can't have two of those. Kevin was the youngest, which was special in and of itself, but not as special as being the boy, which Corrine hated, and couldn't understand why this would entitle him to special treatment, until she had a boy of her own.

Corrine never felt special growing up. She wasn't as old, smart or as pretty as Katherine and she wasn't a boy. She was always in the middle, which makes one feel very middling. It was perhaps not surprising that she fell for the first man who saw how truly special and beautiful she was.

And did she really love him? At the time he certainly made her feel as if she did. Then again Lincoln gave that feeling to nine other women. She spent the majority of her twenties believing that feeling was unique to her and her son before reality set in. The reality that they were alone and anything she wanted she would have to work for it. In fact she'd have to work double, as what she wanted most of all was a house she and Alex could call their own. To that end she took a second job as a Nurse's Aid and worked it on weekends.

Alex came back to the kitchen after paying the delivery man for the pizza and found his mother's head slumped over. At first he thought she had fallen asleep. She often fell asleep abruptly while watching television. When you work seven days a week you take your rest anywhere and anytime you can get it. But something was different this time. As he rubbed her neck he wasn't intentionally searching for a pulse but he noticed he didn't feel one. He called her name and she didn't answer. He called again and again she said nothing. He walked around to the front and tried to rouse her by lifting her head but it slumped down lifelessly. He lifted her head again, called her name and looked in her eyes. They had a yellowish green tint. He realized something very serious was happening and ran for the phone.

By the time the paramedics came it was already too late. Losing his Mother was the worse pain of his life. It was like losing one of his lungs. He never quite breathed the same again and he always felt incomplete. He still felt that way eighteen years later. How can you lose something that you're holding on to? And if you can lose that, why hold on to anything? She literally died in his hands. "Life is—fickle," he said to Zawe. "It can go away just like that, but we're all living by this notion that we can actually own things and own people. The truth is once you can die there's no real ownership. Everything is temporary."

Zawe used to think Alex's belief in not owning anything was something trite he came up with because it sounded pithy and made him look cool when he said it to women he picked up at bars. She looked at it differently now. She wouldn't say she agreed with it but she no longer dismissed it off hand, and more importantly she understood why he came to feel the way he did. He said he was over his Mother's death but his lifestyle and the tears that secretly formed under his eyes said something else. Zawe wanted to hold him and give him a shoulder to cry on but was pretty certain he'd say it wasn't necessary. Still she wanted to be close to him, so she moved to his side of the tub, got between his legs and laid her head on his chest and as a result he held her—hoping that was the end of it, happy her inquiry hadn't dovetailed into questions about his father, because God knows he wasn't ready to talk about Lincoln.

82

Lincoln was a farmer. He liked to sow seeds. At last count, at fifty-eight, he had thirteen children by nine women. On two of them he doubled and on another he had a triple, with Corrine fortunately only a base hit, which came during the seventh and by inning thirteen, Alex had long stopped caring about the game. Technically Alex had twelve siblings, six brothers and six sisters, but if they didn't come from his mother's womb he didn't consider them and cared less if they lived or died. This insouciance was rooted entirely in his disdain for his father as much as one could call him that. Lincoln would win no awards for his parenting. You have to be present to be a parent. Lincoln was adept at making babies but not rearing them. For much of his adolescence Alex wondered how this man who barely graduated high school and never worked an honest day in his life duped all these women (and some of them, like his mother, intelligent and attractive) into having all these babies. As he got older he learned the answer—after all he had inherited it.

Lincoln was the type of person who could fill a room with his presence. Wherever he was he was the center and people gravitated to him like satellites to a planet. He was smart, abundantly charming and had a great sense of humor. He always had a joke and a story to tell and when he'd talk people sat around riveted and broke out in riotous laughter when he finished. If he had ever considered it he would have made a great stand-up comedian.

He had an infectious affability. People liked him and liked being around him and liked other people they would normally never like when they were with him, and when he left, like the down after a great high, he would suck the mirth out of the room. He was a drug and people, especially women, couldn't get enough of him. He wasn't the most handsome man but he had an inherent sex appeal and that confidence Alex inherited. He could chat up any woman he'd see and unlike his son he wouldn't wait for an invitation to proceed. Alex had his mother's genes so he grew up to be the more handsome man, however, when it came to charm Lincoln had his son beat. Alex's mother dated other men after her breakup with Lincoln but despite each suitor's best intentions things never worked out. She hated Lincoln but, like the other baby-mothers, was in love with him, and once you've felt the light of the sun the moon just isn't bright enough.

As a child Alex loved his father as well and looked forward to Lincoln's visits. In the early years he would come on average twice a month and every once in a while he'd spend an entire week. Whenever he was there every day was like Christmas. Lincoln was always full of jokes and laughter. He would watch cartoons and play Nintendo. He taught his son how to box, throw a baseball and make a layup, once, all in the same day. And whenever Dad and Mom got into it, Alex would take his father's side and blame Mom for running him off when he left. Alex was too young to see just how shallow his father's visits really were.

Lincoln would bring a toy for Alex when what his Mother needed was milk and bread. He'd put twenty dollars in his son's pocket when a hundred was needed to pay a bill. Worst of all was when he'd come to her to borrow money. Much like his son later in life, Lincoln didn't work, save for a little weed dealing, and lived off the kindness of women, continuously borrowing from one to pay the other, and sometimes not pay them at all. He was always in debt to someone and lived like a nomad, continuously moving from one baby-mother's place to the next.

A lot of people said Lincoln should have been a pimp given his ability to get women to do what he wanted, but pandering required a certain kind of cruelty Lincoln didn't possess. Lincoln's cruelty was more surreptitious. He preferred to think of himself as a male lion. You know the ones who would make babies then sit back and have the females take care of all the labor.

Alex may have loved his father at four but by fourteen he had seen through the façade. In the end he blamed Lincoln for his mother's death. If Lincoln had been a better father she wouldn't have died. She wouldn't have had to raise a boy alone, and work two jobs saving to buy a house—a house Alex didn't even want. The doctors said there was no real cause to her death that she had been, by all signs, healthy and that unfortunately these things just happen. Alex knew better. It was the loneliness and the exertion that did her in. She died literally and figuratively of a broken heart.

83

"You hate me don't you?" Lincoln asked as he took a seat beside his son on the steps leading to the back door of Katherine's house. Alex didn't say a word or even look at him but Lincoln didn't have to see it to know the boy was seething. "That's okay, I hated my father too. It's kind of a family tradition."

Corinne's funeral had been in the morning and family and friends had gathered at Katherine's house in Nassau County for the repast. Alex would have to get used to Katherine's house as he would be moving here. Katherine had agreed to take him in and raise him the rest of the way as Lincoln was so obviously incapable of doing so.

"In spite of what you might think, I loved your mother." He sounded sincere but his words were so contrary to reality they were patently absurd. Alex huffed and shook his head. "You don't believe me. That's because you're thinking like a woman." For a man, especially a boy of fourteen, any comparison to a female always sticks under your craw. "This isn't your fault. You were raised by a woman and I wasn't around enough to show you different." Reminding Alex of his absences was not the way to endear him to his son.

"You're thinking how can I love your Mother when I have so many other women? That's because you think love is limited. It ain't. You'll learn a man's love is like the universe, it's big, there's no end to it. That's something women just have a hard time understanding. They're always like, how can you love me and be with her, and I'm like—why not? If a man can have multiple children and love all of them, then why can't it be the same with his women? I love all of my kids, I love each of them different, but I still love all of them and it's the same for my women. You may not be able to see what I'm saying now because you're still a boy but as you become a man believe me you will." The only thing Alex could see were the memories of his mother crying over this man, crying over the phone, alone in her room, never in Alex's presence but you can't hide red eyes.

Corrine had suffered from the same affliction as most women: a misguided belief that they could change a man. He already had five children by four women by the time he met her; her being eighteen and he twenty-five. She didn't know this before she fell in love with him but she did before she allowed him to ejaculate inside of her. But like all the others she thought she was different, that her and her child would be the ones to settle him down. Learning you're not special is a slow and painful realization. That was a hard pill for Alex to swallow as Christmas came less and less, and when it did he started not caring as much, until he didn't care at all, until he started to detest it and stopped believing in Christmas and religion altogether.

"You know we're a lot alike."

"No, we're not," Alex answered quickly. "I'm nothing like you."

"Yeah, I said that to my father too. But you'll see."

"No I won't. I don't . . . I don't wanna see you again. Don't come back."

Lincoln took a moment to absorb what his son just said. "Are you sure about that? You sure about what you're saying? And be sure because I don't make a habit of going where I'm not wanted."

"I'm sure." Alex wasn't but he said it anyway.

"Well you've made a man's decision and I'll respect that. I don't like it but I'll respect it. You know right now you might think that I haven't done enough for you, or given you enough, or been there enough, but remember this, I gave you life, and that's a gift you can never pay back." With his mother dead and the gravity of that pressing down on him so hard he felt it might shatter his bones at the moment that gift didn't seem all that special.

And true to both of their words Alex never saw his father again. Funny how Lincoln spoke so much about how he loved his children, yet all it took was a word from a boy mourning the death of his mother for him to forfeit his responsibilities. This burned at first, it burned a lot, but in the end it was all for the best. As a father, Lincoln had nothing to offer and nothing to teach. The only thing Lincoln could teach him was how not to be. Not being like his father, for a long time, was a goal to strive for, but the unfortunate thing about parents is that it's hard to run away from something that's in your DNA.

84

Jasmine Bailey.

He loved her—at least he thought he did.

She was pretty. She was the definition of pretty: fifteen, cinnamon skin, almond eyes, the color hazel, a perfect round nose, dimpled cheeks, budding boobs, butt too, svelte figure with a smile to die for. Everyone loved her; Alex more than most—and she liked him too; she thought he was cute.

They were a couple during the spring of sophomore year at JFK High. He treated her like he thought girls wanted to be treated. He bought her candy and roses—and not just on Valentine's; he gave her a small flower every day. He saved up his allowance and bought her a tennis bracelet; and most importantly, he wrote her letters, beautiful three to five page love letters, where he intimated his soul, which she would later share with her friends and they would simultaneously coo.

She broke up with him before the summer.

Bottom line: she didn't love him, she needed space, she thought he was too suffocating. That hurt. To give love to something you believed deserved it and to have that love dismissed. That hurt—nowhere near as much as the death of his mother but being in such close proximity it increased it tenfold. To add insult and injury he found out she had left him for a nineteen year old gang member. That was the injury. The insult was finding out every now and again he smacked the piss out of her and apparently she loved him. That one did Alex's head in. One man's treasure is another man's trash. That was a painful lesson learned.

85

Cassandra James.

He was seventeen and Cassie was thirty-one when they met at the jewelry counter at Macys two days before Mother's day. He was looking for a gift to get Katherine when, "Women should be getting you gifts," she said, and he looked up a little confused.

It was the first time a woman had ever propositioned him—and she was decidedly a woman, not a girl, not a teenager, not Jasmine; had a great smile, bright eyes, long legs (slightly knock-kneed), smooth milk chocolate skin and a great bust (the best c-cups he had ever seen) and didn't mind if your eyes deviated. She knew where her bread was buttered. She could have had a lot of men, and she did, but she wanted this boy now; lean and athletic, just coming into his handsomeness and his charm. She saw the man he would become and wanted a crack at him early. She gave him a card with a number on the back, and of course he called her, which seventeen year old doesn't fancy an adventure with an attractive older woman. He met her at her apartment—always at her apartment. He was like a doll to her, and though they never met outside she liked to buy him clothes and dress him up and have him model them. She liked to think she was molding the man he would become.

When Katherine saw him with these clothes she asked where he got them and he told her straight: I'm seeing a thirty year old woman (there was no reason for deceit; he and Katherine had always been open with each other) to which she said, okay just always remember to wear a condom. The last thing the world needs is another Lincoln. She also told him to be discrete with his new clothes in front of Bree and Adriana, and above all else not to tell them anything about this woman. She didn't need them coming to her arguing about double standards because God knows she would never allow either of them to have a relationship with a thirty year old man, even Adriana who was twenty at the time.

Yes there was a double standard. The sexes are different and what can be abusive to a girl can be very enriching for a boy. It was enriching for Alex that his first time was with an older woman. He didn't have to endure the awkward embarrassment of stumbling in the dark, struggling to find the hole and blowing his load between her inner thighs like what happened to Ian.

Alex had a teacher. She took him by the hand and guided him in. She told him whenever in doubt let the girl do it. She wants to do it and knows her biology better than you think you do. Once he was inside she showed him how to stroke it, nice and easy, in and out, up and down. This is sex not dancing, none of that wining around shit. She didn't mind that he came within two minutes his first time. She was a professional she expected it. Also being seventeen she knew he'd be ready to go again in five minutes, and he was, but that first orgasm—wow—was quite possibly the most intense experience of his life; so intense he felt like it might take his spine out and leave him paraplegic. He pulled off the condom and it was overflowing.

His second lasted ten minutes and was sweeter because of it but a bit less intense. She came as well but not before more tutelage. Alex was trying to make love, doing it like he saw in the movies, slow and romantic, taking care never to hurt her. But harder she said, and harder again, and again, and he obeyed and her eyes rolled back and her mouth opened and she sort of gasped and howled concurrently and he wasn't sure if she was in pain or pleasure, when he began to realize it was both, and there was the epiphany. She couldn't experience the one without a bit of the other.

She came four times that night. Alex was a quick learner but he wasn't in her bed because of his aptitude. He was there because of his youth; that taut, young body made all of muscle and sinew. He could fuck all night if she desired and on some nights she did. When she was a girl wanting to feel more grown she always wanted to be with older men. She married an older man. Now that she was a woman, and divorced, she felt cheated out of the experience of being with younger men and now couldn't get enough of them. She couldn't get enough of him. Youth is beauty in and of itself. He didn't know it at the time but she was his first Game as he was her Fun.

His relationship with Cassie lasted seven weeks. To date it was still his longest affair. When you have a relationship based purely on sex it's exhilarating in the beginning but can get quotidian quickly. Fucking her wasn't as much fun as it used to be, and with the experience he'd gathered he was curious about other women, and girls, and they were curious about him. Kim was a junior at JFK like he was. He started breaking appointments with Cassie to meet up with Kim, and when Cassie asked what was going on he told her straight.

When Cassie first approached Alex, she never imagined him being anything more than a sexual toy, and for all intents and purposes that's all he was; so her anger at him for being with another woman (well a girl, which made it worse), came as a surprise to her as well. But there she was, pissed as all hell, cursing at the top of her lungs and demanding he return all of the clothes she'd bought. Cassie taught him another important lesson. When people buy things for you, spend money on you or pay you in anyway they believe they are entitled to a degree of ownership commensurate with what they have put out. Also the longer the relationship goes on the more ownership they believe they deserve. Alex didn't like the idea of being owned. Beyond the obvious enslavement ownership also bred attachment. After his mother died and to a lesser extent his break-up with Jasmine, Alex wasn't keen on being attached to anyone or anything. The next day he returned all of the clothes Cassie bought him and, despite her apologies, never spoke to her again.

86

And as much as Alex loved Katherine for the three and a half years he lived at her house he always felt unsettled and uneasy . . . closed in . . . stifled . . . it was hard to breathe; it was hard to explain. He couldn't understand it himself. He appreciated living there and he loved everyone in the house but it never felt like a home, and when somewhere is not your home you always feel like a guest and a guest by nature is transient. When he graduated he couldn't wait to go away to school. His first stop was SUNY Buffalo.

In the beginning being away was just what he needed; a new room, new environment and new people—however, all new things eventually become old (though he would've never imagined so quickly) and by semester's end that gnawing, unsettling feeling started to return. While he was there he made friends and slept with his fair share, but soon he became tired; tired of the dorm room, tired of his roommate, tired of the Hall, the hallways, the stairways, the elevators, the bathrooms, the showers, the toilets, the dining hall, the food, the campus, the people, their faces, the cold, the snow, the snow, the cold, the food, the bars, the drunks, the townies, the Greeks, the Blacks, the Whites—everything.

After freshman year if he didn't get out he felt he'd go insane. He got good grades so transferring wasn't a problem. He majored in Philosophy, which was what people, who don't know what they wanna do with themselves but like reading old convoluted literature major in. Because you can't get a real job with it, can you? But it did get him into Morehouse then Berkeley, after which half way through junior year he said to hell with it and quit, not because he couldn't hack it or Berkeley was any more unbearable than the other two. He dropped out because he decided it was all pointless. He didn't want to become a professional philosopher—if there even was such a thing. In truth he didn't know what he wanted to do. He only knew what he didn't want to do, which was what everyone else was doing. He didn't want a job and he didn't want a career. He didn't even want to be rich. When we're all going to die what was the point of it anyway? You can't take it with you. The Egyptians tried that and they failed miserably. People said the point was to leave it to your children, but Lincoln had a lot of kids and was the world any better because of it? The world was over populated as is. The last thing the world needed was more children, left abandoned and under-loved. Also children wouldn't gel with his growing addictions.

We all have a fondness for new things—new clothes and especially new cars—and he always hated when the newness went away. After you've laundered your clothes they're never really the same again. The colors are faded and the fit is altered. After you've worn shoes more than three times the heels rub down, the toes get scuffed and dirt accrues. After you've driven a car for six months, the new car smell goes away, the oil needs to be changed, the tires rotated, the check-engine light starts popping up, and that's only the beginning of your problems, and they'll precipitously get worse. We all get old but do we have to suffer all of our shit getting old as well?

Life was too short and you only get one of them so he decided he'd live it how he wanted, doing what he wanted. Like Epicurus he believed the pursuit of pleasure was the summum bonum, the highest good. He recognized, however, that to live this lifestyle, to wear the new clothes, to drive the best cars, to spend his hours reading and never wake up early unless he deigned to do so, he would need money. That's where the kindness of women came in, and in spite of his disdain for Lincoln he saw himself becoming more and more like him.

The seminal difference was Alex wouldn't leave a legacy of under-loved children. He wouldn't do to another woman and child what Lincoln did to him and his mother. Nothing terrified Alex more than having a child, not only because he had been hurt by his father but because he knew if he became one, he would do the same. That's why he always wore a condom and always disposed of it himself. He'd never been inside of a woman without latex, never felt the true intimacy of her vaginal walls—and he knew the tricks of the trade, about the times of the month when it was supposedly safe. However, pregnancy wasn't the only risk. The greater danger was doing it without a condom and liking it, and not wanting to go back. That's when errors in judgment can happen and those errors metastasize quickly.

He must admit he'd been tempted before . . . many times. He was tempted right now as Zawe lay between his legs in the tub. He was erect and everything was already wet, and all it would require was a shift and then a thrust, just a shift and a thrust and his whole world would change.

"I think we should get out," he said.

Zawe tilted her neck and looked up at him. "Are you sure?" she asked.

He debated for a heartbeat, before, "Yeah," he replied.

87

Katherine looked good for someone who was dying. Zawe couldn't help thinking if she was fifty-three and was laid up in the hospital dying of cancer she'd hope to look this good. There was still color in her skin, fat in her cheeks and her eyes weren't too badly sunken in. If you didn't know better you'd think she was simply under the weather and would be out in another day or two. She still had a light in her eyes, and she still smiled and she was still vain. She wore her wig and had a scarf tied neatly around her neck. Alex held her hand and Zawe stood beside him.

"You remember Zawe," Alex said to her.

Sounding a little groggy,

"Zawe, yes, yes the one with the good spirit," she said.

Zawe smiled and asked, "How are you feeling?"

"Eh. Nothing a good orgasm won't take care of." Alex and Zawe laughed. "That's how it happens you know. You stop having sex, things build up in you and then the cancer comes."

"We'll be sure to remember that," Alex said while looking at Zawe and she gave him a sarcastic smile.

"We. I like that you're speaking in plurals. You two look good together."

"Yes we do," Alex concurred.

What did he mean by that?

When most people said things like 'we look good together' they meant they made a good couple. But that couldn't be what Alex meant. He didn't believe in those things. So why did he say it and why did he ask her to come here and visit his dying Aunt?

Perhaps the better question was why did she come? It was a simple answer—because it felt good. Being here with him felt good and it felt silly to break something in the present because you feared that it would get broken in the future. When Zawe told Emma she and Alex finally had sex, Emma told her, it was about damn time, to enjoy it and, for once in her life, go with the flow instead of always trying to control it.

88

Going with the flow—that's what she was doing sitting on the edge of his bed watching him get undressed. Still just because you're going with the flow it doesn't mean you can't nudge the boat a bit. "If you weren't doing what you're doing what else would you be doing?" she asked him.

"What?" he replied, pulling his sweater over his head and placing it in the Ian hamper.

"I mean like when you were growing up, what did you want to be? I'm sure as a kid you weren't thinking I wanna swindle money from women and day trade it."

"Well if I'd known you could do that as a kid I probably would have." Now he took off his undershirt and placed that in the hamper labeled Trash.

"C'mon, I'm serious. I mean, I've seen the pictures you take and they're very good. Have you ever thought about doing it professionally?"

"Ahh photography . . . I like it, but no."

"Okay. Well is there anything else you like, or liked to do?"

Why was she asking him these questions?

"Ummmm," he hesitated before saying, "Comedy."

And why was he answering them?

"Comedy? Really?"

"No, not really doing it myself. But I do like writing bits, you know funny observations."

Other than Ian he had never told anyone else this before.

"Have you ever thought about performing it?"

"God no. I wouldn't be funny on stage. But I've given a lot of them to my friend Ian and he performs them."

"Wait, so your friend's set at the comedy club, you wrote that?"

"In essence but he puts it in his own voice and makes it funny." He took off his jeans and placed them in the Church hamper.

"Wow, you're really talented."

"Hey don't start having respect for me now."

He was naked now except for his boxers, which would be off in another second. She had seen him naked before but this was the first time she had the opportunity to enjoy the show. So that was what going to the gym every morning looked like: 190 pounds and six percent body fat. He was an anatomy lesson. He would have made a great nude figure model. You didn't get a body like that unless you were an athlete or very vain.

"I'm going to take a shower," he said.

"Really? Because I thought you were just getting naked for no reason."

"You wanna join me?"

"No. But I wouldn't mind watching."

He smiled, threw his boxers in the Trash hamper and started for the bathroom. She was admiring the firmness of his ass as his weight shifted from cheek to cheek when it occurred to her, "Wait. You just put your underwear in the trash. Does that mean you're going to throw them away?"

"Well it wouldn't be cool to give away used underwear. What else would I do with them?"

"You can wash them," she said astounded that she was even saying what she was saying.

"Yeah, but that would mean going to the laundry."

That one left her mouth agape. "You know what, just go take your shower." Alex laughed and walked off to the bathroom. Once he'd left Zawe walked over to his hampers and opened them up. She couldn't believe what she was seeing. Look at all these good clothes, and very expensive clothes at that, just tossed out like yesterday's rubbish. She knew he'd said this was what he did but hearing about insanity and witnessing it were two different things.

89

Two days later Zawe was at a warehouse in Manhattan's garment district. The offices and showroom of Devon Denim was on the seventh floor. Devon was a boutique clothing brand specializing in high-end hip-hop. It was the kind of brand that sold printed tees for seventy dollars and their cheapest jeans for three hundred. It was clothes for rappers and anyone who'd like to go bankrupt trying to dress like one.

Zawe's friend Marissa worked there as a Purchasing Manager. Marissa had a great sense of style; part hipster part hip-hop. She was the type of person who'd wear combat boots with loose fitting jeans (ripped at both knees), a midriff and a fedora—and she'd pull it off. Zawe always admired her audacity. She tried dressing like Marissa once but couldn't get herself to leave the house. Along with Emma, Zawe and Marissa graduated the same class at Cornell. They were good friends in college but became better friends afterwards. Marissa had actually been the one to introduce Zawe to Gavin.

"Hey Girl. Long time." Marissa said as they hugged affectionately. Their distance had been by design. Other than Emma, Zawe had kept away from most of her friends. These were people who had already gotten their wedding invites and had taken time off for that weekend. She didn't want to constantly be the poor thing and mostly she didn't want to deal with all the questions. "So how are you doing?" Marissa asked.

"I'm good. Actually I'm pretty okay," she said, and for the first time in a long time she was and then it hit her.

I'm over Gavin.

Just like that—right then and there.

That persistent heaviness she'd felt in her chest all these months was gone. Realizing this was a revelation in and of itself. She felt so incredibly light. She felt liquid, amorphous, like she could never be boxed in because she could take the form of whatever space you put her in. She could breathe again. Hell if she wanted to she could breathe underwater. The spectre of their relationship wasn't haunting her anymore. She started smiling and it felt so good to smile she started grinning as well.

"Great," Marissa said and contagiously began grinning too. "So what brings you by?"

"I need you to do me a favor? Can you repackage these for me and make them look brand new." Zawe handed her two shopping bags filled with clothes from Alex's hamper. Zawe had them dry cleaned. She'd even gone through the trouble of fishing their tags out of Alex's recycling bin.

"Um, sure," Marissa said. This wasn't the first time a friend had asked her to repackage their clothes. This was one of the perks of working her job. She had all of the tools needed to package garments for retail: the tags, the tag gun, the tiny pins, the cardboard backings, the clear plastic sleeves; she even had the chemical spray to keep out the wrinkles and give them that new clothes smell. She was infamous for buying clothes, wearing them sometimes up to five times, repackaging them and then returning them to the store for full cash back. This was a perk she shared with her friends, who were usually women returning women's clothes. "But why?" Marissa asked seeing that these were men's clothes and they couldn't be Gavin's. She knew this because she had been in touch with Gavin, and Gavin had assured her he had not been in touch with Zawe. So then Zawe must have been seeing someone else, and he must be someone serious for her to go through all this trouble. But when probed, Zawe wouldn't say anything more than, "I'm just running a little experiment."

90

"You bought me clothes," Alex said as Zawe presented him the garments in her living room that night.

"Yeah, I saw what you were wearing and I know you said when you like something you buy more than one so I figured I'd buy it for you."

"That's so sweet. Thank you." He gave her a kiss.

"Your welcome. Now try them on."

"Ahhhh, that's okay I already know how they look."

"Yeah but I wanna see them on you."

"But you've already seen them on me."

"Alex, I just wanna see if I got the sizes right. You can't try them on?"

"Zawe, I know they're not new."

"What?"

"They're not new. I know you got them dry cleaned and re-packaged."

"What? How could you possibly know that?"

"One, you just told me. Two, I figured you'd try something like this eventually, and three, you just told me."

"Oh my God. You see, you didn't know, you couldn't tell the difference. It's just as good as new."

"No it's not, once you wash something it always loses its essence."

"Essence my ass. You're so full of it." Zawe laughed and

Alex couldn't help saying, "God I love . . . the way you smile." For a moment they both thought he might end that sentence differently. They were both relieved he didn't. Neither of them was prepared to hear the alternative—and it wasn't that they currently felt the alternative but the fact that they were even thinking on those lines was very serious and very scary.

91

It was scary because in the beginning he never imagined this. Seeing her at the gym he never thought about having sex with her and then going on dates afterwards. She was supposed to be a Fun Girl, not a Game and definitely not a, whatever it is this was becoming. Yet here they were sitting by a window in Columbus Circle with the city behind them having dinner by candle light. They were at one of the more expensive restaurants in Manhattan. You could fence the crockery and the tip was another restaurant's entire bill.

It was their first time going out without the pretense of the bet. She wasn't pretending not to want to have sex with him and he wasn't pretending that having sex with her was all he wanted. To top it off he was wearing her clothes. He was wearing his clothes that he threw out that she washed and repackaged and returned to him. He was wearing old clothes. He hadn't done that since he couldn't remember. So why was he doing it now?

He was wearing them to prove her point. There was no difference she said. They were just as good as new. Really? Then why were they itching the hell out of him? Why were they, at times, making his skin crawl. He reached discretely behind his collar and could feel the beginnings of a rash. It went from his neck to his thoracic vertebrae. It was an annoyance but he would grin and bear it, because she was grateful he had made the attempt, and he had an earnest desire to make her happy, because she smiled when she was happy, and he really did love the way she smiled.

92

Later that night they sat on the sofa with her legs stretched across his body while he massaged her feet. A good foot rub was second only to good sex and more times than not a prelude to the latter. She closed her eyes and let out a sound that let him know the latter was very likely. Not that the audible was necessary. They had been fucking every day since the first day they fucked. They were fucking like they were on vacation. Surprisingly she couldn't get enough. This was so unlike her. It was as if she was having a sexual awakening, as if she never knew it could be this good. When she'd had sex with Gavin of course she'd enjoyed it but it had never felt this imperative, nor had she ever felt this desire to impress.

Leaning her head back she looked over her living room, at the entirety of it, and the enormity. In truth the house wasn't that big but for her alone it seemed so excessive. It had three bedrooms she never even entered. This house was supposed to be future-proof. Those rooms were supposed to be for her three children—but Man plans and God plans . . . and the idea of having kids anytime soon now seemed like science fiction.

"Do you think I'm silly for buying my house?" she asked him.

"I don't think you do anything silly," he said.

"Sometimes I think I am. Sometimes I think I bought it just to prove that I could do it without Gavin."

"Did you?"

"Maybe," she sighed and it seemed more significant than a normal exhale.

"Do you miss him?" Why did he ask that? *Why did I ask that?*

The question surprised her as well. "Gavin . . . still . . . no."

That was a good answer. But why was it a good answer? Why did he care? "When did you stop?" *What are you doing? Stop asking these questions.* Nothing good could from these questions. It made him sick inside after he said it.

"Um, I can't say. I'm not sure exactly."

"But you're over it?" *Urgh.* That was even worse. He literally wanted to throw up.

"Yeah, yeah . . . definitely."

"And no regrets?" The vomit was marinating in his mouth now.

"Regrets? No . . . well ummm . . . maybe one regret."

"And what's that?" And now he figured if he was going to throw up it was best to get it all out in one sitting.

"Well, you know I always told myself if I ever caught my boyfriend cheating that I wouldn't go crazy, I wouldn't fight him, I wouldn't make a scene, I'd just walk away, and when I saw the two of them together that's exactly what I did. I held my head high and I walked away."

"Good for you."

"I thought so too at the time, but later on I realized that wasn't what I really wanted to do."

"What did you really want to do?"

"I wanted to beat the shit out of him. I wanted to punch his face and just keep on punching."

93

She remembered how she caught him, how Gavin himself had clued her in. She was at work and he had sent her a text.

'I miss you too. I'm getting hard at work thinking about fucking that sweet fat ass.'

His text gave her a pause.

Why?

It had started out well enough.

'I miss you.'

But then there was the 'too', which was odd since his was the first text in the thread. Still that wasn't cause for an alarm. Perhaps he was joking her into telling him she missed him as well, so she let that go. But then the text devolved into something else, something unusual, something so unlike Gavin in language and tone. Intimating his arousal at work was not the issue. He had done that before and she liked that—but then there was the fucking and that sweet fat ass.

Whenever Gavin and she spoke of intercourse they always referred to it as making love. Primarily because Zawe never liked the word fucking. It always seemed so base and demeaning. Fucking is an action performed by one person onto another, usually by a man to a woman, or more precisely by the party that penetrates. There is the one who fucks and the one who gets fucked. The fucker is dominant and the fucked is recessive. Even when consensual the action is never equal. Getting fucked is never good. Whenever the term is used outside the context of sex it's never in the positive. Getting fucked sounded like a violation as if something was forcibly taken from you. Making love on the other hand was about mutuality. It was about two bodies coming together to share themselves amorously and respectfully. They both give and they both take, neither is superior or submissive. Gavin knew very well she detested the word, so his using it would seem to be in poor taste. Still, although it bothered her, she could overlook it. He was talking dirty after all, and you can't talk dirty without well, talking dirty. 'Make love to that sweet fat ass' just didn't sound right on a multitude of levels.

And now she came to the real issue. 'That sweet fat ass.' If it had only been 'that sweet ass,' she would have gotten down. That wouldn't have been a problem. But Zawe never, ever, ever, liked her ass being referred to as fat. She never liked any part of her body being referred to as fat. She had a fat phobia and would gladly admit it. Gavin knew this, he knew this since year one (they had an argument about it for heaven's sakes) and in year six he should have damn well known better. He could have never thought this text would turn her on—unless of course this text wasn't meant for her.

Like inception the idea invaded her mind and spread like wildfire. Fear makes you hot and within a minute she was feverish. She was so hot it was hard to breath. She had to calm herself down, tell herself she was being ridiculous. It was just a text. It was an odd, misplaced but nevertheless innocuous message. This was no smoking gun. Perhaps he was just being playful. Maybe she was being too prudish. Maybe she should be playful as well. She playfully replied,

'My sweet ass misses you too.'

Then she waited . . . three very long minutes . . . before,

'Hey beautiful. Can't wait to see you at home and show you just how much I miss you.'

His second text was tonally more in tune with how they spoke to each other. He called her beautiful, told her he missed her, and there was no mention of fucking, though intercourse was implied. This was a good text but it didn't satisfy her. It actually made her more inquisitive.

He had sent her a dirty message and she had replied with

her own dirty message, and if they were playing this game why did he change his tone and start speaking romantic? This wasn't a fire but there was definitely a hint of smoke, and though it bothered her she wouldn't ask him about it and she wouldn't even mention it to Emma. She didn't want Emma swaying her opinion one way or the other. She would deal with this on her own. For now she left it alone.

At least until that night when Gavin went into the shower and left his phone out. Zawe had never looked through her boyfriend's phone before. She prided herself on not being one of those women. She didn't know how some women lived like that, with the constant jealousy and mistrust. If she couldn't trust her man she'd rather not be with him. All that being said as soon as she heard the shower come on she picked it up. The questions about that text had been eating at her all day. She needed answers or she wouldn't be able to sleep.

She turned it on but couldn't access the phone because it was locked and required a passcode. She took a guess that it was the same as Gavin's pin for his debit card, and it was, and it was as if she had stepped into a hidden vault. Once she was inside she began to feel guilty. She was betraying his trust and invading his privacy. She shouldn't be doing this but she did it anyway. She had to. The questions were eating her inside out like an ulcer. She told herself she only needed a minute to look through his messages, confirm that everything was fine, that this was all in her head and then she could move on and put this whole silly mess behind her.

She looked through his message folder and there were threads from her, from his mother, his best friend, his brother, her mother *(interesting)*, another friend, another friend and also his Barber. She breathed a sigh of relief. There weren't any female names she didn't know and so no apparent reason for alarm. This had all been in her head. But then something caught her eye.

He and his Barber had texted each other over 4,000 times. 4,000 times? That was more than he and anyone else had texted each other. That was more than he and she had texted each other. What the hell was going on? The fire from earlier reignited but this time it burned even hotter as she not only feared her man was having an affair but that he was doing so with another man.

She was right and she was wrong. Gavin was having an affair but he was not having it with a man. He was having it with this woman named Sophia. And if Zawe thought the text he'd sent her earlier was dirty she would need to recalibrate her definition of the word. These texts were a like priory of porn. It didn't even sound like him. Who was this man?

The texts dated back three months. They met at the barbershop. She worked at the adjacent beauty salon. They fucked two days after they first spoke, which was three months after he had proposed to Zawe and the wedding was six months away. Wedding? There would be no wedding. What an absolute fool she had been, spending so many hours planning a wedding, booking the church, arranging the reception, the flowers, the decorations, the dress, the bridesmaids, the bridesmaids' dresses, the cake, the honeymoon and the house. They were supposed to buy a house together, a house where they'd have their children. She was such a fool. Were they laughing at her? Were the two of them getting their chuckles at how blind she was? No. From what she could see they never mentioned her. He never mentioned her. Sophia had no idea she was the other woman. Which now begged the question who truly was the other woman?

Zawe put the phone down. She had seen enough though she wouldn't address it with him that night. She had proof but she wanted incontrovertible certainty. She wanted to catch him in the act. She kept hearing that Shaggy song 'It Wasn't Me' in her head. Men are adept liars and he would try to tell her that the texts weren't his, say that it was a friend using his phone or some other such bullshit. No, she would have to catch him in the act and not just to prove it to him but more so to prove it to herself. She needed to see it. She needed to see her.

The next day Zawe left work early and went to Sophia's salon. She entered feeling sad and angry and left feeling pissed and insulted. He was cheating on her with that. He was risking everything they had for that. Zawe wasn't a snob but she thought very highly of herself. She knew she was beautiful. Even if she didn't have eyes to see it she would know because people told her everyday. And she knew she was smart. You don't get to an executive position at a fortune 500 company as an African American Woman before the age of thirty if you're not. She was also loyal, generous, in reasonable measures, and she was faithful. She had only had four boyfriends but she'd never cheated on any of them, neither had she ever expected any of them to cheat on her. She knew that some men cheated. She had heard the horror stories from her friends, and friends of friends, but that's all they were, other women's stories, other women's problems. Hell her father had cheated on her mother, and as terrible as that was even Zawe would admit Andrea was not the easiest woman to live with—and Zawe was not her mother. That would never happen to her. After all why would her man cheat on her? Why would he want to? What more could he want that she couldn't offer?

She left the salon stupefied. He had humiliated her but she wouldn't demean herself further. She didn't make a scene at the salon (even as she overheard Sophia and her co-workers going on about Gavin as if he was her man and hers alone) and she didn't make a scene when she confronted them at Sophia's apartment the following night.

She had read his texts. She knew Sophia's address and she knew they were meeting up. He told Zawe he was working late. Working late? It was so cliché it was pathetic and she like an idiot had been falling for it. She hadn't even been questioning it. Chalk that up to equal parts arrogance and naiveté. She saw his car parked outside the private house in Bedford Stuyvesant. Sophia's apartment was on the first floor. It took every bit of strength in Zawe's body to walk to the door and ring the bell. Sophia answered while fixing her robe, a little taken aback to see someone as professional looking and elegant as Zawe standing at her door-step.

"Yes. Can I help you?" she asked.

"Can I see Mr. Chase please?"

"Mr. Chase?"

"Gavin . . . Gavin Chase?"

"Okay. Whatchu want with him?"

"It's business related. Could you call him, it will only take a second."

Both cautious and suspicious Sophia turned her head and called, "Gavin."

After about ten seconds, "Yeah babe, what's up?" he said, and that was his voice. He was there. It was confirmed and he called her babe. He also called Zawe babe. Hearing it made her sick and she fought hard to hide her revulsion.

"There's some woman here at the door for you."

"Some woman? For me? Who?"

Sophia turned and looked at Zawe. "Tell him it's his secretary."

"She says she's your secretary."

"My secretary? Leslie? What the hell is she doing here?"

"I don't know. Why don't you come find out?"

Twenty seconds later Gavin came to the door, fly undone and fixing his shirt. When he saw Zawe he looked as if he had seen a ghost—literally. He was petrified, he was speechless, so it was kind of kind of her to say, "Don't say anything, don't think, don't try. Don't make it worse by insulting my intelligence. I'm going to walk away now. Don't follow me and don't come home—not tonight. Do it tomorrow, in the afternoon, when I'm at work. Then you can go in and pack up all of your stuff, all the things you can carry. The big things you'll get at another time, when I'm not there. I never want to see you again and I never want to hear from you." She took off her engagement ring and handed it to him. "And you should give this to her. I hope you two will be very happy." Then she left. She never raised her voice and she never lost her cool. She couldn't have been any more dignified, and parked downstairs in the parking lot of her apartment building she couldn't have hated herself more. She kept seeing his face and that stupid shocked expression. She kept wanting to punch it, and punch it and keeping on punching. She wanted him bloody so he could feel an iota of the pain she was feeling. She had let him off easy. Stupid, stupid, stupid. She screamed. Locked in her car with the windows closed she screamed. She screamed until she lost her voice, until she coughed up blood, and beat on her dashboard so hard her knuckles turned red.

"I thought you said you were over it," Alex said, seeing the emotions in her eyes as she recounted the story.

"Just because you're over something, doesn't mean it doesn't still hurt."

"Yeah," he said. "I know what you mean."

94

He listened to her sleep. He liked listening to her sleep. He liked watching her sleep even more. Was there ever anything more beautiful?

He inhaled.

He loved the way she smelled and the way her scent filled the room, even when she wasn't there. And it had nothing to do with the toilet. He could spray the Dolce like deodorizer and it wouldn't smell the same. Her scent had a soul and a little went a long way. He came out the shower the other day and her scent was so strong he swore she was there. She wasn't and even though he would see her in a few hours, he felt sad she wasn't there at that moment. He missed her. He sat down and laughed to himself.

"I miss her."

The feeling at the beginning of a new relationship was the best feeling in the world. If Alex could bottle that feeling he would be a billionaire because it was a feeling that everyone wanted and wanted to cherish. You feel so alive because in those moments you have the best reason for living.

Love.

However, love in potentia and love in actuality are very different. Potential love is God, actual love is God and Devil combined. You fall in love with the good but live with the good and bad. But is the good worth the bad? For him it had never been worth it before.

His hand slid down her spine, passed her lower lumbar, rested on her coccyx . . . and didn't pull away. A voice deep in his head was telling him to let go but he didn't listen. For a moment he thought he could lie here, hearing her, seeing her, smelling her and touching her forever.

Forever lasted a few seconds.

Still it had been two weeks and he had done this every night they had been together and he still hadn't pulled his hand away. He hadn't felt so invested in so long maybe never. Was that a good thing or bad? It felt good but what would happen when it stopped feeling so good? He was starting to sound like Zawe. Maybe he should follow the advice he gave her and deal with that when it happened, if it even happened at all.

95

Zawe woke up with a smile and reached over for Alex but his side of the bed was cold and empty. The emptiness jolted her like a shock to her funny bone. He was gone. He had left her in the middle of the night as he had done to less than a thousand other women before. She had always feared this happening and now it had. A look came across her face as if to say, 'I can't believe I allowed him to do this to me,' when she heard a slight creaking sound and the hiss of steam.

She sat up and looked toward the center of the room. Alex was there with the ironing board out. He was ironing clothes. In fact, "Are you . . . ironing my clothes?" she asked.

"Hey. Yeah, I figured I'd let you get a little extra sleep. I picked out an outfit for you too. I hope you don't mind."

"No, that's so, no I don't. Thank you."

"No problem."

Every once in a while things surprise you. Waking up to Alex ironing her clothes was one of those things. It was so unexpected and incredibly romantic in a very practical way. In a way it meant a thousand times more to her than if it had been breakfast in bed. She couldn't help smiling. She smiled during her shower, she smiled on her train ride to work and she was still smiling while having lunch with Emma at a buffet in the city.

"What are you doing?" Emma asked, finding all this unprovoked cheerfulness unsettling.

"Huh, what do you mean?"

"You are like smiling for no reason."

"Oh, I was? Sorry, I was just remembering something Alex said." Zawe started laughing outright.

And what was unsettling to Emma before became downright terrifying. "Holy shit . . . holy fucking shit."

"What?"

"Are you falling for him?"

"What . . . no . . . no." Zawe took a swallow of her ice tea. "But if I was? Would that be so bad?"

"Hell yeah it would be."

"Look I'm not saying I am, but I get him. You know, he basically grew up without his parents. That's why he doesn't want to feel attached to anyone or anything because he thinks eventually they'll all leave him."

"Oh c'mon. You're a psychiatrist now."

"No, I'm not, but I can talk to him. We've known each other for only six weeks but I swear I've talked to him more in depth than I did with Gavin in six years."

"I get all that, but Zawe please don't go there."

"Don't go where. I'm just going with the flow. Isn't that what you told me to do?"

"Yeah. I did."

And that worried Emma to no end.

96

Alex was a bit worried when he opened his door and saw Emma standing in the hallway. He had only met her the one night at the club and later at the side of the road when he helped with Zawe's car, so when security buzzed him there was an Emma (Zawe's friend) downstairs he got a little nervous. Why was she here? Had something happened to Zawe?

"Hey," he said, trying to divine Emma's reason for being there by her body language.

"We need to talk," she said, all business like, and stepped right in without being invited. Alex was a little off-put by her forwardness but also grateful. She had something important to tell him but it wasn't tragic. She was too staid for that. Zawe was fine but this visit concerned her all the same. Alex closed the door and Emma walked into the living room and began pacing.

"What are you doing?" she asked.

"Excuse me?"

"You know, I totally got it with the bet. It was a cute way to trick a girl like Zawe into bed. But dude the bet's over. So what the fuck are you doing?"

Okay, he got it now. This was her one woman intervention. But why would an intervention even be necessary? It wasn't as if Alex was taking Zawe to the dark side and getting her hooked on drugs. Unless of course Alex was the drug. Even still, "I'm not sure that's any of your business,"

"Oh believe me it is. See I'm the one that had to be there for her, for basically six months of crying after Gavin broke her heart, and I really don't wanna go through that again."

Six months of crying? Had it really been that much? And could she actually be over all that in six weeks? "How do you know I'll break her heart?"

"Oh c'mon, this whole thing was about being honest. Don't lie to yourself."

Don't lie to yourself. Funny. These weeks with Zawe have been the most honest he had ever been. He hadn't spoken one untrue word to her. He had never tried to game her or play her. He had attempted to win the bet but even then he never resorted to subterfuge. However, if you are naturally a liar wouldn't honesty be the real prevarication. It was an act against your nature and you can only betray your nature for so long. You know this to be true. Don't lie to yourself.

"Noted," he said. "Now was there anything else you wanted to talk about?"

He asked her a question.

She took some time to consider her answer.

97

It was evening when Zawe came up from the York Street subway station. It was late November and though technically still fall you could feel winter's approach. She could see her breath and smell the cold. It wasn't a biting cold, nevertheless, she and Alex would be taking less walks in the park from now on she gathered.

She and Alex. The way she paired them made it seem as if they were a couple. That thought sent a nauseating feeling through her body, due more to its aftertaste than the initial swallow. A word like that came with connotations and she didn't want that. She had done that before. It didn't turn out too well. She'd rather think of her and Alex as a verb rather than a noun.

Zawe and Alex meant having fun, it meant smiling all day for no reason, it meant no lies and pretensions, it meant communicating (actually talking to each other and expressing their feelings), it meant letting go of the heaviness and feeling light, it meant switching from a stick shift to an automatic and allowing the car to do the driving. Lost in her thoughts she walked on automatic and looked up seven minutes later standing outside Alex's building.

98

Alex was surprised to hear a knock at his door. Other than Ian he didn't get many visitors and they were always announced by the front desk first. He slipped on his jeans and his t-shirt and walked over to the foyer. He didn't need to put his eye to the peephole to know who it was. He felt her through the door, he smelled her, and took in a deep breath before opening the door halfway.

"Hey," he said.

"Hey," she said.

"Hey, you didn't call."

"Yeah I know. I actually didn't plan on coming over. I got off the train and I thought I was walking home but I must have been in a daze because I ended up here. So I figured why not come up and say hi. So—hi." The Security Guard at the front desk had let her up without calling Alex. He had seen her pass through numerous times now and was confused whether or not she was a guest or if she actually lived there. He guessed the latter.

Alex sighed and bit his lip. "You really should have called."

"Okay, sorry. Is it a big deal?"

Alex didn't say anything but his silence and the fact that he hadn't invited her in spoke for themselves. It didn't take long for it all to seep in, and when it did it was as if all the blood in her body fell to her feet. She felt momentarily weak and immobile, light-headed and stupid, so very very stupid.

"Oh my God . . . I'm such an idiot . . . I can't believe I let this happen to me again."

"Zawe—"

"Fuck you . . . just—" she said and was about to leave when she saw something through the crack of the door; something disturbingly familiar. She pushed by Alex and walked straight to the yellow Louis Vuitton bag on the dining room table. She picked it up and examined it carefully. It was a popular bag but there was only one person she knew who had it. "Emma?" she called and turned to her right. Emma was across from her in the living room adjusting her blouse. "Holy shit. Oh my fucking . . ." Too disgusted to finish her sentence Zawe exhaled through her teeth, turned and headed out of the apartment not even looking at Alex as she did.

"Zawe . . . Zawe," Emma called as she went after her. Emma left the apartment and found Zawe halfway down the hall. "Zawe hold up. C'mon—stop," she shouted. "There's no reason to be mad."

Zawe stopped and walked back two meters. "There's no reason to be mad? Are you kidding me? You just fucked—"

"I just fucked what? I just fucked who? Your boyfriend, your fiancée—no I didn't. I'd never do that. I-would-never-do-that. He's not Gavin."

"You don't have to tell me that. I know he's not Gavin."

"Then don't make this more than what it is. This is not a big deal. Alex is just a fling, he's a happy detour, a great lay. You use him for what he's worth then you move on."

Just a fling.

A happy detour.

Use him for what he's worth.

A little less than a thousand.

Not Gavin.

All of the above beat into her head like heavy percussion. Zawe felt punch-drunk and immediately got a headache.

"Maybe you're right," she said between throbs. "Maybe that is all he is, but you knew how I felt."

"And what about how I felt? It's not always about you Zawe. I wanted him too and you know I did. You don't always have to be the one to get the guy."

You don't always have to be the one to get the guy? Those words were very dense and carried a lot of hidden meaning—years of meaning, years of secrets and envy. That's how Emma had been thinking all along. From freshman year every encounter with every guy that's what she had been thinking, which was odd because Zawe had always been in a relationship, and whenever guys approached them, she always turned them down and in fact sent them Emma's way. Zawe had never taken any guy from her. So what was she talking about? Maybe Emma was upset because she had never been the first choice. Maybe she was offended by Zawe's charity—no one ever liked being the consolation prize—but if that was the case too fucking bad. Zawe wasn't about to kowtow to her insecurities, especially not after this. If she wanted to finally get the guy so badly, "Well you got him now and the both of you can go to hell." She turned around and continued down the hall. Emma thought about following when she heard the door shut behind her. When she looked back she saw that Alex had left her bag outside.

99

Why did he do it?
Why does a man climb a mountain?
Because it's there.
Why did Bill Clinton have oral sex with Monica Lewinsky?
Because he could.

He did it to see if he could; not out of desire but curiosity. He asked a question and she didn't give an answer but when he kissed her she kissed him back. She was curious as well but also more desirous—and different. She was different than Zawe. She smelled different; different perfume but also different skin, different pores, different taste, different tongue, more aggressive, more anxious; bigger mouth, smaller lips; wore lipstick instead of gloss; wore no bra and a thong; he could feel it through her clothes; felt her body in his arms, more stomach, more arms, thicker legs, more dense, more liberal; more wanting to put on a show, wanting to please, and she performed and he played par but it pleased him not.

Different used to be a good thing. The differences among women were what Alex always appreciated. The differences was what made sex exciting. When something was no longer different it became familiar. Familiarity can breed contempt but before it does it breeds boredom. He had never remained long enough to be contemptuous, however, that was how he felt when he was done, and Emma felt the same as neither of them wanted to touch the other. There were only two people in the room but this had been a ménage a trois and they both would have preferred to have been with the third.

Alex sat by the window seat in his bedroom. Manhattan was

calling him but he was ignoring her. He didn't feel up to it, he didn't feel up to much of anything. What was this strange feeling in his chest: guilt, regret? He couldn't qualify it. He wasn't sure he had ever felt it before. His doorbell rang for a third time that day. Again he knew who it was before he opened the door. This time he was glad to see her. He didn't see the fist coming though.

"Ow—shit," he said as he stumbled backward.

"Did that hurt?" Zawe asked as she entered the apartment and closed the door behind her.

"Yeah," he winced.

"Good." She took a vase from off its stand and chucked it at his head. He ducked as it sailed by and smashed into the wall.

"What the fuck Zee?" She went for another vase but he rushed her before she got to it and held her by the wrists against the wall. "Zawe stop it."

"Get off of me." She struggled to free herself. "Get off of me."

"Are you gonna stop?" She didn't say anything and after a beat he let her go. She used the opening to punch him in the mouth. "Shit," he grimaced, grabbed her hands and pinned her against the wall again and got in her face. "Oh you got strength for me huh. Couldn't beat on your man, so now you wanna do it to me."

"Fuck you."

"Fuck me. Is that what you want? Is that what you came back for?" He pressed his body against hers and immediately got an erection. He still desired her, very much so. This revelation was as refreshing as it was arousing. He wanted to strip her down and take her right there.

"Get off of me."

She wriggled in his arms and every sway was a wine. He was dancing with a dagger, a dagger she felt as well. He kissed her, expecting a struggle at first but eventually acceptance. After all wasn't that always the game? No, no then yes, yes, then— "oww," she bit his lip and he pulled back bloodied. "Fuck."

"Look at you." She heaved. "You're so sad. Sex is the only thing you know. It's the only way you know how to relate to people. You don't know how to love. Because you can't lease it."

"Look, let's calm down," he said recomposing himself. "I understand you're upset, and I'm sorry you saw what you did. I never wanted that."

"No I guess you weren't being very respectful fucking my best friend."

"I never promised you anything."

"You promised me the truth."

"Then you're the one lying to yourself if you thought I'd change."

"Well, forgive me for thinking you were a human being for a second."

"Human Being . . . I don't know what that is. I'm a man. I like women, many women. I desire them. It is a constant every second of every day nagging. And it's not personal, it's not emotional, it's just biological."

"Oh please, don't give me that biology bullshit. You have a mind. You make a choice."

"A choice men have been making since the beginning of time. When are you going to learn we're not going to change? Stop fooling yourself. Commitment is this game you force us to play that we're predestined to lose, and you wonder why we cheat."

"We don't force you to do shit. Men always want commitment as well. In fact you want it more. You just want it to be one sided."

"I don't want it period."

"No, no . . . not you. That's why you'll always be alone, a sad little boy still crying for his mother. You will grow old alone and you will die alone."

"Don't fool yourself we all die alone."

"You know, for all your bullshit about not owning anything, and always moving and your newness crap, you, you're always the same. You're always the same, and you're not getting any younger. Aren't you tired of yourself?"

Maybe. "Not yet."

"I used to think that you were helping me, that I was actually learning more about men from you. But I see that you weren't really telling me the truth. You were just telling the truth as you see it in your own sick twisted mind."

"What other truth could I possibly give you?"

And with that there was nothing more to be said. It didn't make sense to argue any further because she would be arguing with the wrong person. She turned and went out the door and left him as he had always been—alone.

100

There they were, as far as his eye could see, an ocean of women, a fete of high-heels, thighs, asses, cleavage, lips, teeth and hair—swaying, bouncing, gyrating, clapping—waiting for him to dive in and divvy them up. There were anywhere from a thousand to a million of them (when you're in the thick you can never tell the difference) but for now one would do and she wouldn't have to be special just beautiful. And there wouldn't be any games tonight and certainly no bets. He would be straight forward and to the point. He'd fuck her purely for fun, for diversion, deliberate, disconnected and a bit deleterious.

"Damn," Ian said as he and Alex stood on the first level of the club off to the side of the bar.

"Yep. But it's alright. It would have ended eventually anyway."

"How do you know that?"

"Because I know."

"But how do you know?"

"Because I know me and I know her, and I know me, and in fact it would have hurt her more later."

"So you fucked her best friend to help her?"

"See how nice of a Guy I am." They both laughed. "But let's move on. Zawe's old now." Like acid indigestion it burned a little every time he thought her name; tenfold whenever he said it. "It's time for something new."

Like a robot he began sizing up each and every one of them. They were a racial melting pot: Black, White, Latina, Arab and Asian; sometimes all in one, dressed scandalously and dancing even more so, with a suitor or solo or sandwiched between friends. He wouldn't mind being the meat in that sandwich or the bread or the topping. If she liked you a woman would let you do just about anything to her on a dance floor as long as you did it fast. He would do it hard but had no intention of doing it fast, so he would have to go back to her place or a hotel but definitely not his (he'd had enough of women being in his place today).

He had his pick of the litter but as he had invited Ian out he decided Guests should eat first. He spotted a pretty demur thing standing by her lonesome as her more adventurous friend had departed for the dance floor. He thought she and Ian would make a good fit and he was even willing to take home her friend to make sure that it happened. "You see that one over there?" Alex pointed her out to Ian. "You should go talk to her."

Ian saw her and of course he was interested; twenty-something, shapely and shy. He could imagine spending a wonderful night getting to know her intimately. But for all that to happen he'd first have to approach her and talk to her. "I don't know. When I'm on stage and I have the mic, I can say anything, I can do anything, but to just walk up to a woman like that, I never had your gifts."

"You don't need any gifts, talking to women is so easy now."

"Yeah for you maybe."

"No, for every man. Things have changed. Just look at them,

they're all freaks." Ian looked at Alex disbelievingly. "I'm fucking serious. This is the Slut Generation. They all grew up on video girls, porn-stars and strippers. They don't give a shit about all that old school good girl proprieties anymore. They're all on Facebook and Youtube trying to out slut each other. Remember back in the day when girls would never give head. These chicks take pride in it. In fact they brag about how good their technique is. I'm telling you slut is not the exception anymore, slut is the rule. And it's fucking beautiful."

Ian looked at all of them, in their short shorts and short skirts, short dresses, skintight jeans, blouses; bra-less, bare arms, bare backs, neckline sometimes down to the belly button; belly dancing, booty dancing, dirty dancing—mainstream. Things had changed. Not for everyone (of course not), modesty was still present but it was no longer a virtue. The liberals were taking over and yesterday's liberal was today's conservative. And what would tomorrow's liberal be? How immodest would tomorrow's girl be? The obvious answer was more so. And if you were a man, as Alex said, it was all beautiful— "But then what do you do if you have a daughter?" It just occurred to Ian.

"I don't know I'm not a father," Alex callously replied.

"Yeah but I am . . . I am," and the gravity of that just hit home.

Alex saw the change in Ian's mood but didn't know what to say to him so he said nothing. It was loud in the club but their silence could be heard over the speakers. Fortunately Ian's phone was on vibrate. He felt the buzz and fished it out of his pocket. His eyes lit up when he saw the name on the caller ID.

Ian left to find somewhere quiet to take the call and while he was gone Alex figured he'd find a nice girl for Ian to take his mind off being a father. It was the burden of all men, wanting to fuck every woman yet never wanting anyone to fuck yours.

When Ian returned Alex wasn't where he had left him. He had to search for a bit before he found him sitting at a booth waving Ian over. He had two women with him. One of them was the demur one they had spotted at the bar and the other Ian suspected must have been her friend. The man truly had a gift. Ian had only left him for ten minutes and he had already picked up two women. Before the call, the prospect of bedding one of them would have been enough to make this a great night. But this night was already great and now could only get better.

He got to the booth and Alex began the introductions. Their names were Tiffany and Tais. Tais was the demur one and meant to be Ian's girl for the night. She looked discretely disappointed when she saw Ian. *Whatever.* After his call Ian could have given two shits about what she thought of him. At the moment he'd much rather talk to Alex than her anyway. "Yo that was Jamie Murphy," Ian leaned in and said.

Alex leaned away from Tiffany and gave Ian his full attention. "Yeah? What's up? What did he want?"

"He's creating a new sketch comedy show and he wants me to come on as one of his writers."

"Are you for real?" Alex gave Ian a pound. "That is excellent man." He then raised his glass for a toast. "Ladies I'd like you to join me in toasting my Boy here who just found out he's going to be the head writer on Jamie Murphy's new television show on HBO."

Alex embellished a bit. The show would be on Comedy Central and Ian would be one of seven (eight) writers. Ian didn't mind the fib. Alex had done it to make Ian look big in front of the Girl's, and their eyes did brighten when they heard the news, and Ian still had more news to tell.

"Thank you. Shit is about to pop off. But be happy for us," he said to Alex.

Alex looked a little confused. "Us? What do you mean?"

Ian pulled closer in order to speak clearly over the music. "I told him I had a writing partner and he said it was all good and that we could come on as a team."

"A team? You're joking, right?"

"No, it's for real. It's all set."

"Ian how are you gonna set me up with a job without asking me?"

"What are you talking about? It's not a job. We're just doing what we've been doing, now we just get to do it for a bigger crowd."

"Ian, it's a job. Whenever someone pays you they own you. They make demands on your time and your work. You know I'm not down with that."

"So what are you saying?'

"I think I said it. I can't do it."

Suddenly all of the lights, the music and the drinking began to make Ian feel as if he might have an epileptic episode. He just went from feeling like a king to feeling like shit all in fifteen minutes. He looked so confused he grimaced.

What was Alex's game?

Wasn't this what they had been working toward?

Then why was he backing out now?

Ian needed an explanation and he needed to hear it away from these girls. He excused himself from the booth and asked Alex to join him in a comparatively quiet corner to the side.

"Yo man, what's going on? You know the material I've had the best success with are the ones we did together."

"Hey, I don't know that. I just know I can't take a job. I'm sorry."

"After coming this far you're really gonna leave me hanging. I thought we were doing this together. I can't believe you're being so selfish."

"I'm being selfish? You want me to change up my life and abandon what I believe in and I'm being selfish?"

"What do you believe in? You don't believe in anything."

"Whatever, man."

"Alex, you know I need this, so I can get back with my family and get my daughter out of that neighborhood."

"Hey, don't put your family drama on me. You chose to have the wife and kids."

"Right. And you're free. You don't own anything and nobody owns you. You're so full of shit, man."

"I'm full of shit? Well you never had a problem with me

when you were taking all of my hand-me-downs, right?" Ian didn't say anything. "Exactly. You're the one who's full of shit. Almost jerked off to your own daughter and now you're fucking freaked. Listen to me, you can take her out of the neighborhood but you can't take her out of the times. She's a part of the generation."

Ian took a moment to digest the innuendo. "Are you calling my daughter a slut?"

Alex exhaled. "My man, if you have to ask a question like that then you already know the answer."

Ian stepped to Alex as if he was thinking of taking a swing at him. Alex stood his ground. Ian stared him down, things were tense for a good ten seconds, but then Ian stepped away. As he did he took off his jacket, the 3,000 dollar Gucci, and threw it to the floor.

"Shit." Alex said to himself as he watched Ian squeeze his way through the packed corridor knowing that he had most likely just lost the only friend he had left.

101

But had he really been a friend? Ian thought he was but what had Alex been thinking? Wasn't it obvious? He thought this was all a joke. Everything they had been doing for the last year had been one big game to him and the moment things became serious he jumped ship leaving Ian to steer the vessel alone. Ian had never skippered a ship of this size or magnitude. Driving Brooklyn bound on the Westside Highway he felt adrift at sea. The greatest opportunity of his career was knocking. Jamie Murphy had thrown him a perfect fastball right over the middle. All he had to do was connect the ball and the bat and he was guaranteed a grand slam, but without Alex's help he didn't even want to step to the plate for fear he would strike out. His phone started ringing and he honestly hoped it was Alex calling to apologize and say he was back in. He fished the phone from his pocket and looked at the caller ID. It wasn't Alex. It was some weird 973 number.

"Hello."

There was a bit of dead air . . . about five seconds worth before, someone said, "Daddy."

Because Tiana was the last person he'd expect to call him, at first he didn't recognize her voice. He knew it was the voice of a young girl. But why was she calling him? And why was she calling him Daddy? His initial thought was that Alex had put one of the girls up to a prank. "Hello, who's this?" But when she said, "Daddy," a second time, everything became crystal clear, frighteningly clear. "Tiana?"

It had been years since Tiana called him directly. The fact that the first time she would do so would be after midnight on a Saturday morning and from an unknown number was disconcerting. Whenever a family member called late at night it was rarely good news. *Please God don't let anybody be dead.*

"Tiana."

"Daddy." She sounded distressed.

His heart rate sped up and all the moisture in his mouth evaporated. "Tiana . . . Titi . . . what's wrong?" *Please God don't let anybody be dead, don't let anybody be dead.*

"Dad, I need your help."

102

Ian pulled up to a side road off Main Street in Newark, New Jersey. At that time of the night it was pretty dark and desolate. The only store open was a corner bodega and even that wasn't completely open. The shutters were down and you could only make purchases through a small bulletproof window at the side. That's where Tiana was standing.

Ian had told her to stay there in view of the bodega clerk. Given where she was he imagined it was the safest place for her to be. Newark was a notoriously dangerous city and even more so after sunset. What the hell was she doing out here? Ian only hoped the clerk was a decent man who wouldn't take advantage of a lost girl standing outside his window. By all appearances it seemed like he had been. Tiana told him thank you and waved goodbye before entering the car. Ian waved thank you to the clerk as well before driving off.

It had been five minutes and neither of them had said a word. He didn't know how to start. He didn't know how to talk to his daughter—this semi-woman. He knew how to talk to Titi. He and Titi used to be best friends. He used to make her laugh. Now she cringed when she saw him. The last time he tried to talk to her she shunned him as readily as if he was some strange dude who had tried to chat her up on the sidewalk, which made her calling him of all people during her time of need very puzzling. She was fidgeting, waiting for him to say something. He had better get to it.

"So, you wanna tell me how you ended up out here in Newark?"

She took in a deep breath. "I was with Tyrone and we were

supposed to shoot a movie together—" "—Oh Jesus, fuck me," he blurted. Tiana stopped talking and he had to control himself. This was hard. It was like having the runs and letting out a bit and then trying to re-close the floodgate. But she was opening up to him and he didn't want to lose this opportunity by being judgmental and reactionary. "Sorry. Go on."

"But when we got to the Hotel he had two other guys with him. He said doing Boy/Girl was boring and people wanted to see gang bangs." Ian tried his damnedest to hold in his anger, clenching his teeth to strengthen his sphincter. It had been hard enough to digest that his daughter was already having sex at sixteen, that she was dancing damn near naked on the internet for all eyes to see (damn his eyes, why was it so hard for that image to go away?) but now a gang bang.

"But I told him I didn't want to and he told me if I loved him I'd do it. We got into a big fight. He said he was gonna drive me home but then he kicked me out the car on that street next to the pay phone and the bodega. He took my cell away and gave me some change and said to call him when I was ready to stop acting like a little girl."

Ian remembered his hands around Tyrone's neck and how good it felt to squeeze. What Ian wouldn't give to have that neck in his hands again and the strength to keep squeezing until there was nothing left to squeeze. However, strength comes not only in being able to take a life but also being able to nurture and support it. His daughter had been strong enough to stand up to this man. Now he had to be strong enough to support her, to save her.

He had saved her before.

Years ago when she was eight he'd taken Tiana along with a few of her cousins to a water park in Pennsylvania. Tiana had snuck on a water slide with some of her older cousins. The slide emptied into a pool ten feet deep. Being barely four feet Tiana couldn't swim in water she couldn't stand in. She was drowning, the Lifeguard was absent and everyone else stood around in slow motion.

Ian had been the one to teach Tiana how to swim. Meaning he didn't know how to swim in water he couldn't stand in either, however, when he saw his daughter's head go down and not come back up none of that mattered. He dived in, dived in without thinking, found her struggling at the bottom and had the wherewithal to pull both of them out.

It didn't take CPR to revive her, just a few sturdy pats on the back and a lot coughing. To this day he still didn't know how he'd been able to pull it off. He hadn't been able to swim like that again. He just knew he had to save her. She held him tight and wouldn't let go for the rest of the day and he had never felt more loved or been more proud of himself. Sitting in the car Tiana looked like that eight year old girl again.

"And you called me," he said.

"I didn't want Mom to know."

He nodded his head. "I understand and I'm glad you called. It means a lot to me that you did. I want you to know you can always call me and I'll always be there for you."

After a noticeable beat, "Okay," she said and she smiled.

"I know I haven't been a great father. I had you so young I never knew how to be. Truth is half the time I still think I'm a kid myself. But I'm going to do better."

"Okay." Her smile increased with each okay.

"You and your sister—and your Mother deserve better. I love you, always remember that. So you don't need to go looking for it from anyone."

"Okay." It was a broad smile now.

"And just so you know, I'm getting a gun and if I ever see that boy around the house again, I'ma kill em."

"Okay." She laughed outright now.

They drove on and by the time they got to Queens she had been laughing so hard she told him to stop otherwise she might pee her pants. Just then it occurred to him that this entire episode with Tiana would be pretty funny if he hadn't been the one living it. Porn loving father almost jerks off to his own daughter and then starts seeing all other women doing porn as his daughter. It could make a great sketch. As always one man's tragedy is another man's comedy. He couldn't wait to get home and start writing it—and just like that he began thinking, maybe just maybe, he could do this thing without Alex after all.

103

Alex had never been woken up by a phone call before. Whenever he'd been sleeping and someone was calling somehow he'd always rouse thirty seconds to a minute before the phone rang. It never failed. He attributed this phenomenon to the connection of spirits. Alex wasn't religious but he did believe in spirits, and the supernatural and all of the phenomena man was as of yet unable to explain. He believed when someone called you their spirit made a connection with your own before the phone could—and that was what woke him, her spirit.

The phone was in the back pocket of his jeans, which was on the floor, which he had to stretch through two sleeping naked bodies to get to. It was Adriana. He didn't need to answer to know why she was calling but he did anyway.

"Yeah . . . yeah . . . okay . . . yeah."

He hung up, put the phone down and breathed. It wasn't a pleasant breath. The room smelled like a woman—not in a good way. It smelled of chemicals: of Nair, and nail polish and nail polish remover and hot combs and feminine wash, all of which were in plain view, littered about, along with shoes, and t-shirts, and brassieres and several pairs of jeans. This wasn't so much a room as it was a large closet with a bed. This was the girl from last night's bedroom. What was her name again . . . it started with a T . . . Tiffany, he thought and her friend was another T name he couldn't remember. The only thing significant about her was that she was the girl he had set up for Ian until Ian bailed on him.

It turned out these girls were a package deal, and one never did anything without the other, so he was forced to do them both. Threesomes in overabundance can become a bore. Three's a crowd and whenever there's a crowd people feel the need to perform and the entire ordeal becomes more like performance art than sex. He could hear Katherine right now. What are you doing Alex? When are you going to give up these silly ideas of yours? Is this what your mother would have wanted? Bringing up his mother still hurt even as a fiction. Funny thing was, he was his mother's creation in more ways than one.

All women want a man who will love them and be trustworthy, but when women have sons they tell them to never trust any woman other than their mother. Learn how to cook so that you're not dependent on another woman to eat because women will poison you. Don't eat under any two foot tables because you never know who's been there before you. Never let a woman step over you either figurative or literal lest you become henpecked. And most important be careful who you lay with, and always with a condom, and always dispose of the condoms yourself because there's nothing a woman wants more than to trap a man. With all of the mistrust women instilled in their sons for other women it was a surprise that men ever got married at all.

104

Alex trusted his eyes more than he trusted the doctors. They said the body lying in the hospital bed was Katherine's but he didn't believe it. He couldn't believe it. When he first walked in he thought a mistake had been made and he was in the room of some other dead woman. This woman was so gaunt and pale and shriveled and so very old, at least twenty years older than she should be. When he saw her just two days ago Katherine looked infinitely better than this. But it was her. The wig she always wore and the scarf around her neck stood as proof. It was a beautiful thing what the spirit does to the body. The body by itself no matter how symmetrical or well-proportioned is so very ugly. It is the spirit that beautifies.

105

Alex didn't cry when his mother died and he didn't cry now. Some people feel death in increments. It's a steady chipping away of your soul until a large portion falls off and you one day find yourself keeled over crying uncontrollably.

It hurts when you lose something but if you don't own anything you don't have anything to lose—but you own everything you love. First his mother and now Katherine, later possibly there would be Briana, Adriana and her children. When you don't own a lot the little you lose hurts that much more.

Goodbye Aunt Kate.

106

It was a beautiful casket made of high gloss cherry wood with an adjustable bed and matching pillow and throw. It looked very comfortable and he imagined a vampire would find it very fetching. But dead is dead and the dead don't care if they're in a decorative box or a plain wooden one, or wrapped in a sheet or burnt to ash. Katherine was long gone and funerals were shows put on for the living.

As they lowered the casket, he didn't say any words, he didn't throw any dirt and as most of the other hundred are so people broke into a cavalcade of wailing he still hadn't shed a tear. He did so not out of any foolish desire to be manly or even from a lack of trying. He wanted to cry but the tears wouldn't come. He looked around at all the people there and how they all seemed to gravitate around each other. Briana hugged her husband and Adriana held David and he held the children. Everyone it seemed was holding someone else, everyone but him. He'd have to admit holding someone right now who cared about him would feel nice. Relationships are about having someone who you can take to funerals, she said.

Yes they are.

Goodbye Aunt Kate.

107

Why was he here parked across the street from her brown-stone? He was driving home from the funeral but on his way something happened, he had a mental lapse, turned left when he should have turned right and ended up outside her house. He had been here twenty minutes trying to figure out what to do next. He couldn't find the drive to drive off or to get out the car. He had never been so afraid and yet desperately wanting to speak to a woman. It had only been a week but coupled with Katherine's death it felt like it had been so much longer.

When you speak to someone every day for six weeks it would surprise you how much they become a part of your life and how hollow you feel not having them to speak to anymore. Speaking to her was what he missed the most. In the end they had become lovers but before that they were friends. He needed a friend so badly right now.

He had been calling Ian for days but Ian wouldn't answer and he wouldn't call back. Alex had even reconsidered his position and was willing to help Ian out with writing duties on the show as long as they did it in secret and Alex wasn't officially a part of the staff. He left a message telling Ian just that and even still Ian never called back. Alex supposed a man takes it personally when you insinuate his daughter is a slut. Women were likewise put off when you fuck their best friends.

What was he doing? He couldn't stay parked out here forever. Either man up and go to her or drive off. He exited the car deciding it was better to see her and get cursed out than to not see her and regret it. He needed to see her. Even if she wanted to beat the shit out of him he would drop his arms and let her do it. At least she'd be touching him again and he would feel something and maybe he would cry. He felt constipated with tears. He crossed the street, skipped up the steps to her front door and rang the bell. It didn't take long for the door to open.

A week can be a long time, so many things can happen, so many things can change and sometimes when you call on a woman's door it's a man who answers it. After the initial surprise it didn't take long to intuit who this man was. It was Gavin—the omnipresent Gavin. Like God he had been the unseen character in Zawe's narrative. Alex had heard so much about him he felt like he already knew the man. He just hadn't put a face to the name, and as faces went Gavin would be considered good looking. Not as good looking as himself, Alex thought, but he could see why she'd find him attractive: square jawed, caramel complexioned with a faded dark Caesar and goatee. He had a good build too; not as good as Alex's, more bulk than lean muscle, but for most women he would suffice, and Zawe was like most women. They liked their toilets.

"Hey, can I help you?" the toilet asked.

"Um . . . no, no. I think I . . . I think I have the wrong house. Sorry," Alex said and started back down the steps simultaneously feeling relief and abject disappointment.

He was too late.

Shit.

She was gone.

Fuck.

He was almost at the bottom when, he heard, "Alex?"

After a week hearing her voice again was like finding fresh water in a desert. You could never imagine water so sweet or a voice so stirring. Seeing her was even better. She wore simply a pair of shorts and a t-shirt but she had never looked more beautiful, even more beautiful than at the wedding. The sun was setting behind her and the outline of her bronze skin was golden. She was like radiation and she poisoned you just by being in her proximity.

"Hey. For a second there I thought you had moved."

"No . . . I don't run away from things."

That was a jab and he took it on the chin.

"Yeah, I guess not."

"What are you doing here, Alex?"

"Um, good question. I guess, I guess I wanted to see you. But I can see that you've . . ."

"Moved on."

"Or, moved back. Either way—yeah."

There was so much he wanted to say but at the moment none of it seemed appropriate or seemed like it would have made much of a difference. He was too late. He bit his tongue, turned around and continued down the steps. He was leaving and as much as she had cursed him in her mind this past week she was happy to see him, and he was wearing a suit, and he always looked good in a suit, but it was a black suit, with a black shirt. She had a dreadful thought and involuntarily called out, "Alex?" He stopped and turned around again. "How's your Aunt?"

It took every bit of strength in him to smile and say, "She's good, she's good. In fact she's back home." He was lying and she saw it plainly and knew behind the fake smile he was crying inside, and as much as she hated him, she wanted to hold him and console him, and have him cry on her shoulder, but she wouldn't. She had already forgiven one man this lifetime. She didn't believe she had the strength to forgive another. "That's great. She's so strong," she said. It took a lot of strength on Zawe's part to hold in her emotions as well. She didn't know Katherine very well but of the little she knew she liked a lot. A line of tears escaped her guard—tiny but visible.

"Yeah she is," he said, and he saw it, and it stirred something in him that required privacy. "Well, alright," and then he left.

108

Zawe entered her house, closed the door and saw Gavin standing there with an expectant smile. He was an expecting an explanation. He wouldn't get one. She gave him a peck on the lips and went upstairs.

And how would she even begin to explain Alex, and the bet, and the friendship, and those beautiful two weeks together and how horribly it ended, and the fact that she and Emma were no longer friends, and that she didn't regret any of it. Allowing Gavin back into her house and her life would be all the explanation he would ever get.

And why did she do it? When he called her five days ago and she was on the treadmill at the new gym in Brooklyn Heights why did she answer the phone? Why did she agree to have dinner with him the day after? Why did she have sex with him two days after that? Why was he downstairs now? It was simple really. Why did she go out with him for six years? Why did she accept his proposal?

She loved him—still.

After he had cheated on her, after seven months of ignoring his calls, after Alex, after what she felt for Alex, or rather the illusion of what she felt for Alex, she still loved him. Any thought to the contrary had been a delusion. It had all been about Gavin. She really made the bet with Alex so she could understand Gavin better. Why he did what he did and what if anything she could have done to prevent it? And when Alex had sex with Emma the anger she felt towards him was really just transference of the rage she felt for Gavin.

So she decided to forgive him. She boiled it down to three choices: either forgive him, or remain single and consequently celibate (and after her sexual awakening that wasn't going to happen) or move on and find someone new; someone who was decent, who made her smile and excited her mentally as well as physically. Then she would have to hope he was trustworthy and find a way to trust him in return. That last bit was the hardest. There wasn't a man on the planet that came with a manufacturer's guarantee never to cheat—none—and in that case none of them were any better than Gavin, who she still loved. Maybe fidelity, sexual fidelity, wasn't the most important thing after all. So she answered his call because she supposed it was better to dance with the devil you know. The last devil taught her that, along with a good many other insights into the male psyche, which she would put to good use, because once you know the nature of a thing it can never surprise you or hurt you as much, she hoped.

So was that the extent of her feelings for Alex then? In the end was he merely a learning experience, a stop-gap between Gavins? In the end it would appear so. Then why was she crying? The tears flowed freely down her checks. She was crying for Katherine. No. Not really. She was crying because she knew that Alex was crying for Katherine. She was crying for him. She was crying because she cared, and it made her wonder, as much as she still loved Gavin, if Alex hadn't done what he did would she have ever picked up the phone.

109

He felt it building. He bit his lip to hold it back but it was no use. His teeth chattered and no matter how hard he closed his eyes the tears squeezed through. He tried wiping them away with his hand but they kept coming.

You can't fight fate.

He eventually surrendered, leaned his head against the steering wheel and let go. He cried (no wailing, no sound, just water, yet) so much he felt like he was taking a piss that would never end. It wet his lips, it went in his mouth; it taste bitter, he felt bereft; no Katherine, no Zawe and no Ian, and they weren't like shoes. You couldn't just discard them and get another pair.

He was still parked outside Zawe's house and if he didn't leave Zawe and her man might start thinking he was a stalker. "Zawe and her man," saying that was as bitter as drinking vinegar straight up, painful like a ten minute bout of blue balls. He could have been that man. He could have been the one in the house with her now. At the moment he wanted nothing more than to lay his head on her chest and to feel her breath on his brow. After all it was about having someone to go to funerals with. Those were the moments that meant the most, but those moments weren't cheap. You couldn't get them with any ole fun or game. They required someone special but that person demanded a steep sacrifice. Was that a sacrifice he was willing to make?

He put the key in the ignition. The radio came on and Human Nature started playing.

He smiled and shook his head.

Of all the songs.

Music more than any other art-form affects us the most. It's because of music's unique gift. Its uncanny ability to get into your brain, attach itself to your memories and transport you to a time and place when you heard the song and it was its most significant. He was back at the wedding dancing with Zawe. He had so much fun that night. It could have been the best night of his life, even in spite of how it ended. How it ended was laughable now. He wished he was laughing about it with her.

He began to imagine there was a potion, or some form of hypnosis, or procedure he could undergo that made it so every time he was with a woman it would always feel like the first time. It would always be new and his desire to be with her would never diminish. If he had such a potion he would never desire to be with another woman because he'd be perpetually desirous of the one he was with. Then he would gladly make the sacrifice needed to be the man in the house.

If he allowed it he could see himself falling in love with her. However, to love her he would have to own her and own everything else that came with her. He could no longer live off the kindness of women. He couldn't even live off the kindness of one woman. She wouldn't allow that. He would have to get a job and a mortgage and a multitude of other possessions. He would have to become like everyone else and foreswear other women, and do so without some magical potion.

But if she would allow him to have her, and to have his biological imperatives on the side, then maybe he would, maybe he could, be that man in the house, because what mattered most was having someone to go to funerals with, someone to share the pain with, someone to help take it away. But she wouldn't do that . . . or would she? Maybe that's why Old Boy was back inside. Maybe when she took him back she told him never again but deep, deep inside had quietly acquiesced to look the other way as long as it wasn't in her face and Old Boy agreed. But Alex couldn't do that because it would be a lie and bet or no bet he had promised to always tell her the truth. That's what made their relationship special—and in the end he would either have to lie to her or lie to himself.

As the song played he settled into a smile and the smile brought with it a peace of mind he hadn't felt in months. He was who he was and that wasn't going to change. For better or worse he couldn't change. He exhaled, wiped his face clean and put the car in drive. Manhattan was on his horizon and beyond that was a thousand other cities, with a million other women and they were all calling him. Show me a beautiful woman, he said to her . . . and I will show you a man . . . in pain, she replied.

ABOUT THE AUTHOR

Heru Ptah is a poet, novelist, playwright and screenwriter. As a poet he has appeared on HBO's Def Poetry Jam and CNN with Anderson Cooper. His first novel a Hip Hop Story was published by MTV Books and given a feature story in the New York Times. Heru was also the book writer for the Broadway Musical Hot Feet based on the music of Earth Wind and Fire and the choreography of Maurice Hines.

ACKNOWLEDGEMENTS

I begin by thanking my mother, Venice, the first and most profound relationship in my life; the same love, same respect, the same infinite gratitude applies like the last time. Your hard work and support has afforded me the liberty to live my dream. We got the house, but not the kitchen with the island, so I got work to do. Special acknowledgement to the inner family: Michelle, Shanice, and Jay; and to Marvin, Uncle Mickey, Uncle Ralph, Florizel, Lomalee and your respective families.

To my love, my heart, my backbone and bride to be, my beautiful Monifa Powell, thanks again for coming into my life. You especially know how trying this experience and these past few years have been, and without your support I don't know if I would have been able to see it to fruition. Since I have met you, you have been my greatest inspiration, and without you and what you have taught me I could not have written this book. You taught me love.

To my brother, Tehut-nine; along with Mo' you know the inner workings of my mind and how I have toiled with great love and labor for this project. Thank you again for your loyalty, your love and your nobility—special shout to the wife and kids.

To my father, Anthony Richards, thank you for giving me my life, my breath and my name. Here's to a long and prosperous life. To the Creator thank you for your guidance; even when ambivalent, it's good to know you're there. And finally to any and everyone who has taken the time to read this book, thank you all immensely—much love Heru.